Tell Tale Tit

Tell Tale Tit

Ulla Bolinder

Translated from the Swedish by

Eric Swanson

in collaboration with the author

Originally published in Sweden as *Går i alla gårdar*
by BoD 2015
© Ulla Bolinder 2015
English Translation © Eric Swanson 2022
Cover photo: Pixabay
Publisher: BoD - Books on Demand Stockholm, Sweden
Print: BoD - Books on Demand, Norderstedt, Germany
ISBN: 978-91-8007-946-4

Lilly Olofsson 1961

In October 1957, I came to know that a woman had been found murdered in the village where my older sister Signe lived with her husband and their nine-year-old daughter Ingrid. The dead woman was their closest neighbour.

Signe and I used to talk to each other on the phone several times a week, and she now began to express concern that the police suspected her of having killed the neighbour's wife. She also said that she had a feeling that people were speaking ill of her in the village and that the villagers shared the police's suspicions because she and the neighbour's wife a few months earlier had fallen out and no longer were on visiting terms.

She kept coming back to this, and despite persistent attempts I didn't succeed in reassuring her. She became increasingly anxious and confused. In the end, she didn't answer when I called, and a few weeks later I was told that she had been admitted to Ulleråker Hospital. We have mental illness in the family, but I could never have believed that Signe would be affected. She refused to receive me at the hospital, and when she got home, she didn't want to talk to me on the phone or see me.

However, the thoughts of what had happened gave me no peace, and lastly, I decided to try to find out what could be behind it. By agreement with my brother-in-law, I visited my sister's home on several occasions, which she reluctantly accepted. I talked to my brother-in-law and to my niece, with whom I have always had a good relationship, but I didn't succeed in reaching Signe. She withdrew and didn't want to answer my questions.

Ingrid and her father didn't have much to say about the

matter either, and I didn't get any clarity in what was behind my sister's feelings. Her thoughts that she was suspected of the murder of the neighbour's wife were probably just a symptom of her illness and nothing else.

Journal at Ulleråker Hospital's northern women's ward

9.12.1957: Admitted to ward 11 after application by her husband Erik Lundin, who also signed the life story report. Care certificate issued on 8.12.1957 by temporary district medical officer H. Zetterberg.

The care certificate announces: Pat. has had 14 siblings. The mother has been cared for at Ulleråker Hospital for about 20 years. A sister and a brother have been mentally deranged and cared for at Ulleråker, now healthy. Pat. has a 9-year-old daughter.

Pat. is usually kind, friendly, happy, and home-loving. A dispute with a neighbour's wife some time ago took her hard. She has been afraid of vagrants and wanted to lock the door when her husband, who has employment in Uppsala, was away.

Previously not insane. 14 days ago, been overstrung and seemed absent and confused for a couple of days, then better. Since 4 days, her oddities have increased more and more. Worried, wandering around, sleepless. Has, however, been able to stay alone at home when her husband has been at work up to and including on 6.12. On 8.12 pat. wanted to go down to the Fyris River to see what dead people were in the water. She has walked anxiously back and forth in the very well-kept home and listened and looked out. It was considered justified to call a doctor.

Status praesens in the patient's home 8.12.1957:
Somatic: Nothing remarkable.
Mental: When the doctor has entered the lower floor of the villa,

pat. comes descending from the bedroom with a quilt around her. She moves forward while somehow listening. Explains that she is not ill but complains of pain in the back of her head. Cannot be examined. She explains: "I have not recognized myself, everything is unreal, I don't recognize my sister and not the man either." Behaviour, posture, movements like a sick queen, alternating with fear. Irresolute. Attention slack, distracted. Sometimes perceives correctly. Memory very uncertain, mixes old and new. Thought processes fragmented. Mental disorders. Says: "Someone is saying right now: You should sit at the gate and go up in the air. Come right away." Shouts: "Come right away!" Laughs, explains: "It's Martin Ljung who shouts." So, she says to her husband: "Open the window and shout! What is this? Come right away! Damn oxen!" And after a while: "I see. There are so many people around the house. There are so many people around the house. There are so many men with white hats sitting around the house looking at me." Goes to the window. "They stare me straight in the eyes." So, she wants to go out in the dark, and when her husband tries to stop her, she threatens to hit him and says: "To hell with you!" Returning to the reasoning about Martin Ljung. Then goes anxiously back and forth for a while. "They are staring at me. I see their eyes. At six o'clock tonight there will be a bang and a fight and fylladelfia." When asked, she replies that she married in 1954. "It's eleven years ago." Hallucinations for sight and hearing. Escape of thought. Memory loss. Thought disorder.

The need for care is urgent because it is completely impossible to know what she can do if she were to come out and get the idea to go and look at the dead people in the Fyris River. In any case, her husband must now refrain from his work and guard her.

<u>9.12.1957: Admitted to dept. 8.</u> *Comes from her home in the company of her husband. Orderly behaviour. Smiles and says that her "nob feels a little heavy". Will be home again soon, assuredly for Christmas. Fully oriented. Short and inaccessible for further conversation. Rejects medicine for the night.*

<u>10.12.1957: Conversation (doc. Berglund)</u>: *Pat. comes in laughing with a yellow cap on her head. Talks fairly freely about her psychotic experiences. Has felt "nice" the last few days. Does not know why she has come here. "Must definitely have escaped," she laughs. Comments that she laughs easily, "has been so almost always". Claims that she is warm on her back – just for the day it is icy cold in the expedition because the heat supply does not work.*

Admits that there has been unrest lately. "I have played a little theatre, sung and trolled and acted out a little. You have to do that from time to time. Of course, I have spoken with voices, otherwise you cannot play. They answer me as they should answer." Admits influences of fellow human beings, especially the nearest neighbour influences her. "I see like faces in front of me. If people are talking, I see them." She mostly sees the eyes of each person, for instance the neighbour's wife, and recognizes them by their eyes. Laughs out loud when it comes to actress Sif Ruud, whom she has seen. "She broke her ass twice, but it does not matter, because no one knows about it."

<u>Summary</u>: *Mood elevated and inadequate. Fragmented thought process. Visual and auditory hallucinations, possibly feeling. Influence ideas, a sense of unreality. No disease insight.*
<u>Diagnosis</u>: *Schizophrenia.*

Therapy: Hibernal in combination with insulin coma treatment.
_11.12.1957:_ Seems happier. Friendly and accommodating. However, does not think it is necessary with insulin treatment.

_15.12.1957:_ Does not contact fellow-pat. Does not need any company, has enough from what she "sees and observes" in the room. Talking about someone being on the go with radar, one sees it in the sky. "Some call it stars, but it is a lot of aeroplanes."

_22.12.1957:_ More sociable with fellow-pat. Tolerates the insulin treatment well.

_24.12.1957:_ Picked up by her husband for leave during Christmas.

_28.12.1957:_ Back from leave in good spirits.

_30.12.1957:_ Insulin treatment exposed after 12 inj.

_31.12.1957:_ Discharged on trial to home.

_12.2.1958:_ Requested by letter to her husband Erik Lundin.

_20.2.1958:_ The husband announces that pat. is very caring and careful about what she is responsible for. Is calm in her behaviour. The husband believes that pat. def. can be discharged from present hospital.

_26.2.1958:_ Discharged, improved. /pat. informed/.

My name is Ingrid Elisabet Lundin and I am nine years old. I am turning ten this autumn.
My mother's name is Signe and my father's name is Erik.
I have no siblings.

I have been to a party where the Christmas tree was to be stripped of decorations. It was with a girl named Anita. As soon as we came in, we each got a paper hat that we would wear. Mine was red with glitter on. Then we drank soft drinks and ate buns and cakes.

A little later there was a fishpond. In the bags we fished up there were fruit and sweets and gingerbread hearts with white glaze on them. The fishpond was a blanket that they had hung up in a doorway. Behind the blanket sat Bengt, Anita's big brother, hooking the bags on the fishing line that we threw down.

I didn't know some of the children who were there. Anita's cousins I think it was. I mostly talked to Gun-Britt, who lives next to us. She is two years older than me and is in fifth grade. She is eleven and I am nine. I turn ten in October. Gun-Britt turns in July. With her, in any case, I was mostly at the party.

Before we threw out the Christmas tree, we played ring games, so we got all sweaty. Becke and Stickan went out and threw themselves into a snowdrift when they got too hot.

Once when I was at Gun-Britt's house, we had a pillow-fight in her mom's and dad's beds. Then we also became sweaty. We are not allowed to be in their beds, but that time everyone was out picking potatoes, so no one saw us.

It's rather untidy at Gun-Britt's house. Sometimes the beds in the bedroom are not made all day, and it's full of clothes and things everywhere. I think that's a bit unfamiliar. In the kitchen, they have two canaries that litter. Putte and Stina are their names. And it's full of dirty dishes on the sink and things on the table and clothes on the chairs.

Sometimes when I am at Gun-Britt's, we are in their basement. There they have packs of old weekly magazines that we look through and cut out paper dolls from. I have got Grace Kelly, Gina Lollobrigida, and Elizabeth Taylor from magazines in her basement.

Dad, he reads *Upsala Nya* and *Mål och Medel* and Mom reads *Svensk Damtidning* and *Husmodern,* which have serial stories in them. From Gun-Britt's mom she sometimes borrows *Såningsmannen* and *Hela Världen.* At least before she did, before they disagreed. Mom didn't want to meet Aunt Eivor anymore because she had talked crap about Mom or whatever it was. Then I wasn't allowed to go to Gun-Britt and play anymore. I thought that was wrong because it wasn't Gun-Britt and I who were angry. So, I went anyway. I didn't ask for permission before because Mom just said no.

Gun-Britt's mother is dead now. She was murdered one day when she was out walking in the meadow. First, she was gone, then Gun-Britt's dad found her down by the river. It was the day before my birthday. Two uncles, who were police officers, came to our house and talked to Mom and Dad. But we knew nothing about it because Mom and Dad didn't usually meet Aunt Eivor. I was the only one who did it sometimes when I was at Gun-Britt's house playing.

No one knows who murdered Aunt Eivor. The police have not figured it out yet. It was Stig and Bengt who found her in the meadow. First it was them and then it was Uncle Tore. And then they saw that she was dead.

My name is Bengt Hallgren and I am fifteen years old.
My mother's name is Aina and my father's name is Sten.
I have two sisters who are younger than me.
My buddy's name is Stig and he is thirteen years old.

It was Stickan and I who found Eivor. We were down in the meadow to pull up the raft on dry land. We built it this summer and it became quite decent, so we didn't want it to remain in the river over the winter and maybe freeze fast in the ice.

Otherwise, I don't spend much time with Stickan nowadays. He is quite childish, and he can't shut his gob. You can get quite tired of it.

It took a while to get the raft up and when it was fixed, it had gotten dark. But we know the way down there, so it didn't matter. We made our way. The river glistened and kind of lit up a bit.

It was when we were almost at the cow-track by the gates that we saw her. At first, we didn't know it was her, but we saw that someone was lying there. Stickan became yellow and didn't dare to go any closer, but I took a few more steps. As I said, it was quite dark, but I saw who it was, because she was lying face up. I was completely empty-headed and didn't get it at first. Why the hell is she lying here? Did she stumble and fall over? Is she sick? Has she had a heart-attack and kicked the bucket?

I cautiously approached and listened. The wind was quite brisk, so it was difficult to hear anything but the whispering of the pines and the rustle of the reeds. I coughed to see if she would react, but she didn't. She was lying there without stirring a limb. I thought about going forward and grabbing her, but it was too creepy, I thought.

I went back to Stickan and said as it was, and he thought we should go away from there and pretend like nothing had happened. He was funky and wanted to make himself scarce at once. But I knew it was wrong and said she might live and would lie there and catch a cold and get pneumonia and maybe die if we did nothing. At the same time, I was pretty sure that she was already dead and that it didn't matter what we did.

We went away from there. I was shaking and feeling rotten. It was the first time I saw a dead person in real life, and it felt quite uncanny.

When we got up on the road, I saw that light shone from the kitchen window at Tore's, and I told Stickan that we had to go there and tell him. Then we saw that someone was walking around in the garden and shining with a torch. It was Tore who was out looking. When we had told him that we had found Eivor, he set off down towards the meadow. We saw how the light from the torch swept and scanned as he ran. We waited up on the road until he came back. Then, when he had been indoors and called, we followed him back down.

It was the ambulance that came first. The ambulance guys saw that she was dead and that meant they couldn't take her with them from there. They had to wait for the police.

Two cops in a radio patrol car came first, and then came others. There was a lot of talking and sharing information before they started their investigations, and everything was dragging on, so finally Stickan and I got tired of standing there and went home.

My name is Gustav Landin and I am a Detective Chief Inspector and a Crime Scene Investigator.

I would like to begin by saying a few words about Mrs. Johansson, the tragic victim of this senseless outrage. We have collected pretty much everything there is to know about her life, marriage, family relationships, and other relations. We have also mapped her circadian rhythm and daily routines. These investigations were motivated, among other things, by the spread of rumours that arose after her death, and which presented her in a dubious light. There have also been allegations of tensions between her and relatives. Unfortunately, this can often be the case when evil tongues have a serious crime to be involved in.

Now people generally don't like to speak ill of a dead person, but we have carefully tried to get as objective views as possible, and I can therefore unconditionally deny all negative statements about Mrs. Johansson. She was a thoroughly decent woman, living exclusively for her home, her husband, and her children. She was also an unusually steady person, who had never appeared in any less flattering contexts.

In my understanding, it must be a person unknown to Mrs. Johansson who has committed the crime. The motive is still unclear. It's clear, however, that Mrs. Johansson was found dead early in the evening by her husband in a meadow near the home. Mr. Johansson may not have had time to understand all the details, but it was immediately clear to him that his wife was injured and that she must had been subjected to violence. Shocked and confused, he ran home to the phone and called for an ambulance.

According to the regulations, the ambulance personnel

couldn't bring the dead body from the scene. Instead, police were called. It was a commanding officer's car from the radio police that was directed there. The policemen met with the ambulance staff and Mr. Johansson, who after his phone call had returned to the meadow where his wife was lying dead. A couple of boys were also on the scene but kept a safe distance.

The procedure in the event of a death is that the preliminary examination of the body is done by the radio patrol that first arrives at the scene. It's these police officers who must decide whether it is a case of murder, suicide, or natural death. It has happened that the police interpreted the circumstances as natural, when in fact it was a murder, and if you happen to judge the death as not a crime, and it later turns out that the death was caused by someone else's acting, you inevitably end up in a difficult situation. Namely, there are always the occasional wiseacres among the colleagues, who consider themselves compelled to subsequently criticize and devalue the incorrect assessment afterwards. In addition, senior officers don't always realize the difficulties that may be associated with quickly assessing a death without a thorough examination.

Instead of becoming more confident over the years, I myself have taken an increasingly cautious approach and am less and less inclined to try to answer the question of crime or non-crime on my own. In more difficult cases, I always want to hear other people's opinions as well. Stars, who with a single glance at the dead body consider themselves able to decide whether it is a crime or not, or young inexperienced police officers who become overambitious and instead of immediately arranging effective cordon of the site in a misdirected zeal give in to play detectives and thereby destroy important tracks or upset the primary condition of a crime scene, one would rather be without.

The fact that young and inexperienced police officers will have to answer for decisions that may be decisive for the entire further investigation is a fundamentally objectionable system, which still prevails in large parts of our country. It should instead be the case that the police officers who are first on site only do a short routine examination and then hand over the responsibility to more experienced colleagues. When in doubt, the National Homicide Commission must be mobilized, which has happened in this case. That was how my colleague Gösta Dahlström and I came into the picture.

The National Homicide Commission, which is a reinforcement of the state police's criminal department in Stockholm, and which has access to a number of specialists with ultramodern equipment, turn out to various murder sites across the whole country as soon as a police authority needs and requests expert help with crime scene investigations, search, interrogations and the like. Another very important task we have, is to try to find solutions to older murder mysteries, where the period for prosecution hasn't expired and where previous investigations for various reasons have failed.

I am thirteen years old and my name is Stig.
My big brother is twenty-three years old and his name is Åke.
My little sister is eight years old and her name is Ninni.
Mom's name is Viola and pop's name is Gunnar.
Our family name is Ekström.

Becke and I were there and saw when the pling-plong-taxi and the copper came, and then we went there again. It was Becke and I who found her. When we got to know that she had been murdered, I thought it was much like in the *Alibi Magazine*, which I had just borrowed from my bro. *Drama in the Night*, a detective novel by Öyulv Gran, type of.

Åke, my bro, was also there. He took the car there. He had to park up on the road, because only the ambulance and the police cars were allowed to drive down.

The car that my bro has is a Chevrolet Fleetmaster. He calls it the rack wag, but it's quite decent for a '46, I think. Although I am not an expert.

I am more for trains and railways. Märklin-trains, that is. I have a steam locomotive, a German mail van, and two passenger cars. The parts are damned expensive. A passenger train locomotive runs to forty-five and a Swiss locomotive runs to eighty-three. You have to take it a little easy and wish for Christmas and birthdays.

I like Meccano too. With the tenth construction box, you can build an entire crane. Actually, I have done that.

I am technically inclined, but I also like sports. Bandy in the winter and football in the summer it usually is. Becke is two years older than me and has acquired some other interests as well, but we still have some fun together. Fiddling about with the rag like Nacka Skoglund and Gunnar Gren, jumping on ice floes, fishing in the river, and constructing gadgets. This summer, for instance, we built a raft down by the river. It was that one we had… The same evening we found Aunt Johansson dead, we had been there and pulled it ashore. This spring we will launch it again.

When we heard about the murder, I thought we would be something like Kalle Blomkvist and try to solve the case, but Becke didn't believe in it and didn't want to participate. Some things I do nowadays he thinks are childish, although he did the same things himself not so long ago. For example, he has stopped reading *Biggles* and collecting Alpha images and shooting with a cap pistol. *One must say!* But I will soon stop doing such things myself, I guess.

Before, we played Indians and cowboys quite often. The most difficult thing was when you were in a hurry and had to put in a new roll of caps. The rolls are in small cardboard boxes, and it's important to get them up quickly and put them in correctly and make sure you don't squeeze your finger when the shot goes off.

I wasn't very good at that. I am better at yo-yo. Actually, I am quite a dab hand at that. I have a Kalmar pulley, and I can do some stylish stuff with it. The easiest thing is to spin, that is let go of the yo-yo and jerk so that it spins around at the bottom of the string. It's important that the string isn't twisted too tightly for it to go well. More difficult things to do are the Waterfall, the Cradle, the Semicircle, and Walk the Dog. If you walk the dog, you first throw out a quick spin, then you lower the yo-yo until it almost touches the ground, and then you walk away a bit with the pulley rolling in front of you. When the speed starts to slow down, you make a twitch in the string so that you get the yo-yo up to your hand again. It looks easy but requires quite a lot of practice.

Well, Becke and I still do some stuff together, but it's not what it used to be, it really isn't. For example, we no longer laugh at the same things. *One must say*! And he seems annoyed that I imitate people or tell funny stories that he has already heard. He also seems tired of me reeling off advertising verses. *Take it easy, take a Toy! Easier washing with Surf! Health for the throat – Bronzol!* Things like that get stuck in you and have to come out sometimes. Before it went well, but now he mostly tells me to shut up when I start. He thinks I am too childish and don't fit into his new style.

When he turned fifteen, he got a moped from his pop. It's an Apollo Motorette with Zündapp engine and helicopter frame. It's sharp, I think. Costs around eight hundred and fifty, I have heard. But Becke's old man is rather flush and can probably afford to cough it up. He works on construction. My old man is a raisin wrinkler, and my bro is a toilet diver. No, I am just kidding. Pop works at the post office and my bro is an electrician.

My bro likes rock and sharp babes. That's what Becke has become interested in as well. But there is probably no chick who wants him. His clock is full of red dots, and he has had that for a long time now. No ointments have helped. When he tried a quartz lamp once, he looked like a boiled lobster instead.

My bro went steady with a chick for quite a long time. One almost began to believe that they would get hitched up. But it didn't last. When it ended, he started gliding around in his Chevy again, looking for new broads. There are some places in town where the *raggare* hang out. But the girl he is knocking about with now, he didn't get hold of there.

My bro has trained for a profession, and I intend to do the same. I am thinking of becoming a fireman or a pilot. Directly after school, you may have to work as a delivery boy for a while and perform errands for some store, but eventually I will invest in a good education.

In a family, it's the man who brings home the dough. He is the one who has a job and gets paid. Without his money, there will be no food on the table and the family will perish. It's the man who is most important in the family. The woman is also important, but not as important as he. She takes care of the household and looks after the children, but you can't live on what she does. She must ask for money and doesn't know how much the man has. He is the one who has the power, because he is the one who brings home the dough that the family will live on.

If you play with girls, you are a milksop. You can play with girls if no one sees it, but preferably not. Once, when I played mothers and fathers with a girl, my buddies caught me. You are weak if you play with girls. I was ashamed and started teasing her to show which side I was on.

Girls are generally worse at things that guys can do. For example, they can't hit the ball with the round bat when they play rounders. They must use the flat girl's bat. And they can never hit the ball as far as a guy can. A guy always wins over a girl.

In school, girls can be good at certain subjects, such as reading, writing, and drawing. Sometimes they can even be better than guys. They curry favour with the teacher and sit at home and study to get more gold stars and better grades than the boys. But that's wrong, since the guys are the best. A guy is stronger and can easily beat up a girl if he wants to. It's not fair to hit someone who is weaker, and a girl is always weaker, but the opportunity exists.

Åke, my bro, has beaten a girl once. That's why he was suspected of the murder of Aunt Johansson. And the same night it happened, someone had seen his car on the way down to the river. The Chevy, that is. Everyone knows it belongs to him. But he says he wasn't there, and then you have to believe him.

Ingrid

Now in the winter when Gun-Britt and I play, we are mostly out making snowmen and snowball lanterns which we put candles in, or caves in snow drifts if it's the kind of snow that you can dig in. Then you get snow in your boots and lumps of ice on your mittens. Gun-Britt sucks them off, but I think that's disgusting. And she *eats* snow and licks on icicles. Mom has forbidden me to do that, because she says that the snow and ice can be poisoned by things that the Russians have let out.

When it's cold outside, it steams when you breathe. Sometimes I take a stick and use it as a cigarette. I hold the stick between my fingers as smokers do, and then I suck on it and pretend that what comes out when I breathe is cigarette smoke. It looks like you really smoke then. You feel jaunty and tough when you pretend to smoke.

I like when there is a storm in the winter. Then it zings in the telephone wires and the snow is whirling. But I feel sorry for Dad who must shovel away so much snow when the walkway has got blocked with drifting snow.

In the woods there is a swamp that we skate on when it's cold. But sometimes the ice is so crunchy that it's impossible. In that swamp we catch tadpoles in the spring.

At school, the caretaker floods water on the boys' football ground so it becomes ice. There, the boys play ice hockey and bandy. They have ice hockey skates or whatever it's called. The girls, some of them, have figure skating skates. I have some called Princess, and Kerstin, who I mostly am together with in school, have some named Piruett. But I can't do any tricks. The only things I can do is cut cake and spin a little on the thorns and glide on one leg.

Once when the boys were playing ice hockey, Tommy in my class was knocked over and got a cut in his lip by a skate so it started to bleed. Then he had to go with our master to the hospital and be sewn. Afterwards the lip was thick and blue with black stitches in it.

I go by bus to school because it's a long way there. The bus stops where Stig and Ninni live, so Gun-Britt and I have to walk or bike there. In the winter we walk, because then it's dangerous to cycle. Before it starts to snow, they set up juniper branches along the roadsides, so they know where the ditches are if the road gets blocked with snow. Then the plough truck comes first and then the sand truck. When the sand truck has gone, you can no longer go kick-sledding on the road. Maybe so if they have not sanded all the way to the edges.

When I go to school, I pick up Gun-Britt, and then we walk together to the bus. I live farthest away, because in the other direction there are no children. Only in the summer a girl and a boy live further away. But then you don't go to school.

The bus goes in pretzel hooks and picks up children. When it comes to us it's empty, and when it arrives at school it's full. In the winter, when there is a lot of snow, the bus may get stuck or slip into a ditch. There is a road that goes straight over a field, and on that road it's very icy sometimes. There the bus went down into the ditch once. That day we arrived at school too late.

It must be difficult for the drivers when it's so slippery. A driver called Fransson often sits and swears while driving. And he doesn't tolerate anyone in the bus fooling around. The guys do that sometimes, and then he gets angry and starts scolding them, so he turns red like a peony in the mug. They may have been throwing apple-cores or starting to fight or talking too loudly. Once he stopped in the middle of the road and went to the back of the bus to Uffe, who goes to my class, and twisted his ear. Another time he braked when I shouted because a guy made a horse bite on me. I was about to go off in a faint, because at first I thought it was me he was mad at. But he had stopped because he had seen in the rear-view mirror that Tommy and Uffe had started to slither on their soles after the bus just when they had gotten off. He ran out and scolded them and lifted Uffe up. It's dangerous to slither on your soles behind a bus because you can lose your grip and fall under the bus and be run over, and if that happened when it was Fransson who was driving, he would be blamed for it, perhaps he feared.

A first extremely important question in case of murder is whether the finding-place and the crime scene are identical. In this case, no trail tracks could be observed on the hard ground. If the ground hadn't been so hard, there should have been opportunities to secure shoe tracks and other things, but this couldn't be done.

The clothes of the deceased were found to be in good order. The apron was as it should be, and the blouse and the cardigan were buttoned right up to the neck. But there were some reddish-brown spots on the blouse collar and on the back of the cardigan, which later turned out to originate from the victim's own bleeding. The skirt, the apron, the knickers, and the corset, with properly fastened garters, didn't provide any information whatsoever to the crime scene investigators.

However, a pair of black boots, an empty basket, a torch, and a denture lying next to her body indicated that Mrs. Johansson's death could have been preceded by a fight. Although there were no traces or other signs pointing in that direction. A strange detail was that some withered maple leaves had stuck to her clothes, even though trees of that kind didn't grow nearby. Our theory was therefore that the murder had taken place in a different place than where Mrs. Johansson was found. The murderer must have carried her, despite her sixty-two kilos, or dragged her there and then placed the objects she lost next to her body.

The site was photographed, and the dead body was examined for livor mortis, how far the rigor mortis had developed, if there was residual body heat and the like. As one doesn't always have access to doctors who can be responsible for the first physical examination, the crime scene investigator himself must have a fairly solid knowledge of such things.

When examining a dead body, you start with the head. The torso, the arms, and finally the legs are then examined. All the time you keep careful notes about the condition and position of the clothes, damage and contamination of the clothes and the body, in which directions body fluids such as blood, saliva, urine, and more have flowed, and so on. With the help of these simple observations, it's often possible to clarify whether a person was standing, sitting, or lying down when he or she received a certain injury.

To begin with, you mustn't unnecessarily disturb the dead body from the primary position. Sometimes, however, one has to search the dead person's pockets for identification documents, but this must be done with the utmost care, so that nothing is disturbed or can easily be restored to its original position.

After the dead person has been examined, the detailed examination of the site, which is also usually the crime scene, is started. You take it point by point, so that nothing is forgotten, and photograph from all necessary angles. After that, it remains to complete the photography by making sketches of the current location.

Mrs. Johansson's body was taken to the mortuary late at night. According to the pathologist's statement, which came some time later, she had died of a severe blow to the head, in the curve between the back of the head and the neck. The area around the brain stem is a very vulnerable place, and any serious damage in that area can be fatal.

After the pathologist's statement, the unknown perpetrator appeared in an even more eerie light. This was apparently a cold-blooded man, who probably first had beaten his victim senselessly and then brought the body down to the river, perhaps with the intention of getting rid of it in the water. The act took place early on Thursday evening, between 18.00 and 19.30, probably closer to the first-mentioned time.

The terrain between the country road and the river was combed out by police with dogs. A dog handler from the state police was out with his Alsatian dog who was to sniff at the site but without getting weathering so that it was enough for track hunting. Special two-man patrols went from house to house to hear neighbours and others who might have made observations at the time. Three detectives were directed to investigate nearby barns with emphasis on the so-called pole barn in Kungsängen, which is an infamous haunt for vagrants. Two others were sent to the brickyard in Röbo and other similar "heating cabins" which in cold weather are often used by traveling elements. Alarms spread to surrounding police districts along all major highways. In other words, the murder hunt was at full blast.

Ingrid

I have got new furniture for my room. Dad let me choose the furniture myself in the store. Only the bed, the chest drawer, and the mirror are the same as before. Gun-Britt thinks I am a lucky dog who has my own room. She doesn't have that because she shares with her big sis. She says I have nice things.

I have been given a secretaire, a bookshelf, a table and two chairs. And I have got light green curtains with ruffles and a green bedspread. Before I used to have yellow curtains, but Mom took them down because they had become so faded.

When Dad was going to repaper my room, I could choose from a large book with wallpaper in which kind I would like to have. I could get exactly the one I wanted, and then I chose a pink one with red roses on it. So, that wallpaper I have now.

Next to my room is Mom's and Dad's bedroom. I think there should be a door between the rooms and not just a drapery, because Dad is snoring so I can't sleep sometimes. I have to get up and push him so that he stops. Then he is silent for maybe two minutes, but then he starts again. Sometimes I don't want to get up. Instead, I shout to him to be quiet so that he wakes up and stops.

On the wall in my room, I have a painting with a small puppy on it that Dad bought for me when I was two years old, he has told me. I also have a real dog. Her name is Lady, and she is twenty-eight dog years old. It takes seven dog years to equal a human year, and she is four human years.

Before, we also had a cat. We had gotten him from Grandpa. There was a she-cat that had given birth to kittens up on their haymow, and I could choose one and take it with me home. Then I took Murre. Lady and he were friends and playing. But he is gone now.

There was someone who came with Lady to Dad's job and wanted her killed because she couldn't walk. A nasty man had thrown her down a flight of stairs, so she had been paralyzed in her hind legs. But Dad took her home to us. He knew that I wanted a dog, so he took her home and gave her medicine, and after a while she got well and was able to walk and run again.

Lady has a blue tongue, because she is a cross between a Norwegian elkhound and a Chinese spitz. You can also say Chow-Chow. I have taught her some tricks. She can put out a paw nicely and catch a piece of sugar from her nose. If I put a sugar lump on top of her nose and say *now*, she throws it up in the air and catches it, and if I reach out my hand and say *thank you*, she lifts her paw and thanks me. It was dead easy to teach her that.

I collect dog pictures, but I don't know many dog breeds. Before my birthday, I wished for a dog book that all breeds would be in, but I didn't get such a book, so I don't know how to learn about them either. In magazines, there are only pictures of dogs that I already know, or it doesn't say what kind it is. That's potty, I think.

Last year in the autumn, they sent a dog into space from Russia. It was in a rocket called Sputnik. I don't know what happened to that dog later. They couldn't bring it down to earth again, so it probably died. Her name was Laika. I was angry with the Russians then, because I felt so sorry for that dog who had to sit trapped all alone and be afraid just because they had to experiment with rockets.

It's a good thing that I have got a new bookshelf, so that I can find room for all my books. I have so many. It's Dad who buys them for me. I still have all the ones that I have had since I was little. Before, I mostly read about animals, but nowadays I rather read books like the Kitty-books, where there is a girl who solves mysteries, and the Five-books which are about four children and a dog that chases thieves. Kerstin, who I usually am together with at school, likes the Cherry Ames-books best. Those books are about a nurse.

In Mom's and Dad's bookshelf there are books that Mom doesn't allow me to read. One which is called *Naked* and one which is called *The Housewife's Medical Book.* Mom had hidden them behind the other books, but I found them and read them secretly because I was a nosey parker. But there was nothing special in them.

There is quite a lot you have to do in secret when you are a child. Play doctor, for example, because I am not allowed to do that either. Gun-Britt and I hang blankets over their garden table and there under we are. I don't think that there should be books and games that are forbidden for children. Children want to know everything, and then I think they should be allowed to do that. How naked grown-ups look, and how it works when they do a *certain thing*, for instance. When I was little, I thought that those who were married only did it when they wanted children, but they do it all the time because they think it's nice. That's what Gun-Britt says. That's why they must have rubbers, so they don't get too many children.

It's nice in our house, I think. If I am to list all the furniture we have in the living room, it's a couch, a table, two armchairs, a floor lamp, a piano, a radiogramophone, a bookshelf, and a secretaire. In the secretaire, Dad has all his important papers. I arrange them sometimes to get them in order and read the verses on his telegrams.

There are nice pictures on telegrams. The Swedish flag that blows out from a pole, or a newlywed couple sitting in a boat with sails and flower garlands and angels on it, or three large gold crowns with three smaller crowns under them. They look like faces, with eye, eye, nose, mouth. No, they have no nose. And then there is one with red roses on it.

There are several such telegrams, but I don't remember all of them. Dad got them when he turned fifty. Then he had a huge party in town. They photographed everyone who attended the party, and there are seventy-two people in the picture. On some of them, Mom has drawn over their eyes with a ballpoint pen. It's on those she thinks have evil spirits in them.

My name is Aina
and my better half is called Sten.
Our surname is Hallgren.
We have three children who are fifteen, eleven, and four years old.

I didn't meet Eivor so often, because we live at opposite ends of the village, and you don't really give yourself time to… We have been so busy renovating the house that we haven't had time for much else. It's Sten, my husband, who has done most of it. He is a carpenter, so he has both the skill and the knowledge. Of course, we had to hire someone for the electrical work, but otherwise he has done everything himself, with the help of our nearest neighbour. Gunnar's eldest son is admittedly an electrician, but we didn't think we could bother him with such extensive work now that he… Gunnar himself is a postmaster but not at all afraid to go at it. He helped Sten to tear down the old cooker hood in the kitchen and remove the wood stove. The tiled stove in the dining room also went out at the same time. So now I have an electric stove and no longer have to struggle with sooty pots and pans. It's really nice. And I have got a stainless-steel sink. It's so easy to work with if you compare it to the cramped, rusty sink with a wooden bench that I had before, and which I had to cover with oilcloth so that it would withstand the wet. Now I only have oilcloth on the table, which actually is the real meaning of an oilcloth.

Yes, and all the kitchen cupboards are replaced. The old ones looked too miserable, disgraced and worn out as they were. The glass boxes below are very practical and good for storing spices and groceries in. And they are easy to pull out and easy to clean.

We have covered the cardboard roof with Masonite boards, as well as the mirror doors, and we have painted everything with glossy lacquer paint to make it as easy to clean as possible. We have also laid cork mats on the wooden floors in the kitchen and the hall and replaced all interior windows with connected ones. We have got it bright and nice, with white-painted kitchen and pastel-coloured wallpaper in all rooms. It was so dark and gloomy before. The girls' room is in yellow now and Bengt's is in green. For the bedroom, we chose a discreetly patterned wallpaper in grey and white, which gives both a sober and cosy impression. Yes, I can only say that I am very pleased with how it turned out.

It was actually when we saw how nice Signe and Erik had made it that we started thinking about renovating ourselves. Their house was just as worn down and gloomy as ours before Erik had it renovated. So, you could actually say that was what got us started.

We have never been close with Signe and Erik, so I don't really know what has happened, but we know that Signe has been admitted to Ulleråker. There are those who think that it was Eivor's death that became too much for her so she... Yes, people talk, both about Signe and the murder of Eivor, which is the most horrible thing that has ever happened here in the village. But I myself don't know much. Sten and I didn't spend much time with Eivor and Tore either, but in a small place like this, everyone is familiar with everyone, and you know what you know about people anyway. It's not at all like I imagine it is in town, where you may not even know your nearest neighbours.

But Signe and Eivor were good friends, and the girls played and accompanied each other to school. Both were here at

Anita's Knut's party this January. Losing a mother can't be easy for a child. But Gun-Britt was about as usual, I thought. She danced and played and didn't seem particularly sad.

I am thinking about what a horrible Christmas they must have had. It's lucky that Siv is old enough to take care of the household. Because Tore can't handle it, I suppose. He has his job, and so does Siv, so Gun-Britt and Lennart will probably have to do their share as well. Yes, poor children.

And who could have done it? Tore was interrogated and suspected, but I can't believe that it would be him. He has never been violent from what I have heard. People talk and suspect first one, then another. And that's when you get into the questions of right and wrong, good and evil, truth and falsehood. *You shall not lie! The truth above all!* But if you always tell the truth, life will be very hard and merciless. All kindness and all indulgence disappear. No one hides their thoughts, and everyone says their opinion straight out without taking the slightest consideration for others. What a hard and cold world it would be!

But isn't it better to be upright and honest rather than to walk around and hide behind petty lies and distress lies and friendship lies? It's the truth that will save us from evil. That will free us in the end. How else are we going to make a better world?

And is a suppression the same as a lie? If someone, for example, knows or thinks he knows the truth about a certain thing or person, and if it would hurt several but help no one to tell it, wouldn't the truth in that case do more harm than good? And if the task of the truth is to serve the good, must it not in that case be more proper to be silent? If in a particular case you keep silent, or strictly speaking only withholding a circumstance that can create suspicions for no reason at all – isn't it better then to keep what you know to yourself? Talk is silver, but silence is golden, it's said. Or can it, on the contrary, be harmful to withhold knowledge that could prevent the truth from coming out?

Before I decided, I was fighting a difficult battle with myself. What if it was an innocent person I was putting in trouble! But I couldn't get away from the thought, and in the end, I decided to tell the police everything I knew.

The case is, that our nearest neighbour Viola Ekström firmly claims that her son Åke didn't leave home until eight o'clock on the night of the murder, while I can swear that I saw him leave already a quarter past five. I recognize that big car he has so well, and I also saw him clearly through the side window when he backed out. Viola must have made a mistake about the time or even been untruthful because I am absolutely sure of the time. It was a Thursday, and the girls had been sitting and listening to Uncle Sven in the *Children's Mailbox* on the radio for a while, so it was definitely just after five. I was standing at the workbench in the kitchen and looking out the window when Åke backed out his car and drove away. Sten was away and didn't come home until eight o'clock that evening, so I was all alone to see it, but as I said, I was completely sure of my witness.

I haven't mentioned my observation to Viola and would rather not do so either if it can be avoided. Disagreements can easily arise between neighbours, and I don't want to risk that. I hope she will never have to find out that I questioned her honesty by informing the police of what I saw. And the fact that Åke left earlier than she claims doesn't necessarily mean that he is involved in the terrible thing that happened. But right should be right, and now at least the police have got the opportunity to investigate and get to the bottom of it.

Gösta Dahlström, Detective Chief Inspector and Murder Investigator.

Surprisingly many people are hesitant about the police. I mean, there is a preconception that it's unpleasant to turn to us and that you should preferably avoid it. Sometimes we are respected, almost feared, and sometimes you can meet a near hostile attitude towards us. But we are there to serve society. It should be as natural to want to assist us in criminal investigations as it is to want to help a neighbour who has gotten into trouble.

While the crime scene investigation was still ongoing, the reinforced murder commission implemented an extensive "door knocking operation". We walked around to the farms and asked the villagers about any observations that could be associated with the murder. Many were frightened and suspicious and difficult to talk with. There were many questions to be answered, but it was hard to get any more concrete information. Some didn't even open for us when we arrived.

In the beginning, we met dismissive answers everywhere. "We know nothing, we have seen nothing, we have heard nothing." Behind this was obviously fear. The drama of violence had shaken the whole village hugely. Everyone felt great fear. In many cottages one didn't dare to sleep at night. Several villagers fled to relatives in other places.

We have literally had to *draw* information out of people. A big help for us would have been if people had told us everything at once. We needed to know as much as possible about Mrs. Johansson's living habits to be able to map out her last time in life. But instead of helping us, the public has attacked us and only dutifully thrown us small pieces of information.

Our job isn't just to expose a murderer. Equally often, it's a matter of eliminating innocent people who have had suspicions directed at them. At these inspections, we have too often been met with the greatest reluctance. People need to learn to understand that anyone can be involved in a criminal investigation. One mustn't take this as a personal insult.

Eventually we still got some clues. Some could be removed immediately, while others were processed or will be examined as soon as we have time. It's given that some messages are completely worthless, which the informant of course doesn't have the opportunity to decide, since he or she doesn't know all the circumstances. We are therefore still grateful for all tips.

Both based on the public's tips and our own surveys, we have followed a large number of tracks. In many cases, it has been possible to carry out these investigations without the person concerned having been aware of it. In other cases, the designated person has been summoned to the criminal police and given the opportunity to report on his activities on the evening in question. Some have been picked up and been forced to stay with us for several hours while we have checked their information. So far, everyone has been set free again.

It's unfortunate that innocents must be deprived of their liberty in this way, but it has sometimes been absolutely necessary. The suspects have most often realized our strong reasons for the deprivation of liberty and submitted to our actions without complaint.

My name is Viola Ekström and I am a housewife.
My husband's name is Gunnar and he is a postmaster.
Our oldest son is named Åke and he is an electrician.
Our two youngest are of school age and named Ninni and Stig.

One day a man came and knocked on the door and wanted to talk to Åke. He introduced himself as Chief Inspector Dahlström and asked to come in and wait for Åke who was at work but would soon be home. I couldn't understand what a police officer could want from him, but I let him in. He sat for almost an hour waiting. Åke didn't come, and I was completely beside myself and didn't know what to do.

A few days later, two other policemen came and wanted to talk to us. I will never forget how it felt when the police car was outside our house, and I saw how the neighbours curiously peeked out from behind their curtains. I wished I had been able to sink through the earth. Later I understood that they walked around and talked to everyone, but right then it felt like it was just us, and especially Åke, they were interested in.

In a child, there are both good and bad predispositions. If a boy pilfers, he may develop into a thief. If he lies, he may end up as a fraudster. If he fights, it will eventually make him a perpetrator of violence. Good and evil always fight for domination in a child's soul, and it's the task of the parents to stifle the evil tendencies and strengthen the good ones. If this doesn't succeed, it's usually the mother who is designated as the culprit. It's she who, because of her incompetence and spiritual imperfection, turns the child into a bad egg that lacks stature and morality.

As a child, Åke was lively and a little mischievous. He had

a defiant disposition that made us sometimes have to tighten the reins to keep him on the right track. But he always obeyed our will when it really mattered. And as an adult, he has been hardworking and skilled. After school, he trained as an electrician, which is a decent and good profession. He has also done his military service without any problems. And his car and his driving license he has earned through his own work.

He is interested in cars and understands engines so well that he can easily fix problems that have arisen on both his own and Gunnar's car. No major things, that he lacks tools for, but he finds the problems and understands immediately what needs to be done.

It's so horrible that he has been hit by this awful thing of being suspected of having beaten Eivor to death. My husband is a postmaster and an honest and respected man in the village. But what does it help that we are considered honest when our name now has been drawn through the dirt in this way? It doesn't matter much to us, because we are soon old, but what kind of an impact may it have on Åke's future? His good reputation may be ruined forever, though he has never before fallen foul of the law.

And I know he didn't do it. I can swear with a hand on the Bible that it wasn't him. He can simply not have done it! But people obviously think he could do anything. Lie and steal and murder without conscience. It's so awful.

People don't understand what repercussions heartless and unreflective talk can have for the individual. From the beginning it doesn't have to be major things, but then it's enlarged and the consequences for the individual can be fatal. Due to the police's interest in Åke, people in the village targeted serious accusations against him. He had to appear in the newspapers, and through the publicity our whole family was plunged into the abyss. For a couple of weeks, I barely dared to go outside the door. It was as if I could feel the neighbour's piercing, accusing glances coming right through the walls.

From the road you can see straight into our nearest neighbour's house. I usually see Aina sitting in the armchair under the reading lamp in front of the window with her glasses on her nose and studying a newspaper or a book. She suffers from slightly impaired vision, but no worse than she sees reading and also knitting and sewing by the light of the lamp. But now I couldn't bring myself to pass by there anymore, for fear she would see me. Once I ventured out, I took long detours to avoid being seen.

But the worst was for the children. It was Stig who was involved in finding Eivor, and due to that he initially got some positive attention from his friends at school, but when the writings about Åke began, it changed so that he instead was singled out as the brother of "the woman killer". Little Ninni wasn't spared either, with the result that she barely dared to go to school anymore. As we all know, no one is as thoughtlessly cruel as children.

And that the matter got such large proportions was of course due to the gossip, which went like wildfire through the village and was enlarged and distorted more and more with each time it was uttered. It's of utmost importance that the truth is revealed so that there will be an end to all insidious and all unwarranted rumours and suspicions that threaten to ruin not only ours, but also other people's lives. Åke, who more than others has been exposed to suspicion, is still hoping to be completely exonerated by the police finding the culprit. No one accuses him openly anymore, but the suspicions live on and will not cease completely until the murderer has been captured and has confessed.

The atmosphere in the village was at first quite heated. Here and there you could see groups of people standing and discussing the murder mystery. And when it comes to unsolved riddles, where people get no facts to bite into, the gossip only grows stronger and stronger. Many guessed that Eivor had been subjected to nasty violence by an unknown perpetrator. But when the police at a later stage found that she was untouched in that way, they no longer knew what to believe. If it was an act of insanity, the murderer could be in our midst, and who knew then what could happen!

The atmosphere entailed that many people got safer door locks, but also that everyone began to suspect everyone else. And the criticism of the police has unanimously grown stronger with each passing day without any positive news.

I myself don't suspect anyone. I haven't the slightest idea who it might be. And whoever has done it, he is surely unhappy now and wishes that what has been done would be undone.

There is still a lot of talk. If it's not cleared up – shall we go here then, year after year, and look askance at each other and suspect each other? Should innocents have to suffer just because the perpetrator doesn't come forward and confess? No, I don't want it to be like that. Nobody wants that. But there isn't much one can do about it, more than hope that the police will eventually find the culprit.

At the funeral I cried, and so did many others who knew Eivor and who were present at the burial. When the ringing of bells began, the coffin was carried into the church by two of Eivor's brothers and by Erik Lundin, Nils Karlsson, Sten

Hallgren and my husband Gunnar Ekström.

The church choir sang Stenhammar's *Must Even Be of the Thorns* and so followed in unison the hymn *I Go to Death Wherever I Go*, after which the clergyman spoke about Eivor based on the words in Matthew 10:26: *Nothing is hidden, which should not be obvious, and nothing secret which shall not be known.* Yes, we can only hope that this is how it will be!

At the end of his speech, he touched on Eivor's personal preferences, such as her quiet and honest nature. Furthermore, he expressed the disgust that everyone in the district feels against the crime committed and how the feeling of insecurity spreads for each day that the culprit is still free. With Charles the Twelfth's mourning march on the organ, the service was over, and the coffin was carried out to be buried in the family grave.

The great number of flower wreaths gave evidence of how many there were who in their mind followed Eivor to her final rest. Aina was of course there, and Sten, who participated in carrying the coffin, but I didn't see the children. Aina greeted us a little measuredly, I thought, and avoided looking Åke in the eye. But God have mercy, she can't believe that the rumours about him are true, can she? I thought.

In everyday life Aina usually wears a simple intermediate dress or a patterned cleaning coat, but at the funeral she was of course dressed in black. She had also hooked on a white pearl necklace and earrings in the same colour. Dark colours against white are a becoming contrast, and she has long had a passion for that combination, so she probably wouldn't have needed to procure something new for the funeral. Despite the serious situation, I noticed that some of the men glanced a little extra at her. She is very striking and knows how to behave, and that naturally attracted the men's eyes. Well, not only the men's, because I watched her myself, and to my shame I must admit that I felt a little envious of her in the midst of all distress.

Åke Ekström, twenty-three,
son of Gunnar and Viola,
big brother to Ninni and Stig.

As bloody bad as my mother thinks it is that I am one of the suspects, I can't agree with. She exaggerates as usual. And I am not alone in it. The police went hard on Tore as well, I have heard. As long as the murder is unsolved, there is virtually no one who is free from suspicions.

They also wanted to talk to my ex in order to hear her opinion about me. This I have found out afterwards. But I don't give a shit. It's their job to snoop, and you can't say much about it. Someone had seen my car parked down by the pasture the same evening that Eivor was found dead. It's clear that the cops must find out if it was true and what I in that case had to do there. I don't think it's strange. I didn't deny it either since it was true.

And of course, the hack journalists took just that detail as their starting point when they didn't have much to write about in the beginning. A mysterious car that has been seen at the crime scene – that's what sells.

I was there with a chick. Her old man is a grumpy bastard who doesn't like that she hangs out with me, so we usually meet a little in secret. I have been called a slacker, a bad egg, and a bloody *raggare*. And I am a *raggare*, I suppose – or have been – but I am not one of those who booze and fight or drive around in an old jalopy without a driver's license and insurance. I would never do that. The car should be cared for and kept in shape, I think.

I like cars, and especially Yankees. In a movie, Elvis drives around in a white Imperial Crown. Shiny chrome and rocket fins… a car like that you should have. Or a Ford Mercury with fenders and white tyre sides that James Dean had in the picture "Rebel Without a Cause". When he drove himself to death, he went in a Porsche 550 Spyder, which was probably his private car. Too bad for both the guy and the car, you have to say.

Yes, I like cars. Cars, chicks, and rock 'n' roll. Elvis Presley, Jerry Lee Lewis, Chuck Berry, Little Richard… The rock music is big in Sweden today. It was Bill Haley who brought it in when he sang "Rock Around the Clock" in a movie that was shown a couple of years ago.

Among Swedish guys, it's probably Little Gerhard who has gone the furthest. On his twenty-three years, he has achieved a lot. In school, he had bad grades except in singing. Then he worked as an errand boy, a sailor, a bus conductor, and a sheet metal worker before he invested in music. Now he is Sweden's rock king. Strongly done, you have to say.

Well, talking about me and my chick… I picked her up on the road some time after five. Then we sat in the car down by the pasture and listened to records for a while before we took off to town and went to the cinema. When we came back, we saw that something was going on down in the meadow. I drove her home and went back to find out what it was. By my bro and his buddy, who was already there, I was told that they had found Eivor dead. Yes, damn it all.

When the cops came to our house and wanted to talk, I tried to keep my girl out of it, but they got suspicious when I said that I had sat on my tod in the car and listened to music and then gone to the cinema alone. They had a feeling that I was lying, but they drew the wrong conclusions from it. They thought I was telling a whopper to hide that I had killed Eivor and transported her body down to the meadow. When I finally told them about my chick, and they had talked to her as well, they grasped that I had nothing to do with it. But people who are not familiar with it haven't stopped suspecting me and the bullshit continues as before. There isn't much you can do about it. Mother takes it hard, but I don't give a shit. They may keep going until they get tired of it, the old gossipmongers.

Ingrid

We have had a visitor. It was Aunt Lilly who lives in town who came to us. Before, Mom talked a lot to her on the phone. I thought it was boring when she did that. Now she doesn't answer when it rings, so Aunt Lilly comes and visits us instead. But Mom doesn't want to talk with her anyway. I don't know why.

I think it's boring to be an adult. Then you must work and earn money for food and clothes if you are a boy and cook and clean if you are a girl. Some unmarried aunts also have to work. Aunt Lilly is married, but she has no children, so she works anyway, so that she won't be so bored during the day. She is a stenographer in an office or whatever she is.

When Dad gets paid, I count his money sometimes. He gets them on Thursdays in a brown paper bag. On the outside it says how much he has worked that week and how much he gets for it, and as much as it says, it is in the bag. If it happens to be a two-crown coin in it, I get it. But it almost never is. For the most part, I only get small coins. I have a red moneybox that I have gotten from the bank, which I put them in. Then Dad deposits them in my savings book. Only those at the bank have the key to the moneybox, so you can't open it and see how much you have, and you can't get any money out because there is a thing that covers the coin slot when you have put in coins. It's annoying, I think, because sometimes I need some money. But I get it from Mom or Dad if I ask them.

Mom also gets money from Dad. She has them in an empty Rumford-jar in the kitchen cupboard. I don't know what she is buying for that money. Yarn and cleaning coats maybe, or things she needs when she wants to have a perm.

The grown-ups have so much to do all the time. But sometimes they want to participate in parlour games if you nag a little. Previously, Aunt Eivor and Gun-Britt's big sis used to play cards with us sometimes, but now they can't. Aunt Eivor is dead, and Siv hasn't time because she has got so much to do.

My name is Siv Johansson and I am nineteen years old.
My brother's name is Lennart and he is sixteen years old.
My sister's name is Gun-Britt and she is eleven years old.
My father's name is Tore and he is forty-six years old.
My mother's name was Eivor and she was forty-three years old.

The last time I saw Mom was at half past five. It was a Thursday and we had just eaten supper. We got yellow pea soup with pork and pancakes with jam. It was Mom, Dad, Gun-Britt and I who had dinner together that day. Lennart was with a friend in town.

After dinner, Gun-Britt went up to our room and started with her homework. Dad put on his jacket and hat and went out. I didn't know where he was going. I helped Mom to clean the table and tidy up in the kitchen. Then Mom started with the dishes, and I went up to Gun-Britt and lay down on my bed and read.

At half past six Gun-Britt went downstairs, but she immediately came up again and asked if I knew where Mom was. We hadn't heard her go out and she hadn't told me that she was going to. Gun-Britt and I went downstairs again and saw that the egg basket and Mom's torch were not on the shelf in the hall as usual. I had seen it standing there earlier, with the magazine *Hela Världen* in it. Her boots and cardigan were also gone, so we assumed she had gone to the hen house.

We got up again, and just after seven o'clock Dad came home. There was no coffee prepared for him, so he came up to us and asked if we knew where Mom was. We thought it was strange that she hadn't come in again, because she didn't usually stay long in the hen house. Gun-Britt ran out and saw that she wasn't there. Then we searched the whole house and

Dad was looking outside.

Around eight o'clock we heard him come running across the courtyard. He came in and immediately went to the phone and dialled a number. Then he told us that he had found Mom down in the meadow. He said she was injured and needed to go to the hospital. He hadn't understood that she was dead and had called for an ambulance.

I accompanied Dad when he returned to her. We hurried as quickly as we could. He didn't let me go all the way, so I stopped some distance away and saw Stig and Bengt who were also there. I told them that Mom was injured, and that Dad had called for an ambulance. I really wanted to walk up to Mom to see how she was, but Dad stopped me.

When the ambulance arrived, Dad was told that Mom was dead. He told me and said we had to wait for the police. It was the state police in a black radio patrol car that came. I went home then and told Gun-Britt what had happened. We both cried and couldn't believe that Mom was dead. At night we couldn't sleep.

When Dad came home, he felt bad. He had a headache, and at night he started vomiting. I had to run with the potty between the bedroom and the water closet until I was completely exhausted. It's impossible to describe how awful everything was.

Now it's me instead of Mom who takes care of the household at home. Gun-Britt helps sometimes but never Lennart or Dad. It's women's work, both think. And I have the knowledge, since I have gone to domestic science school, but I am not particularly interested in it. I had planned to get a nursing assistant education and eventually move to my own apartment in town, as a couple of my friends have done. But it will probably not come about now. I must keep working as a sales assistant. It's in a haberdasher's shop. I get on well there, but my dream has always been to become a nurse.

I am also interested in needlework. I have crocheted laces for the bed sheets and pillowcases that I save for my dowry and sewn half the monograms in flat stitch – I don't know yet what my surname will be as married – and hemmed and marked towels that I will have in my future home. I haven't met my husband to-be yet, and there is no hurry with it now that I still must stay at home and help Dad and my siblings. Gun-Britt is only eleven years old, and Lennart goes to the secondary school and can't support himself. After graduating, he wants to apply for a workshop job and study engineering at Hermod's correspondence school while he works.

I wonder a lot about who it was that wanted to hurt Mom so badly. Who is the murderer? He must be here in the middle of us. We can't go outside the door without risking bumping into him. Almost everyone in the village agrees that the culprit is a villager. This is how it's reasoned in the families, and everyone is worried and frightened.

I myself was so terribly frightened one day. It was about four o'clock in the afternoon when I went to the earth cellar to fetch potatoes. Then I saw a man standing there holding his head with both hands. He panted and mumbled silently to himself. In the dark, I couldn't distinguish more than that he was big and tall and wore dark clothes. He didn't discover me, but he really scared me, and I thought it might be him who had assaulted Mom. I ran in to Dad, and when I had told him about the man by the cellar, he went out to look, but then he was no longer there.

Police officers have walked around in the village and talked to everyone to find out what people have seen or heard. We haven't been told what has come out of it and the gossip that is going on can't be trusted at all. I told them about the man at the cellar and about the tramp who had been with us twice the same week, begging for food. I was home once and could describe his appearance. The first time, Mom offered him brown beans and pork, and the second time, he got coffee and buns.

He had been a stevedore before he started wandering on the roads, he said. It was a physically demanding profession that had made him strong and resilient. But then he happened to injure one arm during a load work and could no longer carry heavy boxes. But he wanted to work, so he started making steel wire work and became a pedlar instead. He made mousetraps, clothes hangers, whisks, and hooks and went around selling them.

The people in the cottages were mostly decent, he said, at least as soon as they realized that he wasn't a gypsy. The cities were more varied, but he never stayed there long, because he thought the townspeople were more stingy and more suspicious than the people in the countryside. He often used to stick to small roads and take up accommodation in crofts or on smaller farms. There was no point in asking farmers with large holdings for help, because they would always require reciprocal services and wanted help at the slaughter or mowing hay and wearing himself out for nothing. A meal and permission to sleep in the hayloft wasn't even worth a couple of hours of work shovelling manure or chopping firewood, he thought.

Mom and I didn't like him. We didn't buy anything from him and were happy when he finally left. I used to admonish

Mom and say that she shouldn't let in tramps when she was alone at home, but she didn't think it was dangerous and said that you should help those who are worse off than yourself. She trusted people and didn't think badly about others. The ones she didn't like she avoided. She never spoke ill of others and wasn't interested in gossip. No one who knew her could have been angry with her.

I think it was a tramp who killed her.

At first it looked like this murder would be quite easy to solve, but over time it has turned out to be more difficult than we thought. I don't say this for the reason that we haven't yet achieved a positive result, but because we have realized that there are so extraordinarily few clues to follow.

There are three circumstances in particular that can complicate a murder investigation, and that is when the murder was committed in an attic or in a basement, when the house where the murder took place afterwards was burned down and, as in this case, when the murdered person's body is found at a place other than the murder scene. So, it actually looks pretty dark right now. But we don't despair but continue tirelessly and with the usual confidence, even though we know that lots of work is still ahead of us before the goal is reached.

During all murder investigations, all stray strangers who have been observed at the relevant location are first checked at the time essential to the investigation. The police want to know their antecedents, case errand, and alibi. In this case, routine checks in various police districts revealed that a stray vagabond, who had previously been guilty of assaulting women, had been observed in the village at the time of the murder. Some time before, he had been in the village selling his wares. He got overnight accommodation with a farmer. The next day he continued his business and was offered coffee in a cottage. He then spoke of having spent the night with the farmer in question. Then the woman who offered coffee said that that farmer had threatened Johansson and his family. "The whole bundle should be killed," he would have said. The tramp was surprised but didn't think more about the matter until now when he heard about the murder. We took him to the village and asked him to point out the farm where he had spent the night and the cottage where he had had coffee. But no, he couldn't do this at all. By all accounts, he had lied to make himself remarkable, which not infrequently happens in connection with murder investigations.

As soon as a serious crime takes place somewhere in our elongated country, the police routine requires that you should seek comparisons even with previous incidents of the same kind and that you must at the same time check previously registered criminals with similar behavioural patterns. Hospital records and leave records at Ulleråker mental hospital and the State Alcoholic Institution in Venngarn outside Sigtuna have therefore been examined to check whether any patients who are described as dangerous were out on the day and night in question.

To date, a large number of people have also been inspected by the police in other parts of the country and had their activities regarding the night of the murder investigated. Thorough murder investigations bring with them revelations of much else shady that has nothing to do with the case itself. For people who have something to hide, and therefore intentionally stay away, it will of course be extremely unpleasant with these close investigations. The police stir the pot and turn every stone. A lot of fishy insects then emerge, and things that can't stand the daylight can be scrutinized. There is therefore good hope that this clientele will give us valuable tips and information about the murder in order to restore calm and avoid coming under fire themselves.

Ingrid

After the February holidays, we had a ski competition at school. Dad hasn't bought me any ski boots yet, so I had to go in my leather boots. The bindings just came loose all the time. And I am so bad at skiing, so I came last of all. Everyone had to stand and wait until I arrived. I am much better at skating and bobsleigh. Uncle Tore and Gun-Britt's brother have made an ice track down from the woody hillside where we ride bobsleigh sometimes.

At school outside the refectory there is a rather high hillock that we usually play on when it has snowed and is cold. We try to push each other down. And there is ice on it, so it's hard to hold on if someone comes and tries to take you down. Last week, it was a girl in my class who got a blow to the head when she was pushed down from the hillock. It's dead dangerous to get that. During math class, she began to feel unwell and vomited in the washbasin. Our schoolmistress let her clean it herself, even though she had had a concussion. I think that was wrong. I think our mistress should have done it.

It's mostly the big guys who are pushing. I usually hang around the leg of the guy trying to get me down, because then it's harder for him to get me away. They think I am good at holding on. A guy named Sajne once said that. He and his buddy had to help each other with me. One took me under my arms, and one grabbed me by my feet, and then they carried me to the edge and pushed me down. It's fun to be taken by them because they are kind even though they are old. Kerstin thinks Sajne is slimy, but I don't agree.

When we get to school, we first stand in line in the corridor by the clothes hangers. When our schoolmistress comes, she unlocks the door to the classroom so that we can march in. We have the desks together two by two with aisles in between. I sit approximately in the middle both if you count from the side and from behind. I am sitting next to a girl named Kerstin. It's her I am mostly together with at school.

In Ninni's class, in second grade, they don't have to stand up from their desks when they answer, because their mistress thinks that there is so much slamming with the chairs when they get up. But for our mistress, we have to stand up. She is rather strict but kind.

Ninni's mistress is quite fat and has grey-black hair and a topknot. Once, we had her when our teacher was sick. We had a singing lesson, and when we sang she began to cry. It was because it sounded so beautiful, she said. She thought we sang so *adorably* nice and couldn't control herself. But then she got angry at Uffe and walked up to him and stood by his desk and started scolding him. I don't remember what he had done. She shouted so spit splashed on his desk, and then he said rather quietly: "Make use of a towel!" But she heard and *bang* he had got a box on the ear! I don't think that teachers should be allowed to do like that.

There are both strict and kind teachers. Gun-Britt's master, for instance, is very strict. If someone makes trouble or hasn't done his homework in her class, he gets very angry. Then he may have an outburst with rage. One time he hit the pointer against the master's desk so the pointer broke off, and another time he threw a compasses straight out into the classroom so anyone could have been hit by it. They have to sit straight as ramrods during every lesson so as not to annoy him. If we had such a teacher, I would be scared all the time, because I am not used to adults who are shouting and fighting.

We are twenty-eight children in my class. Seventeen girls and eleven boys. Among the girls, there are three that I don't like. The first is Birgitta, who always is stuck-up and thinks that all guys like her. She is a real guy charmer. Then there is one named Inger who is also uppish. She always brags about how much money and clothes she gets from her dad. But the worst one is Monika because she quarrels with Kerstin and me. When I came to class in second grade she was kind, but then she started teasing and carrying on. Kerstin gets very sad when Monika says something nasty, but I don't, because I know that she is just envious. I couldn't care less what she is doing. I usually tell her to belt up.

A good thing about school is that you get pencils and books for free. I have two yellow lead-pencils and a coloured pencil that is red at one end and blue at the other and a green rubber and a ruler. All of them I have gotten at school. And we have received notebooks and a math book and a reading book and a hymn book and a local history book and a Swedish grammar book.

I have a wooden pencil case with a tiny little abacus in the lid. No one else has such a pencil case. I got it as a Christmas present from Dad once. In second grade, when we were photographed, my pencil case can be seen in the photo. It's on the desk that Tommy is sitting behind. He has his hair plastered up with water, so it looks like a brush in the front.

You could almost say that Tommy and I go steady. I don't quite know how we got together from the beginning. I don't remember. But he always sits next to me on the bus and when we are going to watch movies or filmstrips at school. And I have gotten glass marbles from him. I will never give them away. I have them in a transparent plastic jar that is shaped like a heart.

In the bus, we usually sit in the back seat and put a jacket over us, so that the others can't see when we kiss. Once when we were sitting with our mouths connected the bus went down in a bump, and then I got Tommy's teeth against my lip so it started to bleed. Sajne, who is in seventh grade, teased us then. He has remained in a form twice, so he is rather old. He told Tommy that he should take it easy and not kiss so hard or whatever it was. But I don't think he should comment on that, because they say that he and a girl named Marianne have done a certain thing that adults do. If you have the bootlegs folded down, it means that you have done it, and she usually has. But I don't know if it's true.

There are rowdy guys and silly guys and guys who are cowards like milksops, but Tommy is good no matter how you think. I like his manner and his appearance and his clothes. For the most part, he has grey trousers and a green knitted sweater. First a shirt that the collar sticks out from and then the sweater. Outdoors, he has duffel boots or brown shoes with raw rubber soles and a black leather jacket and a green woollen cap with folded edges. Some guys have caps with tassels, but that doesn't look tough, I think.

Another guy in my class named Mats, I think is a bit in love with me, because he looks at me a lot. But he is the kind of boy who would never dare ask a girl to go steady. Only some guys dare to be with girls. Some don't want to, I suppose. A guy named Anders, for instance, doesn't want to, I think. But everyone likes him anyway because he is clever. We call him the Professor. No one teases him about his glasses either, as they do to some others. He plays the clarinet and knows a lot of good stories. During fun hour, he tells such stories. One story he has told was like this: "It was Pelle who came home from school and said to his mom: Today we have learned to make gunpowder. And his mom said: Fine, what are you going to learn in school tomorrow then? What school? Pelle said." Another time Anders said this: "Baker Bengtsson bakes big, burned buns. How many bs are there in that?" Then Uffe said it was six. "No, that's wrong," Anders said, "because there are no bs in that." In the *word* "that" he meant, since he had asked how many bs there are in *that*. Then Uffe was a little taken aback.

*My name is Tore Johansson and I am employed by Anders Diös
construction company in Uppsala.*
My wife's name was Eivor
and our children are named Siv, Lennart, and Gun-Britt.

When I got home around seven o'clock, Eivor was gone. I had
been over to Harald to discuss a fence he wanted help with
and didn't know where she had intended to go.

The girls were looking indoors, and I went out with a torch
and shone around in the garden. Then Stig and Bengt came
running and told me that they had found Eivor down by the
river.

She was lying just inside the gates to the cow-pasture. At
first, I thought she had fallen and broken something. But I
couldn't wake her, and then I understood that she was ill. It
didn't occur to me that she could be dead. But she never used
to be sick. Yes, she was confined to bed with the Asian flu for
a couple of days last year, but otherwise she was mostly in full
vigour.

It came as a shock to hear that she was dead and that it had
also happened through someone else's acting. My thoughts
began to go round and round at once. Who could have done
it and why? Who could it be? Who has this horrible deed on
his conscience?

I myself became a suspect for having done it. I was called
for questioning, and there were many surprising questions
that met me, especially since I, in my nervous zeal to be helpful, got tangled up in it regarding the timeline. In a strange
feeling that the interrogator wasn't satisfied with my answers,
I tried to improve my alibi.

When a suspect – guilty or innocent – starts playing about

with half-truths or lies, it immediately becomes dangerous. For me, this meant that I was admittedly allowed to leave the hearing as a free man, but the suspicions against me remained – and may still do.

Personally, I don't suspect anyone. Who would it be? The assumption that it could be a villager is so incredible that it can hardly be imagined. You don't want to think so badly about your friends and neighbours. It must be someone from the outside.

After a while, the police made a first arrest. An insane man had been seen wandering around in the village since he had managed to sneak out of Ulleråker. But it was mostly a matter of standard procedure on the part of the police. After an act of violence with an unknown perpetrator, it's primarily insane people on leave or on the run, and itinerant vagrants who are controlled. It turned out that the man had a clear alibi and thus could immediately be sorted out as not a suspect. The police investigation revealed that he admittedly had been in the village the same day as Eivor was attacked, but that he in the afternoon and evening had been arrested for drunkenness and assault, since he had attacked a pedestrian on Drottninggatan in Uppsala and then in police custody continued to be threatening to the constables. Lucky enough for him, you must say, because a better alibi he could hardly have.

I don't know how the villagers perceive what happened. Are they still as upset as I am, or do I stand alone with the entire agony now? I have discussed the matter with Hallgren, whom I sometimes come across at work, but he hasn't had much to say. He doesn't want to deal with women's gossip and other idle chatter, he says.

I have had difficulty sleeping and have often been up and sauntering around at night. I have dreamed about Eivor and woke up, and then it has been absolutely impossible to fall asleep again. But I have received support, and everyone asks themselves the same as me: Who is it that has done it?

We don't know yet. We also don't know if the police have found any new clues. We must try to ferret out the very fundamental intention, I think. It's not that easy to find, but it exists, and if we find it, we may also find the murderer.

It's empty without Eivor and if the children didn't exist, I would give up, I think. At the same time, I worry about them and wonder how they will get along in life.

At school, children and young people have no peace. The examination rush, which starts already in the lower grades of school, makes schooling nervous and anxious. Despite everything that has been said and written about the overwork of school youth, and despite all attempts to find new and better methods, the result has been the same: more subjects, more lessons, more study, more effort. It can't be right that young people during the brightest time of life, and the one who should be the most light-hearted, are burdened by the compulsion to store knowledge that they for the most part won't have the slightest benefit of later in life. Gifted and healthy children may suffer the injury unscathed, but those who have a poor health, or are mentally less well-equipped, will certainly have to bear for a long time the consequences of overexertion during school age.

I don't know how to remedy the shortcomings in the upbringing system. The old school had at least the advantage that the plan was simple and that it contained hints of duty to others, of sacrifice, self-control, contentment, and privation. In all this modern experimentation with new attempts and discussions about the future school, there are no clear guidelines. And today's youth is largely no better than the old school product, only more strained, more self-willed, more hard-hearted and, after all, less suited to see for themselves.

It's clear that the school is far from being alone to blame for the current situation; outside school, children no longer live in a more or less secluded childhood world. Nowadays, the "spirit of the times" requires them to go out into life immediately. Already in primary school, they participate in social life, entertainment, travel and to follow the daily press.

If the children also get a glimpse of the more serious aspects of life, and if they participate in homework and family chores, is another thing that of course is very different for different children in different homes. Many children, and mainly the daughters, are forced to work quite hard at home as well and have to bear their fair share of the burdens at home. On the other hand, there are now, as in the past, many spoiled children who are not required to do the least. Later in life you will find them in the deplorable crowd of disappointed, dissatisfied and "misunderstood" ones, because life spares no one and least of all the one who has only learned to demand but never to go without things.

What is at least certain is that the children come too early in contact with adult life. During the school terms, a life of pleasure is added to the schoolwork, and this by no means only applies to children from affluent homes. Everyone tries to the best of their ability to follow the swirl. Dances and invitations are not uncommon even for smaller children. With the exception of jazz, rock 'n' roll and other Negro dances, in which whites only appear grotesque and ugly, dance and music are pleasant phenomena which I don't in the least envy the young people, but it should be practiced in moderation and at a sufficiently mature age.

On the other hand, we elders mustn't forget our own youth when the previous generation lamented over us and found us close to the verge of ruin. And the current so victorious young people, who think they have discovered so many brand-new ideas, will within a few years shake their heads at the succeeding generation, which in turn will find their parents hopelessly old-fashioned and out of date.

Ingrid

At Aunt Beda's and Uncle Harald's home, they have a *telly* in the living room. All who want to can go there and watch it. In front of the telly, they have placed plenty of chairs, and when everyone has sat down, they pull down the blinds so that you can see the viewing screen better.

On Wednesdays, there are no programs on TV, so then we don't go to Harald's, but otherwise we go when there are such programs that we think could be good. It says in the newspaper before what it will be. I usually watch on Saturdays. Programs I have seen are *Lassie*, *Robin Hood*, the *TV Journal*, and some others.

The other day, I went with Dad into Aunt Beda's and Uncle Harald's kitchen. It was very cold outside, but inside their kitchen it was hot so you could sweat to death. They have a black wood stove in the kitchen because they are a bit outdated. In front of it they had put wellingtons and ski boots and hung wet woollen socks to dry so it smelled awful. Uncle Harald sat by the table and had put one foot on a chair, because he has a pain in a toe. It's blue and is rotting, I think. He may have to go to the hospital and chop it off.

They had an ugly cork mat on the floor and a torn oilcloth on the table, and water ran down the windows because it was so hot. But why isn't water flowing on our windows when it's hot inside our house? Maybe it was because of that wood stove they have because we don't have such a stove. We have a boiler in the basement that Dad fires with wood and coke, but upstairs we have an electric stove with an oven. On top it's black and below it's white. It's like a black lid that you can fold up if something has boiled over and slid down there. And on the wall, we have a fan that you can turn on so that the smell of cooking disappears if you for example are frying pork. We have a much nicer kitchen than Aunt Beda and Uncle Harald, I think.

While Dad and the others were talking, I was looking in an old *Allers* magazine. It's so boring when the grown-ups talk because they talk about such boring things. About the social democrats and the peasants' union and other things that I don't know what they are. And they often talk about the weather. "We will see how long the cold lasts," they say. "We had eighteen degrees below zero his morning, what did you have?" I think it gets so humdrum.

Aunt Beda is disabled. She can't hold her head up but must have it always leaned down towards her shoulder, and her arm on that side hangs straight down and can't be moved. She can't do anything with that arm because it's paralyzed.

Uncle Harald is funny when he jokes sometimes. Once when I was cycling past their house and he was out in the garden, he shouted at me: "Hello there, the rear wheel is turning!" At first, I thought there was something wrong with the bike, but he was just kidding. I had stood up on the pedals to curtsy, but then I sat down flop on the saddle again because I was so taken aback.

He is funny, but I don't like being indoors with them. I can only be where they have the telly, because there they don't fire, and there they have no disgusting dishes with old food standing on the table. Old food should be given to the dog or thrown away, I think, because otherwise blow flies will come and sit in it. At least in the summer they do.

If you have a lot of flies indoors, you can put up glue spirals that they get stuck on or spray them with a little DDT. But we don't do that. We kill them with a fly swatter. Mosquitoes are harder to get hold of because they are so small. You can hardly kill a mosquito until it has sat down somewhere and started sucking blood. Then there may be a blood stain there when you smash it to death.

I don't like blood. Stickan says that Aunt Eivor was quite bloody when he and Becke found her in the meadow. I don't know if it's true. He is just going on about how it was when they found her and thinks apparently that he is tough.

Once an aunt we know was hit when she rode her moped. Dad saw her before the ambulance arrived. She was bloody and lay in a ditch and whined. When I think about that, I feel bad. Then the ambulance came and picked her up. I was in school, so I didn't see anything.

When you hear the sirens from an ambulance you know that something terrible has happened and that a human being is lying somewhere and may be dying. Bleeding so all the blood in the body runs out or something like that. It's scary. If I am not home when I hear the ambulance and it gets closer and closer, I am afraid it's on its way to us. The same if I hear fire engines. Then I think it may be our house that has started to burn.

Why must there be so much awfulness? Murders and accidents and fires and wars. However, there is no great risk of war in Sweden because Sweden is neutral. That's good, I think, because otherwise another country might want all the land of Sweden. Norway, for example, might want it, so they could extend their borders to the Baltic Sea.

If Sweden is attacked by someone who doesn't care that it's forbidden, Dad must go and defend it, because he is in the Home Guard. Sometimes he goes on home guard exercises.

In such exercises, they pretend that it's war, and then they practice shooting so that they know how to do it if there should be a war in reality some time. I don't want that to happen.

At school sometimes, some boys draw swastikas and stuff. They had such things in Germany during the World War II. It was like a sign for their party. And when they met, they raised their arm and said *Heil Hitler*. But it's forbidden now.

This autumn, some girls in the sixth grade started doing a forbidden thing. Almost every break they were doing it, and one day Gugge and I thought we would try it too. Because we had seen how they did it, and we didn't know that it was dangerous. Kerstin was also there. We went behind the school building, where you can't be seen from the windows, and so I did it first on Gugge. The one who does it should stand behind the other one and put her hands on her ribs, and so the other one should take a deep breath and hold her breath, and then the one behind should press hard with her hands until the other one faints.

And it worked. When I pressed Gugge, she became heavy and fell to the ground. Then it took a while before she awoke and sat up.

But it's forbidden now. The headmaster said it in the loudspeakers, so that everyone would hear. It can be dangerous for the heart, he said. So, then we didn't do it anymore. Not me anyway. Imagine if Gugge had died when I did it on her! What if her heart had stopped so she hadn't woken up again. Then I would have been a murderer now, much like the one who killed Aunt Eivor.

My name is Harald
and my wife is called Beda.
The family name is Karlsson.
The scions are named Nils, Stina, Lisen, Gustav, and Greta.

Yes, Tore was here, he surely was, the night Eivor died. He arrived before six and stayed for about half an hour. Exactly to the minute I can't say. One wouldn't have to give the murder a thought if it weren't for the widow Westman's malignant gossip. She hasn't said it outright, but through hints she has made it clear that she believes that it's Nils who has killed Eivor. And for what reason would he have done that if one may ask? He and Eivor had no dealings with each other. What motive would he have had? It's without rhyme or reason. But the old woman has started the rumour, and he can't defend himself against it no matter how much alibi he can present. She has decided that it's he, and people in the village listen to her. Many put her up on a pedestal, which is completely incomprehensible. With the best will in the world, I can see nothing but a frail old crone, who doesn't even smell clean.

If she had at least an ounce of sense in her limited nut. Like all of her kind, she finds it easy to speak, but I have never found the slightest value or the slightest logic in her reasoning. Twaddle, I would call it. She tells long stories that are supposed to represent truth, but that one doesn't know if one can believe in or not. Expands on things far and wide and makes people listen. Surrounds herself with a kind of wilful wisdom and thinks she has the right to point out the ways for others, even though she hasn't the least to do with other people's circumstances. Rebukes and says as she thinks without a thought of the consequences. It's a pain to know how almost everyone in the village listens to her talk as if it were profound and meaningful. Sometimes one is tormented by the mere thought of it. Would she be a wise woman? Like hell she is! Wisdom is obtained from God's own words, in the Book of Books, if one bothers to read and acquaint oneself with it.

And what can one learn from these words? Well, that dutifulness and uprightness bring prosperity. The defeat comes from other things. God intervenes where needed. One may not understand why he does what he does, but one can trust that he will let one's sins find one out. And it's he who decides when one's time is up. No living person can make a difference in that matter.

One may wonder what the widow Westman has to live for. She owns virtually nothing. The rest of us have something, some a little less but still enough, but what does she have? What has she left other than ailments and hunger? It's obvious that she rarely or never eats enough. But she is probably meant to have it that way. The Almighty pays everyone according to merit. Sure, it's a shame about the old crone, but one must always see clearly and not let the sentimentality drag away with the sense. One who spreads false rumours and slanders innocent people deserves no mercy, I think.

It must be revenge she is looking for. It was her son Axel who knocked Stina up the first time, but he denied it and disappeared. When we brought it up for discussion with Olga, she thought we were trying to input something to him that he was innocent of and turned a deaf ear to it. And that the matter came out and gave him a bad reputation, she thought was due to us. So that's probably what's behind her wanting to put Nils away now. To get even with him. But in contrast to Axel, Nils is completely innocent.

Yes, Tore was here, and we were sitting at the kitchen table talking. When he started expanding on things as usual, I tried to offer him a glass of strong spirits in order to lighten it up a bit, but he declined. He wouldn't last long, he said. He isn't addicted to it either, as far as I know.

I myself have a stock of alcohol at home all the time now when one doesn't have to think about the ration book anymore. The government had to kiss the rod anyway and admit the failure. As the only country in the world, Sweden tried to get rid of drinking through rationing. They thought it would be possible to legislate away the abuse. But in the end, they had to realize that the rationing had no effect on the general state of sobriety and that it was pointless to keep the ration book.

It's this bloody toe that makes me have to take a stiffener sometimes. It has got gangrene in it. The big toe is bluish red and swollen and has wounds that run and smell like shit. The doctors say they may have to amputate. So far, I can manage with covers with Burrow's solution and to sit high with the foot, but only the devil knows how much longer.

And nothing gets done. It gets on one's nerves to just sit indoors and stare. And this business with Olga and her false accusations doesn't make things better. One wishes that the bloody witch could fly away to the Brocken, so one got rid of her once and for all.

My name is Olga Westman and I have one year to go until my seventieth birthday.
I am a widow of Anton Westman who is the father of my two children.

If I have incidentally stated that I don't suspect anyone, it's not to say that I don't. I have thought this through, and I have selected one. But it's not my method to express a person's name on mere suspicion. And if anyone wants to believe that the act happened by accident, I am of a different opinion. The one who guided the steps of that man was one with a tail and hooves. Satan it was, and no one else! And it's him we fight when we try to get to the bottom of this.

And we will fight and go to the bottom! If the police don't sort it out, we will do it ourselves. First, we will pillory the villain, and then we will show him the way from here. You have the right to make certain demands on people. We don't want thieves, bandits, and murderers here in the village!

It's a great disappointment that in the midst of us there is such a vile and deeply sunken man. It has grabbed me so I am grieved right into the soul. Now I see that behind the fine facade lurked a wretchedness without limit. If I had the sinner in front of me, I would look right through him and then completely still turn my back. For what has happened first and foremost? Yes, that the word of God is violated. You shall not kill!

The villagers have at first, out of solidarity, refused to acknowledge the painful thought that the perpetrator is one of us. Only eventually, and extremely reluctantly, have the facts been accepted. The murderer and his terrible deed are found among the faithful servants of God! I was extremely upset when I finally understood who it was that must have committed the wicked deed. I was at my wits' end. And he couldn't have done it for nothing. No. He must have been driven to it by evil forces. Satan has used his most powerful weapon against God's chosen. No Christian has developed it himself, nor has the Lord sent it. No, it comes straight from the caves of hell!

And what personal reasons drove him so ruthlessly? Yes, that's what we are going to find out. The murderer must appear, and he will have his punishment and be forced to do penance!

I lie in the evenings and remember what it was like when I was a child. How come? I remember it as if it were yesterday. Imagine that she and I are the same person. I who is lying here now, am the same person as that skinny little girl sixty years ago!

I remember one day when it was snowing terribly outside, just like it does today. I and my younger brother, who was eight years old, were going to school. It was over two and a half kilometres there and then we would still take a shortcut through the forest. Otherwise, it was more than twice as far to go.

Mother sent with us a little more food than usual and asked us to be careful and not sit down in the snow and rest on the road. The snow fell in dense flakes and made the footpaths in the forest almost invisible. They only appeared as narrow hollows in the rest of the snow, that soft and white lay above the ground as far as the eye could reach. The air was full of flakes, and we had to incessantly wipe our eyes with our woollen mittens to be able to see.

And it was hard to walk. The snow went over the ankles,

and under the snow it was treacherously slippery so we repeatedly lost our foothold. But we plodded along with the books in the bag, which we took turns carrying, and panted so we couldn't get a word out. At last, my brother was so tired that he stopped. "We have to move forward," I said. "Miss will get so angry if we come late." I asked him so nicely that he would move on and finally he agreed so we could continue.

The schoolroom was large and desolate with long rows of desks and maps and posters with plants and animals on the walls. At one short side stood the teacher's table, and behind it sat a large blackboard. There was a fire in the tiled stove, but it didn't help much against the cold. We were not used to better and didn't complain, but probably it would have been more advantageous if we had been less wet on our feet when we arrived.

And the hours passed. After the catechesis it might have been arithmetic, and after the arithmetic, we had handwriting for an hour, while the teacher lit a fire and took care of it. Then there was a dinner break with following geography and reading from a book before it was time to go home.

It was still snowing out there. In the forest there was no beaten track and no traces of people who had made their way there before us. But we knew how to go and set off. It was already dark, a little lighter out on the plain but in the forest it was dark, and it got darker the further in we came. My brother took a hard hold of my hand, frightening and dark as it was, but we had gone this way many times before and would certainly find our way home.

But it was snowing and cold, and it hurt terribly in our feet that had become stiff because the socks had been on wet. In addition, we got so terribly tired of lifting our feet high for every step we took in the deep snow. My brother wanted to go into a cottage where a light shone, but I held his hand and continued forward. "We are home soon now," I said. But there was probably a good bit left.

And the snow fell more and more densely. Suddenly I no longer knew where we were. The path wasn't visible, and I didn't recognize any of the trees. I was seized by fear and thought: If we get so tired that we must sit down in the snow to rest, maybe we fall asleep and then we will never wake up again. My brother noticed my anxiety and started crying. He had so much pain in his feet that he couldn't take another step, he said. I had pain too, but I wasn't allowed to cry. I, who was the eldest, must calm down and comfort the one who was younger. I felt so alone, and such a heavy sense of responsibility came over me, because now I knew it was entirely up to me if we were to arrive safely home.

I trotted on and talked to keep my brother in good courage. My hands and feet ached, and I could have screamed for fear that he would sit down in the snow and not be able to move on. I talked about school and the teacher, and the country squire's children, and the evening meal that Mother was waiting with at home. But how would I find home? My brother cried more and more violently, and his cheeks stung from the tears and snow that he desperately tried to wipe away with his soaked mittens.

I don't know how long we were lost, but it felt like an eternity. When I finally saw light through the snowfall, we were completely exhausted and at first, I didn't dare to believe that we were saved. But when we entered the courtyard and I didn't have to be afraid anymore, I couldn't keep the crying away any longer. I cried with such heavy, violent sobs that my brother became frightened. And when we came in and Mother asked why I was crying, I couldn't answer. And then I cried again in the chimney-corner where I stood warming my hands while Mother cooked the porridge and my brother, who was playing with the cat on the floor, already seemed to have forgotten all the hardships. Even when I had eaten and was going to read my homework for the next day, the sobs remained in my throat. Not until I had gone to bed and Mother came to tuck me up did I calm down again. So long did it take for the anxiety and excitement to let go of me.

Oh, my Lord! Imagine that I remember everything so well. It's peculiar, isn't it? It's like it was yesterday.

It's the memories I have left to live on now, both the bad ones and the good ones. They fly around like anxious birds and give me no peace. Many are about Anton, who I married. About himself, he said: "I'm just a gypsy. I'm shit, I'm nothing!" He wasn't exactly evil, but he had no peace in his body. It was a shame because he was handy and knew all the tricks. When he drank, he fought and quarrelled, but in a way, I liked him anyway, strange as it may sound. He shouted and swore, and God help me if there was no food on the table! For long times, we were without it, and that he took out on his spouse.

I tolerated almost everything – I even let him remove it from me a couple of times when I was expecting. He didn't like the cries of infants and could handle such things. Oh, how awful! In the end, it was maybe a little too much, because I became wimpy and started listening to voices.

But everything eventually sorted itself out. Anton went through the ice, and I was left alone with the children and regained my sanity of pure necessity. I tied brooms of birch twigs and went around selling them, and that was what we supported ourselves on. When the children got older, they could contribute to their own livelihood, so we had nothing to complain of.

My name is Beda Karlsson.
I am married to Harald
and we have five children whereof the eldest, Nils, lives here in the
village with his family.

To that extent, it's a pity about Olga that she has had both drunkenness and crime in her family. Anton, her husband, was a notorious beer drunkard who seldom or never had done a stroke of work. He was in prison a couple of times for bootlegging liquor, if it wasn't even for home distilling. And his son Axel was a shady figure who appeared and disappeared again without anyone knowing where he used to be or what he was up to. The only thing you knew for sure was that he was a waster. He was probably not as violent as his father, but he was an idler without a steady job and had a score to settle with the police as well, as was rumoured. He had probably started distilling liquor. He followed in his father's footsteps more and more, even though the gaffer had been dead and buried for a long time, but Olga refused to acknowledge it.

And now she has attacked Nils. It's old grudges that lie beneath, we think. She wants to denigrate him to get revenge. But how she can suspect Nils of the murder is more than we understand. It's downright preposterous. He who is so peaceful! He wouldn't have been able to do it even if he had wanted to. And why would he have wanted to? He has never had any conflicts with Tore and Eivor. But the gossip doesn't take such circumstances into account.

When Eivor died, Tore was here, so it can't be he who has done it either. There are those who believe that, but it's absolutely impossible. He was sitting here at the kitchen table with Harald when it happened. I understand that some may think that his behaviour that night was strange. His silence and fear aroused suspicions. But we who know him know that he hasn't had his hand in this. How can anyone believe he is lying? He has always been an honest and upright man. That night he was so frightened, I have heard, that he couldn't stand on his feet but sank to his knees next to Eivor. But he has always told the truth, and he does so now as well.

And he has always been on good terms with everyone in the village. He has never said a bad word to anyone. He is an honest and hardworking man who has always taken care of his family. Seen in that light, his fate seems so much worse, I think.

Harald and I haven't spent much time with Tore and Eivor. It's probably Erik and Signe who mostly have done so.

Yes, Signe... You really don't know what to say. She who has always been so lively and happy! How is she now? Is she better? I wonder. And the girl child... Yes, it's not that easy for Erik either, but the poor girl has been ill and is perhaps still weak. She was in the sanatorium, wasn't she? Yes. It might have been too much for Signe to have her away for so long. Although it's been a while now, so it may not have anything to do with it. You can't really know, and it doesn't concern me.

For us, it's Olga and her accusations against Nils that are our biggest concern. If we could only, on some conditions whatever, get her to stop talking, there would be some way out later. But to go there and say that we all already know that it's she who is behind it, and get her to admit and explain, goes against the grain for us. If only she could persuade herself to say it on her own and promise to take it back! Then we could just say that we understood her and that she was still the same person for us. Of course, that wouldn't be really true, but I wouldn't hesitate to show understanding and forgiveness if it led to her ending up slandering Nils. Harald takes it harder than he wants to admit, and now with his foot on top of everything else he has all the time in the world to sit and ponder.

It's so wonderful when it's Easter. Then you have eggs and twigs with coloured feathers in, and you put up tapestries with chickens and daffodils on them and eat good food and drink Easter must.

Gun-Britt and I dressed up for Easter witches and went out to get candy and money. We each had a broom with a coffee pot in front where they could put in what they wanted to give. From an aunt we were given Nickel, which is a sort of hard, square candies with fruit flavour that are very tasty. And we also got raspberry jellies. Virgin breasts Mom calls them, but that's not their name, I think. Maybe in her time they were called that. I don't know.

At Easter, Aunt Vera always comes to us. She lives in Stockholm, but she usually comes to us at Christmas and Easter and when Dad has his holiday. Sometimes she sends me cards. It's fun to get cards, I think.

This Easter, she brought me a big Easter egg. Half was lilac and half was silver coloured, and there was a large pink bow on top of it. Inside it was full of sweets. There were punch buttons and those eggs that have something disgusting in them. I gave the eggs to Lady, and she ate them.

Before, there were quite a few who came and visited us, but now Mom only allows Aunt Vera and Aunt Lilly to come. She thinks everyone else is stupid. Dad must go away if he wants to meet others. A while ago, I went with him to some who have a farm. Their names are Aunt Svea and Uncle Evert. It was rather disgusting there because it was so dirty. In the hall there were boots with dung on them and in the kitchen, there was smell of cooking and grease on the stove. The rag rug in front of the sink was tore and the cat's milk bowl was full of dead flies.

We were to drink coffee and eat wheat buns and soft gingerbread cake. They didn't ask me if I wanted fruit drink. I can drink coffee, but I want cream in it, because otherwise it tastes so bitter. But I didn't get any cream from them. And the bun came apart when I dipped it in the coffee. I had to pick up the pieces with my spoon. Then I burned my tongue when I was going to eat it. And there was sticky stuff on the oilcloth where I sat that looked like snot.

Aunt Svea poured her coffee on the small saucer and sipped it from the edge. Mom also does like that sometimes when she thinks the coffee is too hot. And she drinks it with a lump of sugar in her mouth.

When I was done, I thanked them and told Dad that I wanted to go out. But when I was about to slip past Uncle Evert, he grabbed me by the waist and lifted me up on his lap. "I think the girl has grown," he said. It was uncomfortable to sit there, and he had such hard hands. They were dirty too. After a while he put them up under my arms and was going to lift me down, I thought, but he didn't. He just sat there with his hands while they talked. I tried to wiggle away, and when Aunt Svea saw it, she said: "Let the girl go now." Then I finally got to come down.

I didn't like being with them. Only when we were in the cowhouse watching the sucking pigs, I thought it was fun. They were so cute. But Uncle Evert said that some sows bite their piglets to death or lie down on them, so they suffocate. I wonder why they do that.

Dad works at a place called SGS where they slaughter animals. First the pig truck goes around to the farms and picks

85

up pigs to be slaughtered, then they come to Dad's job. I have heard the pigs screaming when they are inside the pig truck. They feel that something dangerous is going to happen. But they must be killed, because otherwise we won't get meat for food.

Sometimes Dad helps Uncle Lindberg, who owns a farm, to slaughter pigs. I think it's disgusting. First, they hit the pig in the head with a club on which there is a sharp spike, so that the spike goes into the pig's brain and he is stunned. Then they throw him into a large tub of boiling water so that they can blanche off all the hairs on his body. Then they hang him up and run a knife into his throat so that all the blood rushes out, and then he is finally dead. Several times I have heard the pig scream when they slaughter him.

I don't understand how Dad can do that to animals. He may think he must, so that no men will think he is weak. He has also killed puppies and new-born kittens. I feel most sorry for the kittens because you put them in a sack with stones and throw them into the river. They hold their breath and try to get out, but they can't, and in the end, they must breathe and get water in them and die. It's so awful. It's not as awful with a pig, I think.

But Dad doesn't slaughter animals when he is at work. I don't really know what he is doing there. Running a machine, I think.

When dad comes home, he washes himself. He is standing in his undershirt at the washbasin, splashing on water. Then he wipes himself with a sack towel. He must have such a towel so that he doesn't soil all the white towels so much.

When he has finished washing, we eat. My favourite dish is potato cakes with lingonberries, but meatballs and small pancakes with sugar on them are also good. Boiled potatoes are boring, but you have to have them for meat and fish.

After dinner, Dad lies down on the couch and reads the newspaper. He is tired after working all day and needs to recover a bit. Then he goes out and mows the lawn or shovels snow or whatever he does. Sometimes he cuts wood with the circular saw, so it jars upon one's ears. After that he comes in and drinks coffee and listens to the news. Then it's almost evening.

Before we had a car, Dad rode his bike to work. In the winter, he had to get up at four o'clock and put firewood in the stove and shovel snow before he cycled away. He left at five o'clock and arrived at six o'clock. Then he worked all day, and after work he cycled into town and bought food if needed. He had the food in a cardboard box on the package holder. Sometimes when there was a snowstorm and the road had been blocked by drifting snow, Mom and I were a little worried when we waited for him to come. Then Mom used to sing *Daddy come home, I know something you will get.* When he finally arrived, he had ice on his eyebrows and in his nose and snow on his hat and coat. But now he drives his car to work and doesn't have to be so icy when it's winter and cold outside.

My name is Erik Lundin and I am a melting worker.
My wife's name is Signe
and our daughter is named Ingrid.

Yes, the police were here talking to us. Signe had been in-doors all evening, and I could affirm that, so they let her go when she withdrew and didn't want to answer any questions. She never goes out nowadays other than to the earth cellar or the potato field.

She has got the idea that she is a suspect and that people talk badly about her in the village. Eivor and she have seen each other all these years and met every week. Eivor came over with eggs, which Signe bought from her, and Signe offered coffee. She herself seldom went over to Eivor, but sometimes that happened too.

Then they fell out and Signe didn't want to meet Eivor any-more. I don't know at all what it was about. I think Signe had started to get sick already then and imagined things that hadn't happened. Otherwise, I don't understand why she would suddenly become so unfavourably disposed towards Eivor.

And now Eivor is dead. But I don't think that people in the village suspect that it's Signe who has killed her. She is just imagining it. People talk, and there are probably those who think that it's a villager, but that it would be a woman, no one believes. For my own part, I believe that it must be an out-sider. No one I am familiar with can I suspect of having done such a thing.

I had to tell the police in detail what I had been busy with when it happened. It was pure routine and applied to everyone.

I came home at half past four as usual, and then we had dinner. Signe had baked small pancakes and cooked vegetable soup with dumplings, I remember. Ingrid had been out playing. After dinner I read the newspaper and rested on the couch for a while. At six o'clock I went down to the basement and looked after the stove and chopped some firewood. When I got up again, we had evening coffee and listened to the news.

Yes, then we saw that there were cars driving down to the pasture, but that was later, when we were about to go to bed. We always go to bed early because I have to get up early. We didn't find out what had happened until the next day. It was Tore himself who called and told me.

After Eivor's decease, he has acted as dutifully as usual and in every way tried to help the police find the culprit. He has given them valuable clues, and he has done so not only because of his grief for Eivor but also for the reason that he wants to assist society.

People in the village have done their best to put rumours in circulation, and at first it was Tore that most of the gossip voices were directed against. There are those who have a little difficulty accepting him and think he makes himself remarkable by having opinions and larding his speech with sophisticated words. That was probably why they threw suspicion on him. For my own part, I have never had anything against him. He has a steady mood and never talks badly about people, and that he would try to make himself superior to others through what he says I don't agree with. He is familiar with things and has definite opinions on most matters, and there is nothing wrong with that. It's just the way he is. One should not judge a person just because he can express himself and is interested in following what is happening in society. That's wrong, I think.

And why would he wish Eivor any harm? Well, it was rumoured that a serious schism had arisen between them, and that Tore had threatened her with death. When people don't know what to believe, they can come up with just anything.

Tore is a decent and upright man who is liked by most people, and in his workplace at Diös he is considered a knowledgeable professional. In the workplace, it has probably happened that he has spoken out sharply at some point when he has felt unfairly treated. As a knowledgeable professional, he knows his rights and doesn't allow himself to be ignored. But he has never been hot-tempered, and that he would have lost his head and beaten Eivor is the last thing I can believe.

Among those who live here in the village, it's probably only Lindberg's farmhand who is known for being hot-tempered – and Göte himself, possibly. But those two had knowingly nothing to do with Eivor.

My name is Jan-Olof Bodén and I am twenty-four years old.
I am a farmhand on Göte Lindberg's farm.

They came and picked me up at the farm, they did. I didn't know what it was about, but I had nothing to hide and followed along and was as happy and nice as I could be in the car on the way there. At first, they didn't say anything, but when we arrived, they said it, and then I understood at once. No, come off it! I thought. How the hell am I supposed to get out of this?

Yes, I just had to stick to the truth, and they had no evidence or anything. They wanted to know what I had been up to the evening when the aunt was killed. I said as it was, that I had been home alone. I don't know if they believed me, but it was the plain truth I told them.

There were three people who interrogated me. They said I was known for drinking and fighting. Notorious, they said I was. But that was mostly when I was younger. Then I was an ace at being lazy. I was too stupid then. I remember one night when there was a revel with a farmhand on another farm. He had managed to get hold of a litre of strong spirits from someone who wasn't so careful about it. He had paid double but offered it anyway. No sheriff came there, and you didn't get sick from it. Should it be so it should be. You forgot your worries and it became warm and nice in the body.

We amused ourselves with shameless ladies, we did. But they are all so unattainable. When you get hot and want to come, they refuse. First, they attract and then they deny. Damn, fucking ladies! They just deny and deny. Because you are not good enough, not beautiful enough, can't do well enough, don't know how to seduce.

I'll fucking show them. They shouldn't think that they rule over me. They shouldn't get out of it. I'll take the wind out of them and force them to give me what I have the right to have. They have no right to deny me when they don't deny others. They should give me what feels most urgent of all. That which almost blows one up if it doesn't get an outlet.

I often think so. Everyone else get it but not me. You hear one wild story after another. Everyone competes to be the one who has had the most experiences. Brag and bluster, they do. But women who let everyone take them they despise. Those smashers are called sluts and whores. But not even from one like that I get it.

I have muscles and am coarser built than most and a head taller than others, I am. I am stronger than most others and can beat whoever I want. When I am out dancing, I grab an arm or a shoulder and squeeze. When they get angry, I hold up my fists and ask if we should fight. In battles, I have power in my blows and win easily. I am a devil at fighting and get everyone's eyes on me. I am a ruffian who is known everywhere. Hated by the old women and despised by the old men I am.

An oldster stood up to me once. I stretched out my arms and tried to get hold of him, but he pushed my arms away and walked a few steps back. With a leap I threw myself over him and gave him a hard blow on the chin. We bashed each other so we lost our balance and fell into a ditch. I came at the bottom but quickly turned around, so that I ended up on

92

top. We started wrestling. I took a hard hold of his hair. A pair of my fingers came close to his eyes. He tried to push my hand away. When that didn't work, he seized me by the throat. I punched him on the head until he let go. It took properly. He walked around with a wrapped skull for quite a long time afterwards.

Those who interrogated me said that I could leave if I confessed. I had nothing to do with it, but I wanted to go home, so finally I said it was me just to get out of there. It wasn't me, but everyone believed it, although I took it back when they didn't let me go. It was spread that I had confessed. It was lucky for me that Göte, my master, went to the police and said that he had seen me through the window to the farm-hand's quarters when he passed by outside. Otherwise, they wouldn't have believed me when I told the truth. Göte is a tough bastard, but he is fair, and he told the truth, so then they had to let me go.

But people still think it was me. I almost thought so myself for a while when I imagined it. They claim that Göte lied for my sake because he didn't want to lose a good farmhand. But that wasn't the case. It was the truth he said.

I am in a bad way now. Sometimes I think I can go nature in advance if it gets into a tight corner. If I feel that life is becoming unbearable, I can probably do it, because I don't want to live like this under any conditions whatsoever. Imagine how nice it would be to rest from the hardships of life. And I think of my parents, who are both dead. If I die too, then maybe, if there is a life after this, I will meet them in a better and rarer world.

The anxiety and the indignation among the villagers grew stronger with each passing day without us being able to report results. "You are looking for a tramp, when you should instead search among the villagers," we were told. That's how it was said among the people who positively placed a farmhand in the role of the culprit. The designated person had behaved so strangely after the murder that the villagers began to whisper behind his back. Some had also seen blood on his clothes. We summoned him for questioning and conducted a house search. Unfortunately, the man couldn't state what he had been up to during the night of the murder. Possibly he had been alone in his cabin or been out on errands. He couldn't provide a more credible alibi for the day of the murder. He didn't remember. In addition, during the interrogations he left no less than four different versions of his activities. His statements were confusing and contradictory, and it was impossible to get a grip of him. It's possible that these many alibi variants were due to memory errors, but it didn't exactly help to dispel suspicions.

Blood on a found jacket further increased the suspicions. You must of course have probable causes for the suspect's guilt before you dare to take action. It's not enough if the reasons convince me personally that we have found the culprit. The reasons must also meet all legal requirements. Undeniably, there was much that indicated that this man wasn't unfamiliar with the tragedy in the village. Several of the answers he gave to our questions were extremely remarkable. On the other hand, it was impossible to establish a truly thorough interrogation with him. Just as he was answering fairly neatly and satisfactorily, he began to waffle about completely different things, and then we couldn't get any further with him. He sometimes left adequate answers but revealed a certain degree of naivety paired with a trait of self-assertion. Over his whole being lay a carefree cheerfulness that contrasted sharply with the situation he was in. His peculiar behaviour during the interrogations and his contradictory information about what he had been up to at the critical time, however, suggested that he had something to hide.

When we had talked through his activities during the day and evening, I had a feeling that something was wrong, and since he couldn't explain in detail what he had been doing, I told him that he was suspected of Mrs. Johansson's death. He emphatically denied this, but the prosecutor on duty declared him arrested. When he entered the cell where he was to stay for a while, he had to undress and put on other clothes that we had provided for him. We sent his own clothes to the forensic technicians for investigation. No one was probably particularly surprised when the gossip started circulating about the designated farmhand.

The next day there was a more in-depth interrogation with him, and then he confessed. I considered that his confession was probably in line with the real situation, but that it couldn't be entirely ruled out that his account had no real basis and was due to his deviant state of mind. As an interrogator, you must always be on your guard against the suspect and especially when assessing the words of an insane person.

The confession he made came spontaneously and was delivered during two interrogations which were more in the form of informal conversations. I was constantly on my guard because false confessions occur sometimes when it comes to serious crimes that have attracted attention.

I never put any answers in his mouth. For example, he described the murder weapon completely without my participation. But since I the whole time thought it was possible that he had taken the blame for the crime, I always asked the questions so that they could never be answered with only yes or no.

We released the suspect after five days of arrest and several hours of interrogation. It felt a little uncomfortable when it turned out that he was innocent. But an official interrogation had been necessary from the beginning, and I don't think he took offence. His last words to me were: "Good to have it done. Now I can return to the village without being suspected anymore." He initially made a very unsympathetic impression on me. I thought he behaved banteringly. But eventually I came to terms with him, and when we parted, I had to some extent changed my mind.

Ingrid

It's spring now and that's so wonderful, I think. The sun is shining, and the birds are chirping, and almost all the snow is gone.

Near where we live, there is an S-curve on the road. There it always floods in the spring. It's the snow in the forest that melts and flows down. And then, when a car comes and goes through it at full speed, the water sprays up higher than the car. It's fun to watch.

Once there has been a car accident in the S-curve. It was one who drove too fast and didn't have time to take the bend. The car continued straight ahead and down into the ditch. Then it overturned and ended up on its roof in the field. When Uncle Tore got there, it wasn't possible to open the doors, so he smashed a window through which they could crawl out. They were able to do that because they were only slightly injured. But I thought it was scary when you heard the thump and saw the car lying upside down in the field with dust swirling around it.

I have been sick. I have had a fever and a sore throat and have been home from school.

When you are not allowed to go out, it's so boring, I think. Especially when the weather is nice it's boring to be indoors. But if you have a fever, you may not even have the strength to be out of bed.

Most of the time when I have to stay in bed, I read. If I can sit up, I might take a tray and do a jig-saw puzzle, or I draw or write in my diary. If you don't know what to draw, you can take a greaseproof paper and put it over a picture in a news-paper and copy it. And you can cut pictures from newspapers and paste them into a book.

When I am sick, it's mostly because I have a cold. I may have been out thinly dressed and gotten cold. Then I get snotty and stuffy in the nose and get thick tonsils. Mom lubricates me with a little Vicks so it should be easier for me to breathe. An aunt, who Mom knows, got her tonsils as big as chicken eggs. She could hardly breathe then, and I am a little afraid that this is going to happen to me as well when I have a sore throat.

When you have a fever, you become rosy and hot as a stove. Once when Mom took my temperature, it was forty and three. If you get over forty-two, you die. Although it's more dangerous for grown-ups than for children to have a fever.

I wish there were no diseases. Some can't be cured, and if you get such a disease you can die. Uncle Henry did, by a disease named cancer.

When I was six years old, I got a disease called tuberous rose. Then I had to stay in the sanatorium. But that disease isn't life-threatening. I missed first grade, because I got sick before I was to start there.

When I was in the hospital, I had some textbooks to write and count in, so that I could keep up. Everyone in the class made drawings for me and wrote letters even though they didn't know me. But I belonged to their class even though I didn't start there at the same time as them.

When I got home from the hospital, I had to take a medicine and go for check-ups at the dispensary. I still do that.

Then you must first be weighed. Then they take blood samples and X-ray pictures. The blood samples they take from your arm. First, they attach a tube to the top of the arm with a thing that looks like a pair of scissors, then they insert a syringe needle where you bend the arm and draw out blood. The tube is put there to make it easier for them to find a blood vessel, because the veins swell when that tube is tight around the arm. Then when the needle is inside the vein, they take away the tube so that the blood flows as usual again and into the syringe.

I was in ward forty-four at the sanatorium. This is where those who have defects in their lungs are staying. An aunt we knew was lying there dying. She had a disease called tuberculosis and they were afraid that I had got it too because it's contagious, and I had met that aunt before I got sick. But I had another illness.

It was rather fun to be in the hospital because you got so many things. I got cards from Aunt Vera and Aunt Lilly and Gun-Britt and Aunt Eivor, and toys and books from Dad. And you could make things there. I made a table mat of bast for Mom and a jar of old X-ray plates for myself. It was an aunt from the play therapy who came and gave me such things to do. But mostly I drew and did jig-saw puzzles and read.

In the ward where I had my bed it was like walls of glass, and in each cubicle, there was a sick child. We went in to each other and played when no one saw. We were not allowed to be up, and one of the nurses was very strict and started scolding us as soon as we disobeyed. But she was no real nurse, because she had no white hat and no brooch with a cross on it under her chin. I don't know what she was. She wore a checked dress instead of a blue one under her apron. Before, I wanted to be a nurse when I grew up, but now I am thinking of becoming a secretary or a stenographer. You can become whatever you want if you just study a lot and get good grades and take your higher school certificate.

Tore and Eivor Johansson are my parents
and Siv and Gun-Britt are my sisters.
My name is Lennart and I am sixteen years old.

The junior secondary school can be applied for from the fourth and fifth grade to the five-year line and from the sixth grade to the four-year line and from the seventh grade to the three-year line. Everyone has the opportunity to earn a low school certificate. If you don't take the chance and try to do better than your parents, you are stupid, I think.

We who go to the secondary grammar school are often so-called dixie dudes, who like traditional jazz and dixie-land and are dressed in duffel coats and cloth boots. Many, but not all of us, have that style.

At my age, you should be able to take some responsibility, I think. You should be able to take care of your clothes, make your bed and clean your room. It's not too much to ask. And you should go to school of your own free will because you want to learn things and get a good education. You should also learn practical things about society and the world and about politics, morality, and religion.

You should have a philosophy of life, I think. Be able to take a personal stand on what is happening and defend your own opinion. Feel a limit within yourself that tells you when it's time to say no and not let yourself be drawn into something. Be able to distinguish between what you say and do in different situations and correspond to a trust. Be able to express anger in words instead of with betrayal or violence. If you can't do that you are still childish, and that's bad for the self-confidence.

Many young people are going astray. This may be due to poor home conditions. It's an advantage to grow up in an ordinary family where all have dinner together every day and where the man works, pays taxes and bills and where the woman takes care of the household and the children. Parents should teach their children how to behave in different situations. How to hold a knife and fork when eating and how to invite a girl to the dance floor. Anyone who knows this gets better self-confidence. Young people who haven't learned the usual social rules try to hide their insecurity in different ways and may become loudmouthed or try to play the buffoon.

People with great knowledge in a certain area, such as those who compete in *Kvitt eller dubbelt* on TV, are admirable, I think. I especially remember Kjell Boman, who competed in history and won ten thousand. It was skilfully done. I am interested in history myself. When the royal warship Vasa was found, I followed it with great interest.

I also find current events interesting, such as the referendum on right-hand traffic in October 1955, when almost 83 percent of the Swedish people voted no, and the total solar eclipse in June 1954. A total solar eclipse occurs very rarely in Sweden. During the nineteenth century, it has happened only four times. The next time will not be until the year 2126. And now in April, the Russian space probe with the dog Laika entered the atmosphere again and was destroyed after spinning 2,500 revolutions around the earth.

Some statistics can also be interesting, such as that around 46,000 traffic accidents with motor vehicles occurred in Sweden in 1955, or that approximately 50 violent crimes with a fatal outcome are committed in Sweden every year.

I am also technically interested. The need for technically trained labour has never been greater than today. So that's probably what I will be investing in in the future. But first I will very likely work for a couple of years. It's not difficult to get a job after school. You can pick and choose. And you don't have to be educated to get started. If you don't get on well, you can resign exactly when you want and look for another job. For me, it will probably be the Post Office. I have had extra work there before, during the school holidays. Then we will see.

I wasn't home when Mother died. I was with a friend in Bergsbrunna and didn't come home until the next day. I have nothing to say about it. I prefer not to think about it. I am trying to put it behind me.

The woman in a family is the one who takes care of the children. She is soft and kind and always on hand when the children need her. She is the one who comforts when they are sad and gives them food when they are hungry. And she is always the one who cooks the food and keeps the home in order. No men participate in the practical housework. While the woman potter about by the stove and the sink, the man sits at the kitchen table and reads the newspaper or takes a nap on the bed in the bedroom. He has been away and working all day and needs to rest in the evening.

And that's how it should be, I think. The woman and the man should help each other so that the whole family feels good. A woman who wants to get an education and a professional work, can't have a husband and children at the same time, because then she doesn't have time for everything that has to be done at home.

My name is Agneta Fagerström and I am twenty-two years old.
I live in Uppsala and work at the Telecommunications Adminis-
tration.

The night Aunt Johansson died, I still lived with my parents,
but now I live in town. I have a small, two-room apartment
with a kitchen. It has both central heating and a water closet,
so I think I live extremely well.

When I come home after the working day and have put on
the potatoes and turned on all the lights and put on a cardigan
and turned on the radio, I feel really satisfied. And when I
have eaten and got the dishes out of the way and made coffee
and turned off all the lights except the one at the radio and
the bookshelf and sunk into the big armchair with my legs
under me and started reading the book I am currently working on, yes, then I feel really fine. I sit there reading and drinking coffee and looking around the room and enjoying.

I am so darned happy with how I have arranged it for myself. Everything shines, because I am careful with what I have,
and I am alone with it too. The old chest of drawers with the
fall-front, which always stands open so that the drawers and
the compartments inside are visible, and on top of it some
old-fashioned porcelain ornaments and a photograph of my
family when my brother and I were little. Between the windows I have a small mirror table and in front of one window
a flower-stand. And then there is the ottoman with all the pillows, and the round pillar table with extension leaf and the
rag rug on the varnished floor, which is shiny and nice. In the
ceiling is the chandelier with its five, small, yellow-brown

cloth lampshades and on the walls embroidered paintings, and the ticking pendulum clock that I have inherited from my grandma. Yes, I really think I have arranged it really cosy and personally for me.

At home I had my own room, which I had decorated myself with a bed, a table, and some chairs. There was a desk with drawers, which I sat at when I did my homework. From the beginning, I wanted a low couch and thought about sawing off the legs of the bed, but it's actually much more difficult to clean under the bed when it's low, and it's more hygienic not to sleep so close to the floor, so those plans I relinquished. Instead, I dressed the bed like a sofa and put nice textiles, which harmonized with the bedspread, on the wall. Then I put poufs at the ends and some colourful pillows that lit up. Dad helped me set up a shelf that was as long as the bed and there I had my radio, my favourite books, and other small things within easy reach.

I have always been careful, both with my belongings and my clothes. All you have acquired are investments that must be taken care of to last a long time. I put shoe blocks in the shoes and rinse my nylon socks in lukewarm water every night and wash them thoroughly once a week. I never forget to change sleeve patches and to put a clean collar and clean cuffs on the dress, and I brush my black skirt with hot coffee and iron it as soon as needed. Every now and then I empty my purse and wipe the lining with a piece of cotton that I have moistened with a few drops of 4711.

Mom had nothing to complain about when it came to how I behaved at home. But you can't get away from the fact that it takes a lot of diplomacy when you live with your parents. You have a strong need to free yourself and prefer to live your life without others interfering. If you don't realize that even as an older teenager you have to follow the house rules with mealtimes and other things, many unpleasant situations can occur. You must also tolerate a certain control, which doesn't have to be rooted in suspicion at all but can be an expression of sheer kindness.

And even if you pay a little for yourself, it doesn't mean that you shouldn't help in the household. After the day's work when I got home, I needed to rest a bit, but my mother needed it too, so I helped her with the dishes. It was work that took at most a quarter of an hour, and then I could, with a clear conscience, devote the rest of the evening to my own business. And I followed my mother's good advice, which meant that I learned to cook while still living at home. I think that can save me a lot of trouble in the future. At the same time, I thought of the old saying that goes: "The way to a man's heart is through his belly."

When it comes to paying for yourself, I think it's a proof of independence to do it when you are out with a boy. I also don't want to end up in debt of gratitude to him. If he has invited me to the cinema or a café, I may feel obliged to pay back with, for example, a kiss at the door afterwards, although I may not feel like it at all. And you have to think a little about your reputation and not seem too willing.

The night Aunt Johansson was assaulted, I still hadn't moved to my apartment in town. We were all home. Lennart Johansson, who is friends with my brother, was also there. He stayed overnight. The police came and asked us about him, as if they suspected that he had killed his own mother. Of course, he hadn't done that!

I think it was an unknown man who killed her. Maybe the same one that attacked me once. On my mother's advice, I told the police about him. Personally, I prefer not to think about it, because it was so awful. It was really nasty, and I had nightmares long afterwards and almost didn't dare to go out.

It was in the summer, and it was about nine o'clock in the evening. I had been visiting a friend and was on my way home. Suddenly I was attacked from behind by a person who grabbed me and hit my head with a hard object, so I fell forward on the road and fainted. When I woke up, I was lying on my back and had a man crawling over me. To keep me from screaming, he put his hand over my mouth so I couldn't breathe. Then he got up quickly and ran away. I managed to get to my feet and had time to see him running towards the train station.

I started screaming for help and two ladies came rushing to me. They had been out together and seen the attack from a distance but hadn't been able to intervene. Now they helped me to go to the hospital, where the doctor stated that I had received a five centimetre long wound in the head that was so serious that I had to stay for treatment. Afterwards it turned out that I had been hit with a large stone. I think it was so darned dirtily done! Unfortunately, I couldn't describe the man's appearance when I was asked, and the police never got hold of him. The only thing I could say for sure was that it smelled like alcohol on his breath.

I understand that one can suspect that it was the same one who assaulted Aunt Johansson. If it had been really bad, I could have been dead now, just like her. I was so darned scared afterwards when I was out alone. I felt safer when I had moved to town, although it really should be the other way around. In a city, so much more happens, I mean. But I am fine now, and I just hope that the police will soon catch Aunt Johansson's killer, who was perhaps the same one who assaulted me.

Ingrid

Sometimes Gun-Britt and I walk on the road and look in the ditches for things that people have thrown out from their cars. Matchboxes that may not be empty and cigarette packets and tablet boxes that you can cut out the front of and paste into a book if you collect such. Once we found an empty wallet and once we found a bottle that had some spirits left in it. Gun-Britt at least said it was spirits. She tasted it, but I didn't want to. The man who had had the bottle could have spat in it before he threw it away. That was disgusting, I thought.

On the main road up in the forest we once found a dirty magazine. It was called *Piff*. It was wet, and the pages stuck together a bit here and there, but we could at least see that the aunts in the pictures were almost naked. I don't know what's fun with that. Gun-Britt said that men buy such magazines when they want to jerk off.

Right now, I collect empty cans, nice boxes, fine stones, Christmas cards, postcards, bookmarks, film stars, dog and cat pictures and soft drink labels.

Last time Aunt Lilly visited us, I got bookmarks from her. There was one sheet with dogs and one sheet with angels and one sheet with roses. It's so fun to cut loose bookmarks. I cut very carefully so that all the white disappears. Then I put them in the box where they should be.

I have my bookmarks in a rather large box that has had chocolate in it. My crayons I have in a grey tin box on which the lid is attached by small hinges and in which there have been cigars. In another box, in which there also have been cigars, and which is made of very thin wood and has like a small lock on the lid, I have pencils, and in a cardboard box in which there has been perfume bottles I have my finery. In that box, it smells delicious like the roses in Dad's garden.

It's a lot of work to take care of a garden. Sometimes I help Dad with it. Weeding and hoeing the gravel path is boring, but it has to be done, so sometimes I help him with that. And on Saturdays when he has come home from work and has driven the car into the garage, I take the big rake and draw stripes in the gravel so that it will be fine for Sunday.

In the autumn, I help Dad raking leaves and moving the piles of leaves in the wheelbarrow to the compost. Once when I did that, I found a brand-new *Hela Världen* magazine there. It was under the leaves and was almost not wet at all. I really don't know how it had ended up there.

Many birds come to the garden. I know what almost everyone's name is. But why are there so many different kinds of birds? And insects. Why do they exist? For the birds to have them for food. But why are there so many different *kinds*? Why are there butterflies and earwigs, for example? Earwigs can crawl into people's ears and lay their eggs there, Gun-Britt says, but I don't believe it's true. And what should all such animals as snails and snakes be for? And all the mammals and fishes? And why are there people? Because God wanted to create them? But why did he want that? There didn't have to be anything at all. No earth and no sun and no moon and no *universe*. It could be empty. But everything exists, and it's so big that a human being is just like a small *dot*.

Last time Aunt Lilly visited us she was wearing a dark blue

dress with white dots. She had bought it from Dea, she told Mom. I don't know what Mom answered. She doesn't say very much to Aunt Lilly. But she offers her coffee anyway and let her be with us.

I think it's fun when Aunt Lilly comes. She doesn't care that Mom is weird, and she talks to me and looks at things I want to show. Sometimes she brings presents for me. I have received books and bookmarks and dollhouse furniture from her. She comes to us because Mom doesn't want to talk with her on the phone anymore. And she hopes that the police will soon find the person who murdered Aunt Eivor so that Mom will stop feeling suspected of it.

We have checked all suspects with the exception of people who haven't yet been identified. Many times, these inspections have looked very promising in the beginning. We have been optimistic and believed in a solution. But it has always ended with the designated or otherwise suspect person being able to present an airtight alibi. Just as important as finding the culprit is, of course, exculpating an innocent person, but this also means dashing hopes for us that the case will be solved.

An important question that is still unanswered is where Mrs. Johansson went on the night of the murder and who she possibly was going to meet. If one could clear up the mystery surrounding that point, we would come a big step closer to the solution. Initially, a man actually came forward already after a week after the murder with a report interesting to the investigation. He had that evening by car passed the crossroads down to the river and then in the dark discovered a man and a woman who were next to one of the ditches. The man leaned forward towards the woman and seemed to speak to her in agitated words. We haven't been able to identify these two people. We also don't know if it was Mrs. Johansson or a completely different woman who the witness observed.

Unfortunately, no witness, who without fail observed Mrs. Johansson at that time, has been heard from. It has turned out to be extremely impossible to find people who have seen her between six and seven. By the last-mentioned time, she was certainly already dead.

The circumstantial evidence in this investigation have been unusually few. There have been no footprints, wheel tracks or other tracks that normally provide some guidance. The little we have found has not been enough to give the expert analyses positive values. This is primarily due to the fact that the act was probably committed outdoors and that the site is not identical to the crime scene. We still don't know where the assault took place, which of course further complicates the investigation.

We have gotten stuck but still work on each new lead. To date, we have listened to over three hundred people, but that doesn't prevent there being additional witnesses who are in possession of valuable and perhaps crucial information without being aware of this themselves. We search for witnesses who during the day of the murder and in the evening may have seen or heard one or more strangers in the village. It's very common for a witness to designate his observation as useless and for that reason doesn't contact the police. But for us, it may be just the piece that is missing in our puzzle. And it takes time to collect puzzle pieces, to hunt up and hear witnesses whose information is to be checked afterwards and compared with other statements.

We have had many suspects, and in a couple of cases extremely careful investigations have been done into their activities on the night of the murder. This has forced us to also declare some people arrested, which is the only legal possibility to detain a person for more than the twelve hours that an arrest allows. A detention can be extended to a maximum of five days.

With this in mind, I would like to point out how important it is that a crime of this kind is really solved. Around every murder there are always bad rumours that point to one or the other, which often means severe mental suffering for the victim of such speculations. The truth is the only thing that can kill once and for all such uncontrolled gossip.

My name is Doris and I am a dressmaker.
I am married to Tage Andersson who is a farm foreman.
Our three children have left home.

The night Eivor was murdered, Tage and I were visiting his sister in Uppsala, so the worst stir passed us by. We didn't find out what had happened until the next day. It was lucky that we were not at home, because otherwise Tage would have been suspected too, I suppose, just like everyone else.

It can be just anyone who has done it. I can find motives for generally speaking every man here in the village if I think about it a little. Yes, no one seriously believed that the lads who found her had anything to do with it, because Stig is just a child and Bengt, who is admittedly both big and strong, couldn't, without Stig having noticed it, have been able to knock down Eivor. No, there were neither opportunity nor motive. And when it turned out that the murder hadn't taken place in the meadow, there was no doubt that the lads were innocent.

In other respects, however, there is no shortage of suspects. Personally, I am convinced that it's an acquaintance of Eivor who has done it. It can even be a woman. But it's the men I primarily suspect.

Stig's big brother Åke was one of the first to be investigated by the police. It was written about his car in the newspaper, and everyone knew it was about him. It was believed that he had knocked down Eivor and with the help of the car transported her down to the river to drown her. When he noticed that she was already dead, he put her on the ground and left.

The motive in his case was assumed to be that she knew something about him that would ruin his whole life if it came to light. His former fiancée, who was acquainted with Eivor's daughter Siv, had told Eivor what he had done and added: "If Åke finds out that I have passed it on, he will kill me!" Eivor may have tried to persuade Åke to go to the police and confess, and when she didn't succeed with that, she threatened to report him.

Well, I don't know for sure, but that's what I have heard. And his so-called alibi isn't up to much, I assume. Young people of his kind can't be trusted. I have read about in different newspapers how they behave. Driving around in their big American cars with open windows and the car radio turned up to the highest volume. Boozing and making out in the back seats, arguing, and fighting. Devote themselves to general hooliganism and vandalization, criminality, riots against the police, and sexual laxity.

Gunnar and Viola should have put a stop to it while there was still time. Now that the boy is of age, it's too late. But so, it has gone as it has gone too. After the newspaper articles, he has been branded as a murderer and it's still there.

Viola has taken it hard. She may think that her noble family should have been spared from all the gossip. But no smoke without fire, I say. And as long as the perpetrator goes free, everyone has to put up with being suspected. Maybe she should think a little about what Gunnar was up to that night. He wasn't at home, anyway. He was out riding in his fancy Mercedes. I saw it myself when I came home with the milk and was just on my way in through the gate opening. Then he drove by and honked for greeting. I don't know where he went after that, but he was out driving anyway. It was a quarter to six. He may have met Eivor on the road later and offered her a ride to where she was going but driven to another place to have an intimate session with her. Gunnar is a real ladykiller, so it isn't impossible at all. He is interested in everyone and doesn't even try to hide it. I saw myself how he devoured Aina with his eyes at Eivor's funeral. And they live next door, so it was certainly not the first time he cast his eyes on her either. She looks good, Aina, in a slightly vulgar way, with her big bust and her wide hips that she wiggles when she walks. "A challenging hip job" as I heard a man describe it once. There is nothing wrong with Aina, but she certainly enjoys the appreciation she gets for her appearance.

Gunnar doesn't look too bad either, with his dark hair and marked features. He is tall and imposing and could easily carry a woman of Eivor's size in his arms or over his shoulder if necessary. And perhaps it became necessary when Eivor opposed his approaches in the car and tried to escape. Maybe he knocked her down to stop her. The suspicions against him are based on the fact that he reportedly had a tough job cleaning his car the day after the murder and that he got rid of a sports jacket and a pair of almost new leather gloves that he often used when he was out driving.

But people talk so much. You have to take what you hear with a grain of salt and not believe blindly in everything that reaches your ears. And Gunnar is by no means the only ladykiller here in the village, I must add now that I am still on that track. An even greater womanizer can probably be said to be

Harry Rosendahl. After his retirement and his wife's decease, he has become accustomed to walking around in the cottages to have a sip of coffee and a chat with the wives while their husbands are away at work and the children are at school. He also doesn't refuse a glass hard liquor if it's offered to him. And he is nice and full of fun, Harry, so it's hard to deny him when he is standing there on the stairs with his hat in his hand and wondering if he can come in. For many housewives, it's a welcome break in the household management to sit down and talk away awhile with him.

Harry was a merchant and a salesman before retiring. It's probably from there he has got his polite and forthcoming manner. You always feel appreciated and respected by Harry, and that's what women fall for. He listens, flatters, and gives compliments. In some places he probably gets more than coffee and a drink in return. But in terms of appearance, he can't compete with Gunnar by a long way. Harry is short and a bit corpulent but still sinewy and strong, and he doesn't hesitate to go at it if needed.

He also visited Eivor's home when she was alive. Once, when I showed up a little unexpectedly, he had accompanied her out to the hen house and was in full swing helping her pick eggs. Yes, he is helpful, Harry, in every way possible. And Eivor belonged to the friendly and compliant kind that willingly adapts to the demands of the environment. She let in vagrants who came and knocked on the door and offered both coffee and food. When she was at home, she never locked herself in.

Eivor was unobtrusive and didn't like to talk about herself

and her own circumstances. Can that be where the explanation lies? That no one knew so well what she was up to when she in her loneliness welcomed both known and unknown men in her home? I don't mean to imply that she was unfaithful to Tore, but if she was good at listening, she surely got to know a thing or two that she could benefit from. According to rumours, she received money from a woman so as not to reveal to her husband that the woman had been intimate with her husband's brother. Another rumour says that a man had confided in her about a crime committed, of which he himself was guilty. A related theory is that she had accidentally witnessed a murder and, under threat of a police report, tried to obtain financial benefits from her knowledge. The same murderer would then have attacked again so as not to end up behind bars.

Surely, there are motives enough, even if not all names are known. The question is also whether there may have been reason for Tore to become suspicious and become jealous. This hypothesis is also included in the great variety of rumours. But according to information, Tore was at Harald's and Beda's home when Eivor met her fate. It could hardly have been he who did it. There were many who suspected him in the beginning, despite his generally witnessed excellence. Through thriftiness and hard work, he has always arranged it well for himself and his family in temporal terms. At the same time, he is a thinking man with intellectual and cultural interests. It's hard to imagine him in the role of a deceived husband who, blinded by jealousy and rage, attacked Eivor and killed her.

Well, what about Harald then? Surely, he avoids all suspicions by Tore and Beda giving him an undoubted alibi? Yes, but if he isn't the one who did it, then it must be his son or grandson! That's how the talk goes. Because it's rumoured that Nils was once suspected of arson and murder. An acquaintance of his, to whom he owed money, was found dead and burned in his bed. At the autopsy, some injuries were found that indicated that he had been subjected to violence. At first it was thought that a thief had done it. Drawers were pulled out and shelves and cupboards had been knocked over. But eventually they started to suspect something else. A witness thought he had seen a running person, who looked like Nils Karlsson, depart from the burning apartment.

Suppose Eivor knew for sure that it was him and tried to extort money from him to keep quiet. That she waited so long may have been due to the fact that Tore now, for perhaps the first time, had got into financial trouble and that Eivor then did the only thing she could to contribute money. And to avoid paying and to save his own skin, Nils killed her.

Or was it his son Ragnar who did it? Not to help his father, because he surely doesn't understand that much, but for a reason quite of his own? The boy is mentally deficient and has caused so much misery over the years that everyone knows what he is capable of. There has been vandalism, arson, and beatings. Once he tried to run over Tage with the tractor. Tage had reprimanded him for a trifle, and Ragnar couldn't tolerate it. As the tractor approached, Tage threw himself to the side at the last moment.

The boy gets outbursts of rage that he can't control, and he is so big and strong that he could easily knock down an adult. A trifle can trigger his anger. And I know that he was out riding his moped the night Eivor was killed. It may have been enough that he saw her coming walking and thought she was in his way for it to happen.

He has no real comrades. The old man Jansson is probably his only friend. He is the one he usually dwells with, I have heard. But what kind of company is that for a young boy? And who knows what Edvin has on his conscience? He has worked hard all his life, which can be seen on his horny hands and crooked back, but he is still strong and can't be placed aside all suspicions. He is unmarried and childless, he has never cared for dames, and he doesn't have so many friends, since he prefers to go by himself. A real grumbler, many say. Some call him the village idiot because of his talk about supernatural beings and perhaps because he has a brother in the madhouse. The fact that he often wanders about in the meadow contri-butes to him being suspected of the murder. He has been babbling about goblins and furry trolls and strange cows that he says he have seen down there. In addition, he claims that he himself has been knocked down there once.

It must have been Lindberg's cows he saw because no other cows graze in that pasture. And who would have knocked him down? The only one I can think of is Lindberg himself, who I know has a grudge against Edvin. It's alleged that Edvin once assaulted him with a bottle tucked into a sock and robbed him of all his cash. For that reason, Göte may have had reason to retaliate. And if he could beat Edvin, he could beat Eivor as well. That he gave Jan-Olof an alibi was perhaps just a clever way of trying to get an alibi for himself.

Göte isn't to be trifled with. Thereto, he has a little too unpredictable temper. One moment he behaves calmly and moderately and as if locked in himself, the next moment he can erupt so violently that he seems completely crazy. One night, his daughter Birgit came running out of the house and continued barefoot across the snow in just her nightgown to seek help from a neighbour. "Dad kills me!" she yelled. Göte denied that he in the slightest way had threatened her. But he disliked that she stayed away from home at night and ran out with boys. When she came home, she was also often drunk.

Sitting at home in the evenings wasn't really compatible with Birgit's temperament and Astrid and Göte found it increasingly difficult to keep her at home. Her desire for amusement and dancing cavaliers finally prevailed. She ended up on the downgrade, where irresponsible rakes and dissolute women became her main companions. For the sake of excitement, she was drawn to places where all sorts of loose people and purely criminal existences dwelled.

She doesn't look bad, Birgit, with her slightly plump figure, which surely tempts the men, and with her long waving hair which she sometimes ties together into a pony-tail hairstyle. But she has a weak character and a fiery temper that is especially evident when alcohol is consumed. Now she has apparently gotten a fiancé, which may have made her calm down a bit, but before that she lived, according to rumours, a very wild and immoral life.

Both Birgit and her fiancé were in the village when Eivor was murdered, and the fiancé was immediately suspected by the police due to his criminal past. The same applies to Birgit's brother Sven, who lives as a lawless man in the woods and commits one summer cottage burglary after another. It may very well be he who killed Eivor.

Another person who was suspected was Lindberg's farmhand Jan-Olof. He was taken in for questioning by the police and pressed so hard that he broke like a dry branch. It's well known that a drunk person commits irresponsible acts, as well as that someone who is unable to hold his liquor tends to quarrel and get into fights. And just because of this, Jan-Olof often behaves wildly. He is a feared fighter who possesses great bodily powers, and when consuming alcohol, he doesn't hesitate to demonstrate his strength. Erik Lundin once said that Jan-Olof had been close to using his clenched fists on him just for the reason that Erik reprimanded him. It happened at a time when Jan-Olof was in the process of driving a herd of cows across the road and Erik was to pass by with his car and had a horn run into the side of the car. When Erik then expressed his dissatisfaction, Jan-Olof became threatening. So, it doesn't take much to arouse his anger. Eivor might have done it without even knowing it.

If, on the other hand, it was Erik who assaulted Eivor, the motive may be that he considered that Eivor's treacherous behaviour towards Signe was what caused Signe's illness. No one seems to know what the betrayal was about, but it's well known that Signe felt badly treated by Eivor and withdrew from her company.

Almost any of the men in the village may have had motives to kill Eivor. Many would rather believe that it was a nonlocal person, such as a tramp who accidentally happened to meet Eivor and who after the act disappeared along the country road under the protection of the autumn darkness. We can scarcely know the motive, they say, and it's perhaps not so important when it comes to a random act without a personal connection. There has been talk of Säby-Kalle, a notorious vagrant of the primitive kind, who has been repeatedly punished for assault. He once lurked behind a tree with a folding knife in his hand, and when another tramp, whom he regarded as having insulted him and who unsuspectingly came by, he rushed forward and cut open the poor man's face from mouth to the ear. Säby-Kalle is cold and emotionless and never shows remorse when he gets caught. According to rumours, he seems rather pleased to be once again housed in a prison where he can receive free food and accommodation over the winter.

Yes, it may have been a vagrant, but as I said, I am myself convinced that it was a villager. Even if you have heard a lot and can guess, there is certainly a lot which is hidden under the surface here in the village that hasn't yet emerged. There is probably more than one person who knows the truth. One or more people know who the murderer is but keep silent to protect him. Otherwise, he would so far have been unable to escape discovery.

Ingrid

Now the summer holidays have begun. On graduation day we got our grade books and went to church and sang. In the church they had installed lilacs and cut birches. First the clergyman talked, then we sang some songs. It sounded so beautiful that Ninni's teacher started crying.

I had a light blue seersucker dress with a bolero on and white knee socks and white shoes. Under the dress I had a foam rubber petticoat so that the dress would stand out. In my hair I had a white diadem and curls from Mom's curlers. If you want, you can put in tin clips instead, but then the hair becomes wavy and it's not as nice as curls, I think.

Mom and Dad were not present at the graduation. I told Dad that he didn't have to come and then he didn't. Mom, I already knew, didn't want to come. She has become unsociable, Dad says. But the other's parents were there and heard when I played the piano at the music show in the community centre. *An der Schönen Blauen Donau* I played, and when I was done everyone clapped their hands.

Almost all summer guests have moved out. In any case, Pia and Maud, who Gun-Britt and I usually play with, have done it. Pia is as old as me and Maud is in the middle between me and Gun-Britt. I think Maud is the kindest. She has had polio and a leg defect and can't run so fast. If you play in piles of leaves in the autumn or eat unripe apples, you can get polio. You can die from it or become paralyzed, so you have to sit in a wheelchair. But I am vaccinated, so I can't get it. And on Maud it only came a little, so she became almost well again.

Pia is adopted. The people she lives with are not her real parents. But she believes so because they haven't told her that she is adopted. Gun-Britt and I are forbidden to tell her.

Pia says that the grown-ups quarrel in her home when they get angry. In our home they never do. Only once when Dad went out to move leaves in the wheelbarrow to the compost did I hear that he was angry with Mom. I don't know why. And when she started to have a towel with cotton wool and tin foil or cellophane against her ears, he also got angry.

Otherwise, they never quarrel in our home. It's just me who gets angry when I don't get what I want sometimes. Then I cry and scream. When Mom gets angry, she scolds, and when Dad gets angry, he leaves. The time he was angry with Mom and went out and worked with the leaves, he did it in order to calm down a bit. It was pitch-dark outside, but he didn't turn on the corner lamp. Then he came in and was all red in his face because he was so sweaty. When he took off his beret, he had a white stripe on his forehead.

I never get licked like Pia, who gets it from her mom. I don't know what they do when they lick children. Do they hit their behind with a cane, or do they give a box on the ear or what do they do? Pia says that her mom pulls her hair when she has been disobedient. But I don't think that can be called licking. I think licking is to hit someone on the behind. You can, for example, have a whip or birch twigs like they had when Mom was little. But I don't think they have such things for Pia.

Pia is great at gymnastics. I am not. I only dare to turn around and hang from my knees in the flying rings, but she can hang on a trapeze and do handstands and turn cartwheels and stand like a bridge and do the splits. I would like to be as agile as she is and be able to do such things, but I have no patience to train myself. Doing somersaults backwards and forwards is the only thing I can do.

When all the summer guests are out and there are many children at home, we play together. We play and play, until we are not allowed to be out anymore. When Mom jingles, I run home. Pia's mom has a whistle that she blows when Pia must go home, and my mom has a bell. It's a cowbell that they used to have on cows in the past. It can be heard very far away. For example, if I am at Ninni's when Mom is jingling, I hear it all the way there. But then she can't hear when I shout an answer.

My name is Dagmar
and my husband's name is John.
We only live here in the summer, in the summer house that my
husband has inherited.
The rest of the year we live in an apartment in Uppsala.
We have an eleven-year-old daughter named Maud.

The hot summer of 1953, when Maud was six years old, the polio ran like a plague through the country. Over five thousand people fell ill. The newspapers had black headlines and the fear spread. Is it the water? Is it unripe fruit? Is it withered leaves?

No one knew for certain. Most people now know that infantile paralysis, or polio as it is also called, is a viral disease that attacks the nerve cells in the spine. The disease is spread via sewage-contaminated water and close contact between people. The symptoms are fever, headache, nausea, and vomiting. At first, it affected children more often than adults.

Fully healthy people could carry the virus without knowing it and go around infecting others. Many were also already immune without knowing it. They had been infected but didn't become ill and received lifelong protection. The worst thing was that no one knew who was immune and who wasn't. There was no vaccine, and all the time you heard on the radio and read in the newspapers how important hygiene was. It was also learned that the numbers of respirators were not enough everywhere. We lived under constant threat.

Maud had been out of sorts for several weeks before she fell ill. I was hoping it was a common cold, but I was so worried about her. And one day it got worse. She was feverish and vomited. During the night she got worse, and in the morning when she would go to the toilet, she didn't get out of bed. She was stiff in her neck and couldn't walk. We called a doctor, and he could immediately tell that it was polio.

The ambulance came and picked her up. They placed her on a stretcher and carried her out through the apartment door and down the stairs. The neighbours in the yard hung out the windows and stared.

At the hospital, they constantly measured her blood pressure and heart rate. If she were to get worse and find it harder to breathe, she would have to be put in a body respirator, or iron lung as it is also called.

But she survived and was moved to the North Pavilion where she had to stay for two months. During all that time, we only got to see her through a glass pane when we came to visit her. She became so terribly sad every time we had to go and she wasn't allowed to come home with us, that I could barely stand it. I know that many parents stopped coming to avoid making their children so desperate, but I couldn't do that. I went to the hospital every day and tried to convey to her that everything would be fine in the end, although deep down I wasn't at all sure of it.

The doctors didn't have much knowledge about how to treat polio at that time. Massages and pool baths were given, and patients got bone plaster, leather corsets, and arm splints. They did the best they could.

And Maud slowly got better. The paralysis in her legs largely went back, and she could come home. Our apartment had been contaminated with a special gas, which was to work for several days. But it was as if Maud herself was infected with the plague. Some children were forbidden to play with her, and it was preferred that she stood in one corner of the yard while the others played together. We experienced similar situations when we were out walking. If we were about to meet an acquaintance on one side of the street, he or she crossed to the other side. When we entered a store, the customers got out of there in a hurry.

But I am so grateful that she survived and was almost completely recovered. There were so many who died or were harmed for life.

Sickness, war, and death… I know there is a strong belief in the future now, with hopes of a better standard of living for all, but for me that optimism is overshadowed by the threat that the Cold War will be transformed into a nuclear war. You read about the constantly ongoing arms race between the nuclear powers, with increasingly powerful nuclear weapons, and there are constantly crises in different parts of the world. The Korean crisis, the Berlin crisis, the Hungarian crisis… Many see Soviet communism as a threat to democracy. When Chrusjtjov started the so-called de-Stalinization, opposition to communism intensified and riots broke out in both Poland and Hungary. When the Russians invaded Hungary, it felt as if Sweden had been attacked as well. Fundraising was started for Hungary in the schools and many Swedes got involved.

The United States, the Soviet Union, and the United Kingdom have carried through a large number of nuclear test explosions in recent years. Chrusjtjov's announcement that he intends to end the Soviet bombings isn't believed by many. It's just propaganda, it's said. And here in Sweden, politicians have discussed the need to acquire their own nuclear weapons. "Should neutral Sweden work for peace by preparing for war or renouncing nuclear weapons?" is the question.

I, and many with me, live in a constant fear of the future. We have been in a world war, and even if our country was spared, we now know how mad leaders can overthrow both their own and other's people straight into the abyss. It's not easy to feel calm and carefree when you know that there is reason to worry about what is going on behind closed doors in laboratories around the world. In the newspapers you can read about the terrible consequences of a nuclear war. And even if the bombs were not dropped directly over Sweden, toxic clouds would travel around the world and wipe out all life. Therefore, there must never be a new war!

Ordinary bombs do damage within a relatively small area. Not many people lose their lives by an old-fashioned bomb. But in the event of an atomic explosion, thousands die within a fraction of a second, and in the immediate vicinity everything is transformed into smoke and dust. There are no ruins, no wounded, and no corpses – everything is powdered into nothingness by the terrible heat.

During the "Blitz", London was rescued by a volunteer force that fought the fire and took the wounded to hospital. In wars of the future, there will be no firemen or hospitals. The heart of a big city like London or Stockholm will simply be wiped out in an instant in a flash of light and fire.

And there is no defence against this weapon or against the terrible evolution of radioactive gases. It's a diabolical force that has unleashed the boundless inventiveness of man. The crucial thing is how the battle between evil and good will end. Other civilizations have perished because they didn't want to learn in time. What we didn't learn from Hitler, we must learn from Hiroshima! Because we didn't want to face the truth courageously, we allowed fascism to spread in Europe. If we close our eyes to the dangers once again, not only Europe but the whole world will be destroyed, and all life will be wiped out.

So, we live in a time of both hope and fear. I am a person who really wants to both know and understand, but for long periods I have avoided reading newspapers and listening to the radio. I have tried to shut out the outside world to create as safe a life as possible for me and my family.

Dangers lurk everywhere. With the murder of Eivor, I have realized how fragile security can be in other ways as well. Against my will, I have read about the murder in the newspaper and my thoughts on it have been that it must be about a man that Eivor was acquainted with and who had arranged a meeting with her and tricked her away to a designated place where he more or less undisturbed could perform his deed. Of course, it could also be the case that it was Eivor herself who earlier in the day had asked for a meeting, and that the man had accepted without a thought of violence. When she then in the evening, perhaps demanded money from him or threatened to reveal what she knew about him – then his reaction may have triggered a so-called impulse murder, which wasn't planned at all from the beginning.

My husband doesn't believe in my theory and says that I have read too many detective novels and let my imagination run riot. But he hasn't heard things about Eivor in the same way I have done. For example, I have been told that she once received money from a married woman in the village not to tell her husband that one of the family's children wasn't his, which Eivor had accidentally found out. The woman herself had offered Eivor the money, but just that Eivor accepted it, I think shows that... Yes, it was very strange, I thought.

And there was a man, she has told a neighbour-wife, who carried a secret that tormented him so badly that the anxiety pressure finally forced him to unburden his heart. He had told Eivor that every night he relived eerie scenes from a crime he had once committed. I didn't know more, and how much more Eivor knew wasn't clear. But after her death, I couldn't help thinking that she might have pressured that man for money so as not to reveal his secret and that he eventually got tired of paying.

But it's certainly as my husband says, that I have too lively imagination. The reality is not like in Stig Trenter's and Maria Lang's books, he says. "No, sometimes it's even worse," I say. "It can also be the case that everything is just idle talk," he says. "Yes, but what would be the reason for lying like that?" I say.

The question is also whether I should go to the police and tell them what I have heard. But if it is like my husband says, that what has been said may not be true at all, then I don't want to contribute to blacken Eivor's reputation.

Sometimes we don't know what to play. We usually play hop-
scotch or compete to see who dares to jump over the most
stone stair steps or who comes farthest when we jump from
the swings at speed. There is soft sand there, so it doesn't matter if we fall. Below the kitchen stairs, where raspberry bushes
have grown before, there is a rather high cement edge, and
there we play grocery store sometimes. Then we dish up dan-
delion leaves for fish and pieces of bark for meat and pork and
spruce cones for sausages.

If there are several children out, you can play mothers and
fathers. Mother is the most fun to be, because then you clean
and cook and do the dishes and put on the coffee pot if a
neighbour comes to visit. When you are a child, you mostly
are out playing, and when you are a father, you just go to
work. When he comes home in the evening, they eat. These
are almost the only things you do when you play mothers and
fathers.

If you want to know how many children you will have
when you grow up, you can pick up small stones in your
hands and shake them and say: "How-many-children-will-I-
have-when-I-grow-up?" Then you throw the stones up in the
air and let them fall down on your hands, and as many stones
that end up on them you will have children.

In the past, before there were rubbers, the families had a lot
of children. Mom, for example, has fourteen siblings, so her
mom, who is my grandma, has given birth to fifteen children.
I have never met my grandma because she is dead or whatever
she is. She is gone anyway. But Mom's Dad exists. When I was
little, we went to visit him sometimes. He lives in an old croft

in the woods. Two of my uncles live there too. They take care of Grandpa because he is so old that he can't manage himself.

I would never want to have fifteen children. I don't know if I should have any children at all. I think it hurts a lot to give birth to them and I would feel so stupid when I was thick, because then everyone would understand what I had done. Children also cry a lot when they are small, and you must look after them all the time. So, I don't know. Maybe when I am thirty, I will have one.

Before, we used to play with dolls sometimes, but nowadays we almost never do. We are mostly out playing. My dolls are named Ville, Gulli, Elisabet, Eva, and Lillemor. Eva is a pee doll made of rubber that you can feed with a baby bottle. She has small plastic baby pants that you can put cellucotton in, but I have no cellucotton, so I put toilet paper in them instead, and when I give her water from the baby bottle, she pees. But the water also comes out where the legs are attached, and not just through the pee hole, and that's potty, I think.

Lillemor is made of celluloid or whatever it's called. Gulli is made of fabric. She has clothes that are sewn to her body. It's not so fun. I have had her the longest. No, I have had the teddy bear the longest. He has no name because he isn't a doll. When I was little, I combed him on the back of his head, so all the fur was worn away there, and instead of purchased eyes, he has black buttons that Mom has sewed on him. He isn't very neat. He should probably be yellow actually and not grey.

Yes, and then it's Elisabet. I got her as a Christmas present when I was seven years old and had been at the hospital and came home for Christmas. First Dad asked me what I wished for Christmas, and then I said a doll who could walk and say mom. She should have long curly hair and sleeping eyes, I said. I almost didn't think there were such dolls, but I said it anyway.

Then on Christmas Eve there was a big parcel under the Christmas tree, and I told Dad that I thought it was the kind of doll I wanted in it. No, it wasn't, he said, because it was rubber boots for Mom. But I didn't believe him. I wasn't allowed to squeeze the parcel, because then I could feel what it was. And I didn't squeeze, but I still knew there was a doll in it.

And it was. Just such a doll I had said I wanted. She had a red sailor dress and a similar hat and white socks and shoes. The only thing that wasn't nice was that she had hinges that were *visible* at top of her legs.

Then it's only Ville left. He is my only boy doll. He is unusual because he is made of soft and hard mixed. His head is hard, but his body is made of fabric. And he has a gadget in his stomach that makes him scream when you turn him over.

Mom has sewn clothes for my dolls. For Ville, she has sewn a red suit with a black fur collar and gold buttons. They are not made of real gold, but they are gold coloured. In the middle they have an anchor.

There are a lot of buttons in Mom's button box. I look in it sometimes and remember what clothes the buttons have been on. Some small white ones that feel like cardboard come from my old bodices, and some that are mother-of-pearl shimmering I have had in a floral dress that Mom sewed for me once. Some come from old cardigans that Mom has undone. There are also large, speckled buttons from Dad's overcoat and some brown ones with fabric on from Mom's winter dress. Some burgundy shiny buttons are from my teddy coat that I had when I was little. The whole box is full of buttons, and most of them I don't know where they come from. Mom doesn't know either.

My name is Barbro
and my husband's name is Sture.
Our surname is Jansson.
We have a daughter named Gunilla and a son named Björn.
We have had the summer cottage in the woods for almost ten years.

It's too bad, this about Eivor's death. I don't know what to say about it. I didn't know her very well, but we had met, and at Erik's fiftieth birthday party she was my neighbour at table, and I talked quite a lot with her. It's inconceivable that she is dead and that she died in such a horrible way. Who could have done that to her? I don't understand.

And Signe... I had closer contact with her than with Eivor, and Sture and Erik also used to meet a lot. It's so sad, I think, that she has become ill. I knew nothing, because during the winter we have virtually no contact with the people in the village, but so I went down to her as I usually do, to greet and show that we had moved out, and then she didn't open for me. I knew she was home, because just before I had glimpsed her in the garden, and when she didn't open, I was completely put out and didn't know what to do. I didn't understand what was wrong. I found out later, but not being let in felt so awful, because I interpreted it as if she had a grudge against me, and I couldn't for the life of me understand what I had done to make her feel that way.

But otherwise, we thrive well here in the country. We have always done that. There are a couple of boys of Björn's age that he can play with, and Gunilla is so small that she hasn't started playing with other children yet. Older children, such as Rut's and Dagmar's girls, are not so interested in attending to her, and you can understand that. But we all spend time with both Bergfeldt's and Dahlin's, and we have done so for many years, so we all know each other. I have good contact with Dagmar in particular. Rut is a little too… light-minded in my opinion, and some of her ideas I have difficulty understanding. Not because you have to like everything equally to be good friends, but it's Dagmar I still get along best with.

The other day, for example, Rut and I came to the question of when it might be appropriate to give children sexual information, and then I thought that… Her ten-year-old daughter had played doctor with some boys and had lacerations on her stomach, she told me. That's how we got into it. Personally, I believe that one should at least in brief and general form provide information as soon as the children themselves begin to ask or wonder about such things. A mother who follows her children's development will surely understand when the right time for more detailed explanations has come. Incidentally, the information should rather come too early than too late, as the children receive information in any case, but then perhaps from doubtful and uninformed sources.

I think an important basic rule that must never be deviated from should always be to tell the truth. A child who has once noticed that the mother's information isn't true may never regain its trust in her, and then it's not just about what she says about sexuality. If the mother can't give a clear message, it's better that she admits that she doesn't know, rather than trying to save herself with evasions. Nor should she disappoint the children by belittling or ridiculing their questions and small trusts or, even worse, telling them to other people, perhaps even in the presence of the children themselves.

Finally, and perhaps most importantly – the mother should never talk about sexual issues in an ambiguous way or refer to the relationship between a man and a woman with obscene jokes. Sitting and whispering with girlfriends and grinning at "spicy things" is unforgivable, and in the presence of the children it's a pure sin. The children's future view of sexuality depends to a large extent on the spirit that has prevailed in the home, I believe.

Rut and I didn't really agree that this is the way it should be. She called me the apostle of gloom and said that it doesn't harm the children at all to occasionally hear small equivocal jokes and allusions to sexuality. And I have noticed that she herself doesn't hesitate to behave like that.

We also have different views when it comes to other care and attention regarding the children. Some parts of what she advocates sound very cold and emotionless in my ears. To me, for example, it's obvious that you don't give the children a beating. You don't beat your friends, so why would you beat your children? But at one point, Rut said: "When the children are old enough to talk to, you may not need to hit them. But when they are so small that they don't understand anything, you have to slap them sometimes to make them obey."

I think obedience is an eerie word. This means that you force the children to do things that they don't understand or are against their own will. Even trying to educate by constantly saying "No!", "Naughty, naughty!", and "Don't!" I think is wrong. It offends and inhibits the children. If you as a parent instead have a distracting and encouraging attitude, you can usually reach a consensus that feels good from both sides.

I remember a mother who let out her one-year-old girl alone in the yard with a stern admonition not to go out on the street. When the little girl did it anyway and was returned to the home by a rescuing neighbour, the kid got a box on the ear with the words: "Haven't I told you not to go out on the street!" To treat children in that way I think is disgusting. I have seen Rut give her daughter a box on the ear, and therefore I can't help wondering how the girl really feels, and whether she may have been harmed by Rut's strict approach.

Ingrid

Last night I went with Gun-Britt and Pia and two guys who are children of some summer guests to Lindberg's barn. It was Gun-Britt who wanted me to go with them. There is hay there that you can jump in. On a farm near school, there is a haystack that we played in before. We jumped and dug passages and made caves. But it was forbidden later because the hay can fall so you get buried and suffocated.

When we were in Lindberg's barn we didn't jump because the guys just wanted to neck. One guy named Björn was with Pia and one named Ronny was with Gun-Britt. Before, Pia was in love with Stig, but he wasn't in love with her and said that she should go home to her mom or whatever it was. Then she got angry and started liking Björn instead. She let him touch her tits. They have started to grow on her even though she is only ten years old. On me they haven't started to grow yet.

And Gun-Britt and Ronny were carrying on with something. It was just me who had no one to be together with. I had to sit and watch. We heard some men outside, and then we lay in complete silence so they wouldn't discover us, because we are not allowed to be in that barn and play. I peeked out through a narrow opening in the wall and told the others when they were gone. Then Ronny said: "Come and lie down here too, Ing-rid!" Gun-Britt was lying on one arm, and he wanted me to come and lie on the other. When I had laid down, he said: "Now one feels good! A chick on each arm!" "Is there anything to do on them then?" said Björn, sticking his head out of the hay. "Yes, damn it!" said Ronny. He swears even though you are not allowed to, and I am just saying what he said. Then he did something under Gun-Britt's skirt, so she folded up and screamed. "Yes, I can hear that!" said Björn and laughed. We lay there and carried on until we became all sweaty.

When it's very hot outside, we sometimes go to the bathing place in Graneberg and swim. We cycle there. I have a red bike that Dad has bought for me. It's a second-hand girl's bike.

At the bathing place there is a rather small sandy beach and then a long bridge out. It's shallow at the bridge, but then it's so deep that you don't touch the bottom. I don't like not bottoming, because I can't swim so well. I usually stay where it's shallow and play with the bathing ring that Gun-Britt sometimes brings with her.

First, you lie on the blanket in your swimsuit and get fried. Then you should go into the water. It's the worst the first time, before you have dipped. I usually walk slowly. At the bottom, there is mire that trickles up between your toes and some sharp stones here and there, so I feel for every step. My legs become stiff and cold as ice if it's not so warm in the water. Sometimes it's so cold that you get goose-pimples all over your body and shiver and get blue lips when you have been in for a while. Then it's not so fun to bathe.

There are plenty of children in the water. Sometimes big guys come and push you, so you fall into the water and get water in your mouth and nose. I think that's disgusting. Because the water isn't clean. If I need to pee when I am bathing, I pee through the swimsuit straight into the water, and others can do the same. Then it comes into you when you get water in your mouth.

I am afraid of big guys who run at full speed out on the

bridge so it rocks and dive into the water so it splashes a long way. Some are so careless. Sometimes they jump down where it's shallow, and then it can happen that you stand exactly where they come. Some smaller guys are swimming underwater and standing on their hands and doing somersaults and things like that, and sometimes when they are down below the surface, they grab your leg and try to pull you down. I am afraid of that too. I wish guys were not allowed to bathe in some places, so those who want some peace and quiet could be there for themselves.

My name is Rut Bergfeldt.
I am married to Egon Bergfeldt
and we have a daughter who was christened Pia.

Eivor and I have been acquaintances since childhood and as long as we have had the cottage, we have socialized every summer. We rent it from Eivor and Tore. And their youngest daughter and our daughter are almost the same age, so the children have also spent a lot of time together. It has been nice.

Eivor and I went to the same school. That means I have known her for almost my entire life. I can't believe that she no longer exists. That she is gone forever!

In the summer we have met several times a week. We usually have coffee together, either down with her in the villa or up with me in the cottage. Used to, I mean. Tore and Egon both work, except during the three holiday weeks. Strictly speaking, it's not that far for Egon to go from here to work, so we usually move out before his leave has started. And Egon and Tore also get along so well. Poor Tore!

Eivor knew everything about me. I had no secrets from her. For example, I told her about my problems with Egon when Pia came to us. I think many men find it difficult when children come into the family, no matter how it happens. Surely, it is like that, isn't it? You can't give them all your attention anymore. Besides, you are so tired, because you have to get up in the middle of the night and feed the child. Pia was only a few months old when she came to us. I tried to get her used to not eating at night from the beginning, but it took a while before she got used to it. Eight hours of sleep are needed for both the baby and the mother and the neighbours!

When she got a little older, I noticed that she wanted something to do when she was awake during the day, and then I got to learn the trick of letting her have fun on her own in the playpen as much as possible. I gave her a rattle and some other little things to play with. Anyone who picks up her baby and carries it on her arm as soon as it screams will later have ample opportunities to repent her indulgence! It's an old and proven experience that the less you deal with an infant, the kinder it becomes.

But that didn't stop Egon from feeling neglected. It's probably jealousy quite simply, which men feel when they are no longer allowed to be the centre of attention. In any case, Egon became irritable and quite demanding. Shortly after Pia's arrival, I couldn't really cope with the physical intimacy, and I told Eivor about it. It helped to just talk about it.

She was very good at listening, Eivor. No chatterbox, as I am. Sometimes I think that was what made us get along so well. I am talkative and outgoing, while she was quieter and more introverted. She kind of stood a little outside, while I always place myself in the centre. She was so calm and soberminded. I never saw her upset or cry. Surely, that's strange, isn't it?

I myself cry all the time. I cry when I see a sad movie at the cinema, and I cry when I see pictures of cute little animals that no one takes care of. When the Russians sent the poor space dog up in a rocket, for example, I cried rivers. And when Pia was little, I cried when *she* cried, even though she was sorry because I had scolded her. And I cried when she did a thing for the first time, like when she said Mom or drew her first stick figure. Ridiculous, isn't it? But I can't help it. I cry when I am happy, and I cry when I am sad.

But Eivor wasn't like that. She always seemed so calm and sober-minded. Not as up and down as I am. I am about like a roller coaster. Start well but fizzle out, that's me!

Not even when we were young did she get excited. For example, she never fell head over heels in love with someone like I could do. She was kind of… patient, you could say. Good at waiting and seeing. See how things would develop. She was very calm.

And she never got annoyed with her children. Not like I get with Pia, when she is obstinate and doesn't want to obey. She was very patient and never lost control. Never that I saw her give her children a box on the ear or a slap on the butt when they had behaved badly. I simply didn't understand how she managed it.

And with Tore… Yes, how can I describe how she had it with him? Egon and I, we disagree and quarrel sometimes, but she and Tore never quarrelled. They were like two old workhorses that went in pairs and almost never bumped into each other. Each one took care of his own part and trotted along in his own furrow, you could say. Eivor was good with vegetables and eggs, and Tore took care of the firewood and the potato field. Yes, and so the whole household was her department of course.

In any case, I never saw them cuddle and coo. Not even when they were young. But maybe it just wasn't their way. You never know how others feel. And when the children came, they both also took it easily and naturally. When Eivor was expecting Siv, she was huge, I remember, like such a toy with a lump of lead in the bottom that stands up again when you overturn it. But if someone had overturned Eivor, she would probably have needed help to get up again!

All her deliveries went well, and I, who lacked experience of both pregnancy and childbirth, of course asked a lot about it, curious as I was. And she answered kindly, though she wasn't really interested in talking about it, I think. She was like that, Eivor, that she would rather listen to others than talk about herself. Sometimes I suspected that she had secrets that she didn't share with me. Last autumn, before we moved into town again, I got the feeling that she was carrying something, but I never brought it up with her. Of course, I regretted it later, when I found out what had happened, because it could have had something to do with the murder. But we were just about to move into a new apartment, so I had a lot of other things to think about right then.

When we returned to town, the residential area itself was still not completely finished, but many of the houses were ready to move into. It was crowded with construction workers outside, and you could hear the rumbling and squeaking of excavators and trucks all day long. The ground on the future yard was just a mess of mud that you had to get through as best you could.

But our new apartment was wonderful. It's located on the fourth floor and has all modern comforts, such as a refrigerator and a bathroom with bathtub and shower. There was no refrigerator in our previous apartment, so that's a big improvement. And we have decided to buy a washing machine. It will be one with a separate centrifuge, which is admittedly expensive – it costs one thousand three hundred – but it will be worth it, because I am so awfully tired of cleaning after others in the laundry room.

And it was so fun to decorate the new apartment. For the kitchen we bought a larger dining table with a Perstorp laminate tabletop. When I set the table, I put tablets in braided plastic under the plates, so that it will look a little festive. And in the bedroom, we now have a Dux double bed with a bed-spread in yellow cotton fabric and ruffles at the bottom and two bedside tables – one on each side – and a teak dressing table with a three-part mirror and an associated small chair.

The living room is furnished with a sofa, two armchairs, an elongated coffee table, and a floor lamp with three different coloured shades of fabric. On one wall we have a shelf – it's a string shelf – for books and ornaments and below it a side-board with sliding doors. On top is the radio, of the Luxor brand, for which we gave two hundred. I listen to the radio a lot when I am home, because it's such good company, I think.

The third room has been given to Pia. Before she came to us, when Egon was still a poor student, we lived out of fashion in one room and a kitchenette. In the room there was a tiled stove that you had to get firewood for, as well as for the iron stove in the kitchen. The draughty windows faced a backyard with garbage cans, and the toilet was out in the hallway, where it was always cold. When we were to wash ourselves properly, we heated water in pots and bathed in a large zinc tub on the floor. Having it like that was fine as long as we were young and childless, but since Egon got a permanent job and we decided to try to have children, we wanted to live more comfortably. At that time, we could also afford a new and modern apartment. It was so different to have our own toilet and hot water and a bathtub... In the beginning, I lay and lounged in the bathtub for ever, I remember. It was like coming to heaven, I thought. But it was only a two-room apartment, and now that Pia is so old, you prefer her to sleep a little more separate from her parents.

We are so happy with our apartment and enjoy it so much that it almost felt difficult to leave it when we moved out this year. Otherwise, I always long for the country and the cottage as summer approaches. But this year it hasn't felt quite as usual. Of course, it has to do with the terrible thing that has happened here lately, because you can't help wondering if it's someone who lives here permanently who has done it. And in that case, it may not be safe for the children to be out playing in the evenings, I think. But you can't keep on worrying all the time either, so I try to push away the thoughts of it as best as I can.

Ingrid

When I was little, we had summer children. It's a boy or a girl who lives in town and needs to come out in the country and get some fresh air. Girls who were as old as me came to us. One named Britt-Marie and one named Åsa. Once Britt-Marie stepped on a rusty nail, so it went almost straight through her foot. Then she had to go to the hospital and get a tetanus shot and a bandage. It was in the meadow down by the river, where Stickan and Becke found Aunt Eivor, that Britt-Marie stepped on the nail. It protruded from a board lying on the ground. When we got home, Mom put on some iodine, but it didn't help, so she had to go to the hospital.

Cows and horses graze in the meadow. These are the cows we get milk from because they are Uncle Lindberg's cows. Gun-Britt and I pull up grass for the horses when they are in the meadow and play that one is hers and one is mine. I have ridden a workhorse once when an uncle led it, but otherwise I have never ridden. Gun-Britt hasn't done it either.

When it's time to pick potatoes, Dad borrows Uncle Lindberg's horse and runs with the plough so that the potatoes come up.

It's rather difficult to control a horse. If you want him to stay, you say *ptroo,* and if you want him to start walking, you gee him up and slap a little with the reins on his back. The most difficult is when you want him to turn around and get to the right place with the plough. Then I almost feel sorry for the horse sometimes, if he doesn't quite understand how Dad wants him to do.

In the meadow, juniper bushes and rosehips grow. What is inside rosehips can be used for itching powder. I know that because I have seen a girl who has got it on her. It was a guy who brought it with him to school and put it on her back, and she jumped around and screamed.

And there are lots of flowers in the meadow that we pick sometimes. There are cowslips, pasqueflowers, meadows saxifrages, babies'-slippers, cat's feet, harebells, lady's yellow bedstraws, northern bedstraws, snake's heads, and buttercups. If you hold a buttercup under someone's chin, you can tell if he or she has grubbed a lot of butter.

Snake's heads are protected. Once when we had picked such ones, before we knew it was forbidden, we had made a huge bouquet, and when we went on the road a car stopped and those who sat in it asked if they could buy the snake's heads for two *kronor*. Yes, they could. We sold them. Because they smell bad when you take them in, but those in the car probably didn't know that. Pee lilies Gun-Britt calls them.

When we are down in the meadow, we sit in Uncle Harald's rowing-boat sometimes and wait for a big barge to come and make waves so that the rowing-boat sways, or we sit on the bridge and splash our feet in the water. It was at that bridge Stickan and Becke had their raft before Aunt Eivor was murdered.

My name is Pia and I am ten years old.
My mother's name is Rut and my father's name is Egon.
We are summer guests here.
In the winter we live in town.

Here in the country, there are no playgrounds and no shops and no cinemas as in town. You just play here or go swimming. I usually play with a girl named Maud, who also lives in town in the winter, and with two girls named Gun-Britt and Ingrid who live here all the time.

There are some guys too. One named Björn, who also lives in town in the winter, and one named Ronny. Another, who lives here regularly, is named Stig. He has cropped hair and walks around and imitates *Kalle Stropp* every five minutes. "One must say!" he says in a squeaky voice. I think he is foolish.

There are all kinds of people living in the country, and they are not quite like us. People out in the sticks are not as modern as people in town. For example, they take milk directly from the cows and don't buy it in the store as we do. And they don't have refrigerators to put the food in so that it doesn't rot.

Ingrid's mother is crazy. It's a little scary, I think. Last summer she was as usual and now she is crazy. I don't want to go in to Ingrid and play now, because you don't know what Aunt Signe can come up with. She says such strange things. Ingrid also doesn't want us to play in their house. She may be ashamed or feel stupid to have such a mother.

And Gun-Britt's mother is dead. Last summer she was alive and now she is dead. It's scary too. It was a man who came and killed her with a stick or what he had. She was murdered, and the police haven't caught the one who did it yet. He may come and murder more if he wants. He can also take children.

A few years ago, a little girl in Stockholm was stuffed in an old suitcase and thrown into a lake. She had accompanied a dirty old man who offered sweets. Then he murdered her and stuffed her in the bag.

Meeting dirty old men and running across the street without looking are the most dangerous things there are. All mothers are afraid that their children will do that. And that they might get polio. You can die from it or end up in a wheelchair for the rest of your life. Maud, who I usually play with in the summer, has had it, but she got well again.

At home in town, we usually play hide-and-seek in the attic. We climb over the nets and hide among the things that people have in their cubicles. If a mother comes up, we lie silent like mice.

In the basement we play ghosts. There is a dark corridor there, that we sneak around in. Sometimes we play postman's knock. The boys stand in one room and the girls in another. Then you knock on the door and ask for handshake, hug, pat, or kiss. The girls almost always choose handshake, hug, or pat. The guys always choose kiss.

The only one we are afraid of is the caretaker. Everyone is very scared of him. Around all the carpet-beating-racks and between the houses there are bushes and lawns that one isn't allowed to walk on. *Keep off the grass!* it says on a small sign. But we play there anyway, and then the caretaker can come and chase us out of the bushes. If he gets hold of someone, he can give a box on the ear. The same if he finds us in the attic or in the basement.

In the basement there is also a laundry room, where my

mother can wash and mangle. She cleans the laundry room very carefully every time so that no one can say that she doesn't clean up after herself.

Mother cleans regularly. And she sews and knits. Sometimes she has a sewing circle, and then she invites the aunts who come to us for coffee and cakes. Every time I must go in and greet. I have to walk around and take each aunt by the hand and curtsy, so that they will see that I am polite and well-mannered. Otherwise, Mother will be ashamed of me.

You mustn't say "you" to adults. "Aunt" and "Uncle", are what should be said. And you mustn't talk unnecessarily or interrupt when the adults speak. You should be quiet and not contradict, even though you may not think the same. The adults are always right. And you mustn't squabble and not shout or swear, because nice girls don't do those things. You must be obedient and always do as the adults say. You should be kind, helpful, and polite and open doors for them and get up for them on the bus.

I have to do errands for Mother and clean my room and always come home on time in the evenings. And I must always speak the truth and stand for what I have done. I mustn't cheat and try to dodge. If I have done wrong, I must apologize and promise never to do so again. It always comes to Mother if I have done something stupid, and then I am scolded or beaten. I get a scolding when I have gotten dirty or had my clothes torn or come late for dinner. Mother punishes me, and it's for my own good, so that I will learn how to behave.

There are so many rules to keep in mind. You have to come in time to the meals and sit nicely at the table so that the underpants are not visible. You should have a good table manner and not smack or slurp when you eat and not burp at the table or talk with food in your mouth. If you need to cough or sneeze, you should cover your mouth. And you should wait your turn and not take food before everyone else. You must eat everything on the plate, because throwing away food is a shame. One must think of the poor children in Africa who are starving. And you mustn't leave the table without permission and not bring food or a sandwich out.

There is so much to remember all the time. I try to do the right thing, but sometimes I forget and then I get scolded by Mother.

My name is Gunnar Ekström
and I am a postmaster.
My family consists of a wife and three children.

We consider the accusations against our son Stig that have been made to us to be completely unfounded. I can't imagine that he has participated in any sexual games and physically injured a girl. According to the girl's mother, the injuries were of a minor nature, but that it was Stig who gave her the injuries, I consider to be completely out of the question. I have had a serious conversation with him, and he emphatically denies any knowledge of it.

At his age, it's natural to try to appear fearless and tough to impress older comrades. He also tries, like so many other boys, to get a little extra drama out of life if given the opportunity. That was the reason he decided to play a little private detective after the murder of Eivor. He looked for traces in the terrain around the site and bragged about his investigations, which he thought could be of help to the police. His excessive interest in the matter meant that even then I had a conversation with him. In his zeal he has a tendency to become thoughtless and rush away, but deep down he is a weak and cautious boy, who could never harm either a human or an animal. Mrs. Bergfeldt's accusations against him must be based on a misunderstanding between mother and daughter or even be a deliberate lie on the part of the girl. Townspeople can sometimes be a bit… nonchalant.

The youth of today enjoy a completely different freedom than previous generations. You have the freedom to study and train for generally speaking anything, and you have the freedom to get where you want with a moped, a motorcycle or a car. You also have the dubious freedom not to have to conform to the parents' previously natural authority.

The responsibility for the children's upbringing has increasingly passed from the parents to school psychologists, curators, family counsellors, and youth leaders and is no longer based on influencing and actively deciding but on understanding. It's believed that even in harmonious homes there may be a lack of interest and understanding of the problems of children and young people.

Many have adjustment problems that may be due to an upbringing without fixed norms and values, and which are expressed in general laxity and flabbiness. Juvenile delinquency is increasing alarmingly. Car thefts in particular are a major problem. I think I have read that we have a world record in car theft in this country.

What, then, is ultimately behind the growing youth problem? Is it the move to the cities or the schools' excessive classes or the mothers' gainful employment or the parents' diminished authority?

Probably a combination of the lot. But new phenomena in society don't release man from responsibility. The parents' responsibility isn't only to provide for the children's temporary well-being; it also means showing interest and giving guidance and love. And love without discipline weakens and breaks down as surely as discipline without love. Honesty and responsibility are important qualities that I have tried to teach my children. And I have succeeded in that, I think. Therefore, I unconditionally believe in Stig when he assures that he has neither played with nor injured the girl Bergfeldt.

In the same way, I completely trust Åke, my eldest son, when he declares his innocence regarding the murder of

Eivor Johansson. Of course, he has nothing to do with it. Evil tongues have tried to blacken him, but everyone who knows him better knows that he, despite his… youthful hobbies, is both a well-behaved and trustworthy young man.

It's his motoring interest one has fastened on. Some experts believe that one of the reasons for juvenile delinquency is the development of technology and the increased leisure time of young people. Many boys and girls become shy of work and prefer a vegetative and parasitic existence to an orderly and regular work. And that, of course, is true. The vast majority of today's so-called car borrowers are probably members of this youthful leisured classes, which prefers irregular and work-free living.

It's also indisputable that there is a connection between number of cars, engine interest, and car burglary. We mustn't forget that young people are exposed to the same intense motor propaganda that makes adults get a car, even though the economy in many cases doesn't allow it. The Swedish youth is obsessed with technology, and nothing can stop it from trying the charm of speed. There is also a psychological and sexual connection between puberty and speed sensation that makes the "motor devil" easily take over.

Stealing a car today is largely risk-free. Many of these young car thieves pose a serious danger to traffic and to other people's lives, but this risk factor obviously doesn't attach much importance. And admonishing doesn't help. Many belong to the "tough" type who behave superiorly, snazzy, and often provocatively impudently. Talking seriously with these car marauders is doomed to fail. As far as the police is concerned, it can also not be very constructive to see a car thief, who has been caught with great difficulty, be released after a short interrogation with only an admonition from, on the part of the prosecutor, to behave better in the future. There is no medicine that works on hardened juvenile delinquent.

What can then be done to get a car thief, who without respect for other's life and property, has completely smashed a stolen car up and caused death or long-term suffering for one or more people, to compensate for the damage he has caused? You can't demand compensation from someone who has nothing. It's far from certain that the young car lunatic is even of working age and has an income with which he can pay fines and damages. Despite the fact that the issue has been the subject of deliberations both in the preparation of the Criminal Code and with various authorities, nothing has yet been done to remedy the authorities' documented indulgence when it comes to trying appropriate countermeasures. The sinners are still free from all financial responsibility.

Another strong contributing factor to the problem is the lack of police in our major cities and population centres. A large part of the police department in charge of law and order, who previously regularly patrolled our streets at night, have been used for supervision and to direct traffic. Burglars, car thieves, and homosexual gangs can therefore live more or less undisturbed without risking being caught red-handed. Of course, this deplorable state encourages criminal elements to increase criminal activity.

However, we mustn't forget that the vast majority of our young people use both increased leisure time and technical development in an exemplary manner. The educational institutions and vocational schools are full of ambitious and curious young people who are working on their improvement and further education. It's estimated that ninety-seven percent behave well, and society doesn't have to worry about them. It's the other three percent, who are responsible for the negative image and who create the problem with juvenile delinquency, that is so difficult to master.

And now this terrible murder story that casts its shadow over us… The case will probably never be solved, I guess. The police don't seem to have the slightest clues to follow. I have consulted with the chief investigator a couple of times and been told that the investigation is largely at a standstill. And as long as no one is caught, the gossip and the speculations continue. Many innocent people have been affected. We ourselves had a hard time for a while, but now I think the worst is over.

Ingrid

I have had a lot of mosquito bites this summer. In order for it not to itch so much when I am to go to sleep, I have to put on Vademecum. We have that bottle in the bathroom cabinet. If I am to list all the things there are in the bathroom cabinet, it's razor, razor blades, shaving brush, shaving soap, iodine, Maniol, hand cream, Vademecum mouthwash, Sunsilk hair shampoo, mosquito oil, wound ointment, soaps, talc, scissors, gauze bandages, adhesive plaster, elastic bandage, toothpaste, toothbrushes, Keratin hair lotion, a gadget that Dad removes wax plugs in his ears with, fever thermometer, cotton wool, nail clipper. Dad must have a special clipper, because his nails on the big toes are yellow and thick and can't be removed with an ordinary pair of scissors.

I know exactly what things we have inside all the cupboards, because I look in them sometimes for empty cans and boxes that I collect. In the cupboard in the dining room, Mom has nice plates and bowls and deep dishes and glasses that she only brings out at Christmas or when there is a party. Then there should be a certain kind of glass for beer and a certain kind of glass for snaps if they are to drink that. Snaps is a kind of spirits that looks like water. It's almost just uncles who want it because aunts get dizzy from drinking it. Dad doesn't want it either, but he drinks it anyway, if there is a party or some men come and visit. At least before, when we had visitors sometimes, he did.

In the kitchen we have a broom cupboard where the cleaning things and the shoe polish and the silver polish are, and then Mom has a small shelf in another cupboard with our medicines. There are my vitamins. They are called Decamin, and I take them to make me feel fit. I usually get empty Albyl boxes and jars that have contained Andrew's fruit salt. Once I got an empty cigar box from an uncle.

In the larder, there are only boring things like milk and potatoes and cream that have become rubbery. At the bottom we have small beer and lager beer and soft drinks.

Sometimes I go with Dad to town and shop. First, we go to the grocery store. There you buy flour and sugar and coffee and cheese. The cheeses are large and round and placed on white towels. If you don't know from the beginning what kind of cheese you want, you can taste a slice of each. And if you don't want unground coffee, they take the coffee beans in a scoop and pour them into a large grinder and grind them. Then they open it at the bottom and let the coffee run down into a bag. Dad knows the uncle who owns that store. His name is Uncle Simon.

Then we go to the fish shop. Inside there are aunts with woollen cardigans and big aprons on them because it's cold in there. Water is flowing on the windows. I don't know why. Where does it come from and where does it flow down? The fish are in wooden boxes with ice cubes on top of the counter. On the cutting boards where they clean the fish, it's full of fish scales and blood and guts.

Then we go to the butcher shop. It's called charcuterie. There they chop off pieces of meat and pork chops from dead animals that they have slaughtered at Dad's job. They chop and cut and saw. For those who want minced meat, they put pieces of meat in a grinder and grind them to pieces so it becomes minced meat. The uncle in that store is called Uncle Tillman. He is wearing a white boat hat and a white apron with blood on it.

Finally, we go to the tobacco shop. There Dad submits his pool coupon. He does this every week, but he never wins any money, because he always guesses wrong. But once, when he had forgotten to hand over the coupon, he was twelve right. That's the most you can get. Then he would have received seven thousand *kronor* if he hadn't forgotten to submit the coupon.

I usually buy a comic book in the tobacco shop. On the way home I sit and read in it while Dad drives.

Dad's car is called Vauxhall Velox. Sometimes I help him wax it. When he has put on the wax, I rub it with the shammy-leather until it becomes shiny. But I can't go on for so long because it's very laborious to wax a car.

There are a lot of car brands, but I only know a few. Dad has a Vauxhall, uncle Tore has a PV 444, Uncle Ekström has a Mercedes, Uncle Andersson has an Opel Olympia, Uncle Hallgren has an IFA and Åke has a Chevy.

Sometimes, Gun-Britt and I sit on our gateposts and write down car numbers. Those who have A and B on their cars live in Stockholm, those who have C live in Uppsala, and those who have X live in Gävle. Otherwise, I don't know. Sometimes we just sit there and wait for the cars and guess what colour the next one will have.

Some guys collect pictures of cars, but I don't. One in my class named Björn says that there are almost a million cars and buses and trucks in Sweden if you count them all.

Once we went on holiday in the car to Kalmar. Then there was a bottle of mosquito oil that burst so everything ran out on the map in the glove compartment. When we were on our way home, Mom became car sick and vomited on the road. It was beetroot salad because she had eaten that.

I think Mom is a little scared to go by car. As soon as she sees another car coming from the side or she thinks that Dad is driving too fast, she brakes with her feet. But there is no brake pedal there, so the car doesn't stop. And she says that toxic gases come from cars. But I think it's fun to go by car. Sometimes I lie down in the back seat and look at the telephone wires that go up and down. They don't, but it looks like it when you look at them from inside the car when it moves.

When Dad was young, he had a motorcycle instead of a car. There were almost no cars at that time. We have a photo that shows him when he is sitting on the motorcycle and wearing a leather hat and big gloves.

Åke, Ninni's bro, is a *raggare*. He has a car instead of a motorcycle, and the girls who ride with him are called *raggarbrudar*. But now that he is together with Solan, she is the only one who goes with him.

Bengt and another guy have mopeds that they drive around and speed with in the evenings. Two girls usually go with them on back of the mopeds. I don't know what those girls' names are because I don't know them. They don't live here. One day, Gun-Britt and I decided to spy on them. There is a barn that you can drive into, and there they usually are. When we got there, they were sitting on a tractor platform and smoking. We saw them between the boards on the wall.

I have also smoked once. That was when Gun-Britt and I cycled to a place called Sundby and met a girl named Marianne and her sis. They asked if we wanted to go with them down under the bridge, and when we had done so, Marianne took out a box of John Silvers and asked if we wanted to share it with them. We would get four and they six. Her sis had matches, and she lit them. Marianne and the others inhaled, but I didn't dare. I don't know how to do it, either.

It looks tough to smoke, I think. When I grow up, I will do it for real and wear the kind of clothes that tough girls have. High-heeled shoes and a tight skirt and a leather jacket and stuff. And I will use make up and have nice jewellery. When I am about fifteen, I will start with that.

It was lucky that Marianne's sis lit my cigarettes because I don't dare to strike a match. Once when I was little and did it, I burned my thumb, and since then I don't dare. I don't dare to say that I don't dare either, because it's silly to chicken out for such a thing at my age. I don't want them to think I am yellow-bellied.

It's dangerous to smoke, some people say. Aunt Vera's husband, who is dead now, died of smoking. I met him when I was little, but then he got sick and died. He was an artist and painted pictures.

When it's summer, Aunt Vera usually comes to us. That's fun, I think. She doesn't act like some other grown-ups, who joke so you feel stupid when you don't understand what they mean, and they may laugh. "Oh, how big you have become!" they say, and then they may tease you a little and ask how you are getting on with your fiancé, even though they know that you can't have a fiancé when you are little. That's nasty, I think.

When Aunt Vera arrives, she has high-heeled shoes and nylon stockings with seams in the back and a fine coat or a fur-coat. In the winter she has a fur-coat. Instead of shoes in the winter, she has boots with galoshes.

I am allowed to look in her purse sometimes. It smells good in it because she has powder and perfume and lipstick there.

On herself she has necklaces and bracelets and earrings and a watch of real gold. But it's not because she is rich that she is fine but because she lives in Stockholm.

My name is Vera Winblad
and I am Erik Lundin's sister.
I am a widow and live in Stockholm where I work for a mail order
company.

It was as if the whole of Stockholm was boiling while waiting for the final match. It was to be played at Råsunda football stadium, and it was between Sweden and Brazil and concerned who would become world champions. The whole of Sweden looked forward with great hopes to the result, but in Stockholm it was probably noticed more than in other places, I would think. The hotels were fully booked up and all the restaurants exceeded all bounds with people who had travelled to the capital to watch the match. It was to be broadcast on television as well, but not everyone has acquired a set yet, so for most it was radio or reality that mattered. Sad that we lost!

The week before I was at Gröna Lund and listened to our famous court singer Jussi Björling who performed on the big stage. He sang *Blomsterarian* by Rachmaninov and *Aftonstämning* by August Söderman. There were over twenty thousand people there and listened to him, I was told afterwards.

That same night, a twenty-six-year-old woman was murdered in a basement corridor in Fruängen. The eerie thing is that she was also at Gröna Lund that night. On Friday morning, she was found dead in the basement of the house where she lived. She had been sexually abused and strangled. At the crime scene, the police found a cigarette holder that was later shown on television. It was the first time the Swedish police used that opportunity in connection with a murder investigation. During the viewing, everyone who had seen a person use a similar cigarette holder was asked to get in touch. Especially if that person suddenly didn't use the holder anymore or had bought a new one, this information was interesting, they said. There was a cigarette butt of the Boston brand in the holder, and since there can't be so many heavy smokers in Sweden who use just that kind of holders, the murder commission hoped that the showing would give many clues. I don't know how it turned out.

This spring, another young woman was found murdered in Stockholm. She was lying naked in a crevice in Västberga, which is about three kilometres from Fruängen, and she was discovered by two little boys. She too had fallen victim to a strangler. In connection with that murder, the police are looking for a Morris, which a witness saw near the scene.

Otherwise, there are no special similarities between the murders according to what has been read in the newspapers. The two women were also of completely different kinds. One was a well-behaved girl who supported herself through organized labour, and the other lived as a prostitute. The police don't think it's the same murderer, but you can't know for sure.

The newspapers always give a lot of space to murders, and this has happened this time as well, especially considering that the murders have occurred so close to each other and both have a sexual connection, which usually increases the readers' interest. It has also been speculated that the same perpetrator is behind both cases, but the police have so far rejected that theory.

One understands what pressure the police must work under, with a feeling that the murders should be solved as quickly as possible. It mustn't be in the way that women begin to avoid going out for fear of being assaulted and killed.

It's awful that there is so much evil and violence everywhere. Even here, in my peaceful little childhood village, it has happened now. I was born and raised here, together with Erik and my other siblings. Erik was allowed to take over the house after our parents, since he stayed and took care of Mother when she became a widow. She was old and sick and needed help. But at that time the house didn't look at all like it does today. Erik has had it renovated and modernized.

I have known Tore and Eivor for as long as I can remember. Tore also took over after his parents. In his case, it was the father who was left alone and lived in the house for as long as he lived. Eivor took care of him, in the same way that Signe took care of our mother.

I myself moved to Stockholm already as a young woman, and there I met Henry, my future husband. We got married just before the war. He is gone now, and I haven't...

In Stockholm, we noticed the war in many different ways. Every night, for example, there was a blackout. You had blackout paper for all the windows and out on the street it was pitch black. There was no light as far as you could see.

For the population, it was home defence exercises. You would, for example, practice going down to the shelter when the alarm came. Then, when the sound "all clear" was blown, you could go up again. Many thought it was unnecessary to practice, since you already knew how to do, they meant.

There was a shortage of food and what was available was rationed. The children received extra rations, so the families with children had many ration cards to keep track of, but it was still scarce for everyone. Shipping was cut down, which led to no goods coming in, and when there was no food to buy, it didn't help how many cards you had. There wasn't much coffee, but lots of surrogate, and the flour in the bread was mixed. You could buy coupon-free sausage, but you didn't even want to think about what it contained. Fish was also in short supply, as it was life threatening to go fishing due to all the mines in the sea. When there sometimes was herring to buy, for example, the queues were winding long outside the market halls.

In any case, we had peace in this country, and we were grateful for that. But once we thought the war was upon us. It was in February 1944, when Soviet bombers dropped bombs on Stockholm, Strängnäs, Södertälje, and Stockholm's northern archipelago. As if by a miracle, only four people were injured. But the material destruction was great, especially on Södermalm in Stockholm.

Two people were injured in Stockholm. One was a waitress who had her back torn by shards of glass, and the other was a man who was thrown into the street by the enormous air pressure and broke his shoulder. In Strängnäs, several bombs fell near the regiment and two conscripts were hit by shrapnel and slightly injured.

My husband and I lived in Täby at the time, but I had a co-worker who lived near Eriksdal, and in that area thousands of windows were smashed so many families had to evacuate their homes. It's said that where the newly built Eriksdalstea-tern had stood, there was only one large pit left. My co-worker was shocked by the bang, but she stayed in her apartment and scarcely patched her windows with blackout paper.

No one really understood what had happened until the next day when you could read in the newspapers that it was Russian bombs that had been dropped. Shards with Russian letters were found both on Södermalm and in Strängnäs, and eyewitnesses had seen aircraft approaching at high altitude from the east. Soviet authorities denied this, of course, and the official Swedish explanation was that the bombing was done by mistake. But we were often worried and wondered how long we would be able to escape the war.

In Täby we also had a tragic murder that year. I read about it in the newspaper and thought it was so awful that I have never been able to forget it. It was a wife who was found dead in her home on Centralvägen, very close to where Henry and I lived. A twenty-year-old daughter was also injured, and it was uncertain whether she would survive. Another daughter, who was no more than ten years old, discovered what had happened and rushed over to the neighbours to ask for help. The police were quickly on the scene and could establish that a violent battle had been fought in the kitchen. On the floor were knives, frying pans, and an iron that had all been used as tools.

There were three more children in the family, namely an older daughter and two sons, who were sixteen and seventeen years old. Pretty soon, the seventeen-year-old son admitted that he had killed his mother and abused his sister. He said that his mother had scolded him for not being able to pay the instalments on a bicycle and that he had become so angry that he had hit her in the head with the frying pan and the iron. Then he had stabbed her repeatedly with a knife. When his sister came home, he also knocked her unconscious with the iron and stabbed her several times before fleeing. Fortunately, she survived.

When I think about it now in connection with what happened to Eivor, I can't help but wonder if it was a trifle that triggered her murder as well. That may very well be the case, and in a way, it makes it even worse. But I know nothing about it. In any case, I can't imagine that she had any enemies. And no one believes that Signe would be involved. The idea that she is a suspect has come out of her own head. It's a delusion, quite simple. It's not possible to sort it out with her, I suppose, but it's certainly unfortunate that she withdraws and isolates herself for no real reason.

For Erik, my brother, her illness has meant a big change. He doesn't talk about it, but I notice how painful he thinks it is. He must experience Signe's personality change as a great loss. I know how much he appreciated her happy disposition before she fell ill. Now she lives enclosed in her own world and can hardly be reached. That she can still take care of the household is pure luck. I don't know much about mental illness, but I think that there is largely no cure. No. But a mental illness isn't a life-threatening illness anyway, and you have to be grateful for that.

Cancer on the other hand... My husband got lung cancer, and that's what he died of. We had no children. Maybe that's why my niece has always meant a little extra to me. And now... It's hard to really know how she takes it. This with Signe, I mean. And that with Eivor too, of course. She hasn't talked to me about it at all. I suppose she is just pushing it away. I guess that's how children do to survive. And trying to force something should probably not be done. No. The best thing is surely to just let it be.

I have no one to discuss it with and it feels difficult sometimes. My brother doesn't like to go into it, and I don't want to intrude. I understand that he, just like me, wants nothing better than to help little Ingrid over this. But it's not easy. We simply have to do our best and hope that will be enough. And I really hope that the police will succeed in finding Eivor's murderer so that there will be an end to all rumours end and so that Signe will no longer have to walk around and feel suspected.

As it's fortunately unusual in our well-arranged people's home that people kill each other, a murder in Sweden always attracts attention, both among the local population and – through the press – among the public. The general police instruction states so beautifully that "there should be a mutually trusting and good relationship between the representatives of the police and the press", and this is of course desirable. An at least equally important sentence I think the following is: "Excessive reticence on the part of the police can often do more harm than good to the police activity."

In the past, the press was regarded by the police as an unnecessary evil, which should be kept out of police work as far as possible. That view has probably now given way to a more benevolent attitude, which means that the police instead count on the means of mass communication and the publicity as a natural and effective part of the investigation work. From my own experience, I know that in an investigation there is sometimes material that could be useful for the inquiries if they were published. Actively utilizing the opportunities for publicity could in these cases be of pure service interest on the part of the police. In a large criminal investigation, moreover, it always emerges circumstances which can be of great general interest and which, upon publication, neither harm the investigation nor the integrity of individuals.

Nor should anyone imagine that it's possible to keep the press completely out of the subject matter. A modern newspaper possesses resources that give journalists great opportunities to obtain much information through their own investigations. But clues that crime scene investigators encounter must in principle never be made public. All initiates must observe total silence to avoid fatal injuries.

In general, however, I believe that the police should benefit more from the press than is currently the case. Without contact with the public, all police work comes badly off, and it's with that contact the press can be helpful to us. Factual information can sometimes even counteract too wild speculations.

The spread of rumours in this case became very extensive from the very beginning. The gossip has gradually run in ever wider circles, which has required its special controls and implied extra fag, which has often proved to be wasted effort. Personally, I have heard a large number of people without getting closer to the solution. Conflicting information has appeared in a steady stream. Some have certainly had significant things to tell but not wanted out with them. Others have concealed important information despite several urgent interrogations. All this has contributed in an unfortunate way to the fact that the mystery is still unsolved.

We have heard hundreds of suspects and a dozen of these have been arrested and detained. So far, there have been mainly four people that we have described as particularly "hot". However, the evidence has been incomplete. But we still hope to dispel the mystery and follow each new idea with the greatest interest.

It has not been possible to determine the motive for the murder. If we knew that, a lot would have been won from the beginning. Is the murderer a wandering peddler, who at an instant impulse was driven into a murder with robbery? Or is he one of Eivor Johansson's acquaintances – unknown to her relatives and to the neighbours – a "friend" who cunningly planned his act?

We have also lacked valuable technical evidence, such as fingerprints and a murder weapon. At first it seemed like we didn't have a single clue to follow. Immediately after the murder, intensive investigations took place every day for almost three months. Every desolate croft, every barn, lodge, and hayloft were carefully searched. All vehicles were inexorably stopped for checks, and a thorough combing of the entire area where the murderer could possibly remain was done. But the result was zero.

However, rumours spread in full sail in the village. Here no one wanted to believe that there were no tracks to follow. No, here they instead felt great resentment that the police didn't directly catch the culprit. And so, one pointed out various personal enemies in the neighbourhood – without a grain of evidence. The police carried out many checks of several villagers who had been out in the terrain that evening, but no one appeared to be particularly suspected at that time.

Anonymous letters pointing out various murderers have of course also occurred. Signatures such as "A friend of justice" and the like have contributed various tips.

In other words, this murder has involved an unusual amount of elimination work, because so many people have been pointed out. In some cases, the criminal record has spoken its clear language and sharpened the suspicions, but all of them have still finally been released thanks to their alibis, which must also be considered a certain success for us. Our task is to arrest suspects and then control their activities and then, as a first instance, release or convict.

Despite our enormous work effort, the murderer is still free after almost a year. It may look dark, and it may seem like we have taken too long. But we don't give up. New interrogations have been held, and new checks have been carried out. However, it's still an open question if and when the culprit can be arrested. Of course, the solution seems to be increasingly remote with each passing day without positive news. But we don't intend to let go. The culprit will sooner or later get caught.

Ingrid

On the twenty-fourth of August, school began again. It's fun to get new books and put paper and labels on them and lay new paper in the desk, but then you get used to it.

We got a schoolmaster called Borg. We will have him in all subjects except handicraft and physical training. In PT we have one named Kent Eklund, and in handicraft one named Anna-Greta Olsson. The boys have woodwork, so they have another teacher. It would be fun to have woodwork, I think, because then you can do carpentry and make cutting boards and work with stains. But girls only have handicraft. I am sewing a nightgown now. It's yellow with red roses on it. Before, I sewed a craft bag, a needle pad, and an apron. After the nightgown, I will start on a cloth. We will learn to sew different kinds of embroidery stitches.

Sometimes when we have gym, we go swimming. We go to town, where there is a bath with a large swimming pool. Everyone who can't swim must learn it. In the beginning, you wear a swimming float, then you have to manage yourself. I haven't done it without a float yet because I am so bad at swimming.

I don't like swimming at the bath because it's so noisy there. And it smells of chlorine so you can choke. They put it in the water to make the germs disappear. *The bugs*, Tommy says. And you can get pushed into the water if some big guys come and run. It's dead dangerous to be pushed, because you can fall backwards and hit your head on the edge and die.

The food at school is the same old food as usual. Rye-flour porridge, semolina pudding, and black pudding are the most disgusting. I can hardly eat that. But today we got brown beans and pork. *Yum-yum*, Tommy said. When I walked past him and some other guys, he tried to trip me up. "What is it?" I said. "Ischlibedisch," he said. It's German and means I love you.

It's fun that school has started again. Master Borg is kind, but he has a mania for hymns. Every time we have religion, we must memorize a part of a hymn. But it's pretty easy. And he doesn't get angry if you happen to say something wrong or don't remember. He has no darlings either, as some other teachers may have. He doesn't like study horses better than others. But I am not a study horse. I just need to skim through the homework a bit, and then I know it. I don't have to sit long and read.

When Mom was little and went to school, the teachers were very strict. Then they had to stand in the corner or go forward and put their fingers on the master's desk and be beaten with a ruler for the slightest mistake they made. If they talked during a lesson or didn't know their homework off pat, for instance. Once Mom had to come forward. She didn't want to, but she had to, and then the master struck on her fingers with the ruler the worst he could. So, it's fortunate that one goes to school now, at this time, and not in her time.

During the breaks, we skip or are on the climbing frame and turn around. Sometimes we exchange bookmarks. I have mine in a large chocolate box with paper in between. I have old-fashioned ones apart and those with glitter on them apart. Around the square ones I have a rubber band. Some of them are boring, with different kinds of birds or wild animals. Flower baskets, angels, and hearts I think are the finest. And flower girls who represent a dog rose or a snowdrop. These I have with glitter on them. My finest old-fashioned one is a hand holding a book that says "Hearty Memory" and a crib. You know that they are old because they are a bit brownish on the back.

Kerstin likes royalties, puppies, kittens, and nice girls with curly hair and ruffle dresses. It works well to exchange with her because we don't like exactly the same. I have exchanged a very nice one from her. It's a pigeon with a red ribbon around its neck on which hangs a heart and a letter. Behind it are pink roses and forget-me-nots. For that, she got two rounds – one with Princess Margareta and one with Princess Birgitta.

At school, we sometimes put a bookmark in a notebook on which the sheets are folded. But then you get no fine ones, or nothing at all if it's empty in the compartment where you insert your bookmark. So, it's better to exchange in the usual way. It's so wonderful to feel the smell in the box and browsing through the bookmarks, I think. That's almost the best I know.

Film stars are also fun. I have fifty-three pictures. If I am to list a few, they are Tony Curtis, Gina Lollobrigida, Brigitte Bardot, Sophia Loren, Grace Kelly, Cary Grant, Gary Cooper, Burt Lancaster, Johnny Weissmuller, Lassie, Elvis Presley, Tommy Steel, Rock Hudson, Rita Hayworth – some names I say as they are spelled and not as they are pronounced – Humphrey Bogart, Lauren Bacall, Gregory Peck, Kim Novak, Audrey Hepburn, Anita Ekberg, Elizabeth Taylor, Danny Kaye, Marilyn Monroe.

And then we have our poetry books. Mine is pink with birds and flowers on the cover. First, someone named Barbro in my class has written. *I was going to pick flowers and tie a wreath for you, but the ground was frozen and there were no flowers.* That one is beautiful, I think. Barbro has warts on her hands, but she can't help it.

Then comes Inger's verse. *Learn the difficult mystery of life, to love, forget and forgive.* I don't like her so much. She is a real stuck-up girl who is bragging about everything all the time. Self-praise is no recommendation, but she apparently doesn't know that.

On the next page, someone named Kristina in my class has written. She is squint-eyed but rather pally. *May your path be flower-strewn, may joy never be lacking, may love then be your reward, this is my warm prayer.*

I have let our former schoolmistress write too. *To love and to be loved, that is the highest poetry of life.*

And here is one named Gunilla. *I wish you happiness, shoes that don't press, no worries and light when it gets dark.* She has had her appendix removed. At first, she was very ill, then she had to go to the hospital and have an operation. I have also had an operation once, but I don't remember it, because I was anaesthetized. That was when I was in the sanatorium when I was seven years old.

The next person who has written is Ingela. She has Pat Boone as her idol. She thinks he is handsome and keeps talking about him. Here is her verse: *Here to the world once came a little baby three inches long, she screamed bu, bu, bu, who was it, well it was you!*

Then comes Ninni's verse. *Three little words for you, don't forget me.* She has written in block letters because she hasn't learned handwriting yet.

And here is one named Anette. She has cold sores. Gun-Britt has that too sometimes. Why do you get that? I don't know. Once Anette wet herself at school. Then the boys teased her and called her mother's darling and cry-baby when she cried and wanted to go home. Here is her verse: *Fall in love often, get engaged sometimes, but for Christ's sake get married as seldom as you can!*

Well! Here it's blank on several pages and then comes Yvonne's verse. She is the one Monika is together with. *When you walk the path of life, I wish you happiness and prosperity.* Yes, she may do that, but Monika doesn't. She just wishes me misfortune and bad luck. So, she won't be allowed to write in my poetry book. She can drown herself, I think.

Here is Gugge's verse: *You are the rose, I am the thorn, therefore I write in the corner.* She loses her shoes all the time because she has insteps-raisers in them so that she won't be flat-footed, and therefore they don't stay on her properly.

Guys, most of them, think poetry books are silly, but I have asked a few if they wanted to write in mine, and some wanted to. Staffan for example. This is how he wrote in my book: *This way guys, come and buy tickets, the highest prize is Lundin's daughter!*

This verse is written by Gun-Britt's big sis. Her name is Siv. *When you pick flowers, pick one for me, when you count friends, count me too.*

And here is Tommy's verse. It's the finest in the whole book, I think, because it's unusual. He has made lines with a nail after a ruler and then he has written on the lines to make it look straight. This is how it is: *Against calumny be calm and safe, it should not give you pain, for what is said behind your back, it does not hit your heart.* Calumny means that they are talking crap about someone. Does he know that they are doing that about me? Do they do that? Who do it? Monika and her mates or someone else who doesn't like me? I don't know. But he might want to comfort me a little with that verse, I think.

Then comes Gun-Britt's verse. *I want to sit in your memory, on a tiny little stick, but if the stick gets too short, I fall out of memory.* But I will never forget her, because I have played with her ever since I was little and met her at least a thousand times.

Then there is a girl in my class named Margareta who has written. She has long hair and braids. I also had them when I was little, but Mom cut off my hair so that I wouldn't whine so much when I was combed. She saved it, and now I have it in tissue paper in an empty chocolate box. *Roses are red, violets are blue, strawberries are sweet and so are you.* She was the one who suffered a concussion when she was pushed down from the hillock.

And Kerstin has written like this: *What would the sky be without stars? What would a wedding be without bridesmaids? What would Sweden be in all its glory, if Ingrid did not exist?*

At the end are Uffe's and Anders' verses. Here is Uffe's: *If your heart breaks, fix it with Karlsson's glue.*

On the last page is Anders' verse, because it's such a verse that you should write last. *At the end of the book, the fool is writing, name and date upside down.* But he is wise and no fool. At least *I* don't think so.

There are some fools in the remedial class, but we usually never join them. Or they are not exactly fools. They are a little backward, so they don't understand everything. And in the village, there is one too. He is the child of Aunt Britta and Uncle Nils who owns a farm.

*My name is Britta Karlsson
and my husband's name is Nils.
We have two children – Solveig who is eighteen years old
and Ragnar who is fourteen.*

Ragnar was born with the umbilical cord around his neck and had a brief lack of oxygen. At the hospital it was said that he wouldn't get any harm from it, but I was worried and constantly compared him to Solveig's development. I thought he was so late in everything. He spoke badly, for example, but it was because he had had a hearing loss from all the ear infections he had had, which had affected and delayed his speech development, we were told. I didn't really believe in it, but I had no one to consult with and tried to push the anxiety away as best I could.

He demanded constant attention. I could never go anywhere or go shopping, because I got completely exhausted by guarding him and preventing him from running out into the street among all the cars. Whatever I said or did, he didn't obey. Nothing worked and no other children wanted to play with him. He was so rowdy. All children can be little rascals, but he was worse than others, I thought. He constantly disagreed with Solveig and other children, and he kicked and fought.

Solveig has been ignored a lot. I think I overprotected him. He was at the centre all the time and she always came in the shadows. I told Nils that I couldn't take it anymore, because Ragnar made demands that I couldn't meet. Nils told me to put my foot down, and I began to do so, so that it returned fairly to the normal, but he was so terribly hard, and particularly to his sister.

I have worried a lot about her too. Mostly because she is a girl and can get into trouble with boys. It can happen that a young girl becomes pregnant even if she hasn't had her first menstruation and received proof that she is sexually mature. A moment of desire, curiosity or thoughtlessness can change her whole life and, in many cases, ruin her youth and perhaps her whole future. Even if the interaction between the sexes has become freer, this doesn't mean that the responsibility has become less. There is nothing as tragic as unwanted children. Not only for the mother herself, but even more for the child, who doesn't receive the care, attention, and upbringing to which it is entitled.

And I have warned her about hanging out with boys who use alcohol. Getting married to a drinker, like my mother did, is almost the same as committing a crime, I think. Especially when the vice is completely obvious and can't be hidden. Not even with a man, who without being a drinker is known to use alcohol, has a woman the right to marry. All the beautiful notions of the noble task of saving him, and all his assurances and promises of improvement as long as she doesn't abandon him, are no foundation to build on. With great certainty he will betray her hope and confidence. Anyone who has once started drinking will never get loose. And a man who is so pathetic that he hangs himself on a young woman for his salvation isn't worth the slightest sacrifice.

There is almost no disaster that is greater for an individual and for a family than drunkenness. A ruined body, a weakened and humiliated soul is the end of the drinker's career. And the worst thing is that he at the same time brings misery and distress over his wife and children, who it is his duty to protect and provide for.

Nils and I have done the best we could to help Ragnar, but it hasn't always been easy. When he was little, he did so much mischief. Once he shot with his slingshot into a neighbour's window, so it burst and we had to pay. Another time he and some other boys lit a fire in the woods. He was then six years old. He never harmed any person, but he was cruel and harsh with animals. He could go behind the cows in the barn and snatch their tails or scare the piglets in the pinfold, so they screamed. Once he cut off the cat's whiskers and burned off a piece of its fur with a match.

When it was time for him to start school, he didn't pass the school maturity test and was placed in a remedial class. He had difficulty sitting still, and it took him a long time to learn to read and write. He did better in a small class, so it was the right decision, but he was never allowed to start in a regular class. Now he is fourteen and his schooling is over. I have him at home all day. Nils has bought him a moped that he drives around on, and we let him do it, even though he isn't old enough. It makes him calmer we have noticed.

When he gets angry, he can do almost anything, and afterwards he remembers nothing of it. He says that everything becomes black for him. And he gets so terribly strong when he is angry. Afterwards, he is completely exhausted and must go to bed. He once chased a neighbour with the tractor. It's said that he had intended to kill him, but that wasn't the case. He stopped the tractor before anything happened.

Everyone gets scared when he threatens to kill people and burn things down. He doesn't notice himself what power he has and doesn't understand why people withdraw from him. There isn't a single person here in the village who doesn't know who he is. He is known – or infamous I should say –

and has been called both vicious and backward. It has felt awful many times. The worst was when he chased Tage with the tractor. That's when I got sick.

I worry about him all the time. He is easily led and is tricked into things by both boys and girls. There are many examples of this. And he often misunderstands what is happening and doesn't get what people are saying to him. I take it so badly. There are those who say that we should take it easy and wait and see. Even if he isn't an Einstein, he may be able to fend for himself when he grows up, they say. But how should he be able to have a job and start a family and live like everyone else in society? I don't understand how it could be possible.

I know that there are those who believe that it was Ragnar who attacked Eivor. Maybe not with the intention that she would die, but as a result of him losing control of his short temper. I have asked him where he was that evening, but I haven't received any proper answers. Not that I for a moment think that he has something to do with it. That I asked was only because I thought he might have seen something when he was out. The only thing he has said is that he was out riding his moped.

I have pondered and asked myself over and over again why anyone would wish so badly for Eivor that she had to die. She who lived such a quiet and considerate life. Everyone I know has only good things to say about her. So, it's completely incomprehensible that it ended in this awful way for her.

Ingrid

On Saturdays we have a funny hour at school. Last time, Kerstin and Gugge sang *Tuttan and Ingeborg*. It's about two girls who disagree. After the song, Anders played the clarinet and Hasse came forward and told some riddles. One was like this: "What is it that goes up and down but never moves?" Nobody knew it, so he had to say the answer himself. It was the stairs. But if it is an escalator then? In Stockholm, where Aunt Vera lives, there are such stairs. Another riddle was like this: "Where do the rivers have no water and the towns no houses?" That was the map. Last of all, Anders did a magic trick. He conjured so that a coin went through a table. *Abracadabra* and so it was through! I really don't know how he did it.

I have a book with magic tricks in it, but what he did isn't included. My best trick is when you put a match on a handkerchief and fold it and let the one you conjure to break the stick inside, and when you unfold the handkerchief again the stick isn't broken. I got that trick from my magic book.

You are not stupid if you don't understand magic tricks, because they are meant to be inexplicable. But some people don't understand things so well because they may have a brain defect. You can feel sorry for them. Once when Ninni was mean to a guy named Ragnar because he didn't understand a thing, I defended him. He is fourteen years old and a little backward. "Do you have eggs in your hat?" she said to him. But he can't help that he doesn't understand everything, and I told Ninni that.

At home, if I have no one to play with and Ragnar might come, I play with him sometimes. I pretend that he is my horse and put a harness on him and let him walk with a rake between his legs and harrow. Or he can be a dog and run on all fours. Then I put Lady's old necklace and leash on him.

Once when Gun-Britt and I were playing with Ragnar, we got to see him pee. He peed on a stock, so it splashed. Boys can pee on what they want, but girls can't. For girls, it only comes straight down where they sit or on their feet or skirt.

Ragnar has a very long tongue. It's so long that he can put it up against the tip of his nose. And he eats pieces of snots. I could never do that. I can eat snot, but not pieces of snot. They are so disgusting. Dandruff is also disgusting. And earwax when you see it in people's ears. I see it in Gun-Britt's ears sometimes. And on Dad, there is dandruff on his shoulders when he wears his black jacket. Why is there so much that is disgusting?

Once Ragnar has lit a fire in the woods, that almost became a forest fire. If you play with fire, you pee in bed at night, says Aunt Vera, but I don't believe that. I think it's the same as when they say that it will be beautiful weather when a cat sneezes, or that it will start to rain if you kill a spider, or that you will get seven years of misery if you broke a mirror, or that someone is going to die when you hear a cuckoo in the south. It's just tales.

My name is Ragnar and I am fourteen years old.
My mother's name is Britta and my father's name is Nils.
I have a big sister who is called Solveig.
My grandfather's name is Harald and my grandmother's name is Beda.
I stay with them sometimes. Otherwise, I am mostly in the woods.

I learn things about nature in the woods. I build huts, and sometimes I make a fire. The fire calms me down. I can sit for hours watching the fire and throwing sticks into the flames. Once there was a forest fire. I helped to put it out because I didn't want the forest to burn up.

In the winter you can't be outside all the time. Then I go to visit Edvin. He is my friend. He is rather old, and I help him shovel snow and carry in firewood and stuff. Sometimes he tells me about things he has been through. He believes in trolls and has met several. But that's a lie.

I am helping Dad with the farming. I drive the tractor and plough and harrow. It's fun. When I grow up, I want to be a farmer or a road worker, so that I can tire myself out properly every day. I like to work hard. I can start early and work all day if I may. I don't need anything to eat either.

I am mostly by myself. I am a lone wolf who doesn't want to be with others so much. It's most comfortable to be alone. It's calmer when there are no others who can tease me, so I get outbursts. I can try to fight back when I feel it's coming, but for the most part I don't have enough time. It's coming so fast. I usually tell them to be careful and stop teasing, because otherwise I can get angry. Some don't believe me and continue anyway and then I get an outbreak.

I don't want outbreaks. When I get angry, I start to tremble and find it hard to talk. I get weird and tense. It gets black and then I don't know what I am doing. I scream and stomp and hit and throw maybe a plate or something. I keep going until all the anger has gone out of me. Then I am completely exhausted and just want to sleep.

I know I am worse than others. At school, I had a hard time keeping up with reading and writing and arithmetic. I had a hard time learning. When I was at home with other children, I broke their things. If I got a toy myself, it always broke on the first day. It just happened. I had to take it apart and look for what it looked like inside, and then I couldn't put it together again.

I can never be still. I have to move my hands and pull my fingers and touch things. I always must have something to fiddle with and get worried from sitting still.

I can never do things just enough. I am harsh and violent. Sometimes I hurt others without wanting to. I like my moped and my mother and my sister. If someone is mean to them, I get angry and want to fight. It has happened once, and then I walloped properly. Girls mustn't be beaten. Not old ones either. I have done it three times, and then I had to regret it.

I know I am no good. I can't speak so well and not read so well and not write and count. And I do stupid things that make others sad. I try to resist it and think before I do something stupid, but sometimes it doesn't work.

Last April there was supposed to be a fire, but it started to burn before it was to be lit. When we were going to put it out, someone pushed me, and I got angry. I grabbed him by the neck. Then they said that I had tried to strangle him.

You only get scolded. If you think you have been good and done something good, they complain about something else instead. They don't want to think that I can be good. So, I have stopped trying.

My name is Solveig Karlsson
and I am the daughter of Nils and Britta Karlsson.
I am eighteen years old and I have a brother who is fourteen.

I think parents should be fair and understanding so that you can talk to them. They don't have to be completely abstainers, but they mustn't drink, and they must be youthful in their way and look decent so that you don't have to be ashamed of them. The mother shouldn't work outside the home, and she should be happy and pleasant so that the father gets in a good mood when he comes home in the evening.

All that I think my parents mostly correspond to. The only problem in our family is Ragnar, my brother. When he was younger, Mom devoted all her time to him. For my own part, I always had a bad conscience about being able to do more than him, and I was ashamed that I didn't love him. Or rather because I hated him, because that's what I did before. He always took his bad mood out on me, and he could hit me very hard. I screamed as soon as he came near, and if he grabbed me, I always started crying.

Later he had epileptic seizures, and I certainly felt sorry for him when he lay on the floor shaking, but I could never feel that I liked him. My friends thought I was weird not being attached to my brother, but they didn't know how he was towards me.

Ragnar will never be able to live like an ordinary person. He does his best, but it's not enough and there are always people who don't understand and treat him badly. When it comes to work, he must adapt to what he can handle, and he has many obstacles in his future that you don't know how he will succeed in overcoming.

Nowadays, at least we girls can do pretty much whatever we want in a career. We don't have to be housewives. Now a technically interested girl can become a good engineer and the scientifically interested can become a doctor or a researcher. The artistically minded can train as an artist or ceramicist – or why not as a home decoration expert, fashion designer, beauty expert, or hairdresser, because those professions can also be considered artistic. Yes, there are lots of professions for us girls to choose from. Even for the practical, there are many interesting and well-paid jobs.

Many girls think that it's unnecessary to get an education because you are to marry anyway. But getting a vocational education and experience of gainful employment can be a good insurance against unforeseen events.

Some of my friends dream of becoming a model, an airhostess, or a film actress, but the most common is to work in an office, in a store or in the postal service. For my own part, I invest in becoming a hairdresser. I go to vocational school. The apprenticeship is three years and the periods in school are interspersed with internships.

A girl who wants to work as a hairdresser must have a sense of form, style, and lines, and have a good touch. She mustn't be trembling or left-handed and not suffer from hand sweat or have thick fingers or wrists. She must be able to work with light, flexible hand movements in order to be a driven haircut. You must also be clean and tidy, and you must have strong feet and legs, because it's tempting to stand a lot. Yes, and then you must have the right way with the customers. A casual and elegant demeanour makes an impression, and it doesn't hurt to be considerate and accommodating so that the customer is happy and feels that you know how she wants it.

If she wants to talk, you should be able to do that, and if she wants to sit quietly, she should have it that way.

Right now, I work at a salon that is open nine to six on weekdays and nine to five on Saturdays. We are ten girls – two learners, seven assistants – trained ladies' hairdressers, that is – and one at the reception. As a learner, you can sweep, wash permanent coils, and wash dishes and bowls for colouring. There are twelve places to tidy up. The washbasins should be cleaned, and the mirrors polished, and it should be dusted and dried with a damp cloth everywhere. Everything should be perfect.

After two or three months, you may start taking care of customers and washing their hair. The hands crack from the shampoo so that the blood flows and you have to lubricate with Vaseline and lie with cotton mittens on at night. And it really takes effort to be up and running all day. When I come home in the evenings, I am so tired that I hardly know my name. I lie down directly on the bed with my hat and coat on and just want to cry. Then it doesn't feel good at all, but the next day it's just as fun to go there again.

I think our efforts are worth just as much as the students'. The journeyman's certificate should be valued as highly as the student grades, I think. We take a practical student exam, I usually say. I think taking a theoretical student exam is more pressing than taking a practical one. On the day of the exam, there is an oral hearing in front of censors in several subjects, and if you don't pass, you are ploughed and have to sneak out of school through the back door. It must feel like a nightmare when you know that relatives and friends are standing in the schoolyard waiting with flowers to congratulate you.

For me, it's a natural thing to wash my hair often. The American girl, who is known for her beautiful well-groomed hair, washes her hair several times a week and rolls it up as hairdressers do. Once a month she has it cut at a skilled hairdresser, who cuts it in a way so that she can do it on her own for the rest of the month. It shouldn't be cut too short but just so long that she can wrap it around her fingers when it's to be rolled up in curls. The hair must be quite moist, and every small part of it must be combed out properly, before it's rolled up for a nice result.

When it comes to the eyes, if the eyes feel tired and dull, you can put a plant or flower compress on the eyelids. You first sew small bags of gauze and fill them with either dried rose petals or other dried plants. Then you take two of the bags and pour boiling water over them, and when the bags have cooled you put them on the eyelids. Such a treatment is really excellent if, for example, you are going to a party or a hop. It makes the eyes relax and look bigger and clearer. Then you can mark the eyebrows with an eyebrow pencil and apply mascara on the eyelashes and eye shadow on the eyelids if you want.

Since it right now, when it comes to make-up, is so modern to emphasize the eyes, the lipstick should be discreet but so that the lips are still highlighted. I usually first draw the contours of the lips with a lip brush. It requires a little practice, but since beautiful well-shaped lips always seem attractive, it pays to sacrifice some time to learn the technique. If you use lip brush, you also get access to the third of the lipstick that otherwise remains in the sleeve, and you can save a lot of money. When the contours are drawn, you can fill in with the lipstick if you don't prefer to draw the lips finished with the brush. Then let it dry for about ten minutes, press a face napkin against the lips so that the excess fat is absorbed and powder the lips just lightly.

Yes, it's beauty care that is my great interest and I want to work with that in the future. Siv, one of my friends, wants to train as a nurse. It has always been her big dream. But now that her mom no longer exists, she has had to postpone it to the future. It's too horrible what has happened to her mother, and I feel so sorry for her and don't know what I can do to help her. I have a bad conscience about the fact that I have my own future so well defined and have not encountered any obstacles. It has gone exactly as I have imagined. And as soon as I have got a permanent job as a hairdresser, my fiancé and I will get engaged.

Before I met Åke, I thought that my husband to-be would be taller and a few years older than me. He should be careful but not shy, calm and confident, punctual and reliable, polite without exaggeration, a little homely and moderately jealous. I thought he would have clear ambitions, his own opinion, and a fun hobby, and that he could dance, take care of a baby, or put on an apron to help in the kitchen. And he wasn't allowed to drink, not to brag about past conquests, not to look too much at other girls when we were out, and not to be wasteful with money. That's how I imagined him, and that's how Åke is. I know that for sure now that I have gotten to know him properly.

I hesitated to tell my parents about him, because Dad always thinks, as soon as a boy is interested in me, that he is looking for just one thing. He thought so about Jan-Olof, and he thought so about Åke as well when he found out that we used to meet. And Mom has always preached that I must take care of myself, which in plain text means that I should abstain from sex until I am married. But I am actually not a little kid anymore, who can't take care of myself! Both Mom and Dad must simply accept that Åke is my fiancé now. And he has promised to be careful.

The fact that Åke was suspected by the police before didn't make things better. But he was with me when Aunt Eivor was murdered. We were at the cinema in town. On the way there, we drove past Uncle Hallgren in the IFA, which was in front of us some distance through the village. It was about half past six. I don't know if he saw that it was us, but otherwise he can affirm that what we have said is true.

I was never interested in Jan-Olof. He was running after me for a while and wanted to take me out to the movies and dance, but he wasn't my type at all. He drank and fought, and I don't think that a boy should do that. Mom has warned me about that too because Grandpa was as he was. So, Jan-Olof was nothing to me. He also had no vocational training, as Åke has. It was a terrible luck that I didn't get involved with him, because after the murder of Aunt Eivor he got crazy and ended up at "the thunder". At Ulleråker Hospital, that is. He tried to hang himself, I think, or if he jumped into the river. It was all the gossip that nearly killed him, Mom says.

Ingrid

A while ago, a boy in Gun-Britt's class died. He was run over by a train. It was about it in the newspaper.

Sometimes I think about what it would be like if Mom or Dad died. Everyone says they are afraid their mom will die, but I am not. I don't know if I would be sad. When Gun-Britt's mom died, nothing was noticed about Gun-Britt afterwards. She was just as usual, I thought. She wasn't sorry. Though she might have been sad when no one was watching. I don't know. But it might be just as well to have another mother, I think. And if both mom and dad died, Aunt Lilly or Aunt Vera could come and take care of me.

There is quite a few that die. *Peg out*, Tommy says. An uncle we knew had a heart attack and another died when he fell from a roof. And then there is Aunt Eivor and Uncle Henry and an aunt named Märta who has died.

When I am going to die, I want to die in my sleep, so that I don't notice it. I don't want a terrible disease, and I don't want a car accident to happen so I have to lie and bleed first and be afraid that all the blood will flow out of my body. I want it to go smoothly.

When you are dead, I believe that everything is black and that you don't know that you exist. Like when you sleep but don't dream. Some believe that you will go to heaven or hell when you die. They believe in God or the Devil. In hell you must burn in a fire forever, and in heaven you have to sit on a cloud and play the harp. But I don't believe that heaven and hell exist.

Although I believe a little in God. In the evenings before I go to sleep, I always say my prayers. After the real one I say:

201

Thank God that I am healthy, and that this day has gone so well. Protect Mom and Dad and Lady and Murre, if he lives, and everyone I know, so they can live and be healthy. And if possible, do so that I don't feel sick and must vomit. Amen.

So, I pray. I have been thinking of quitting, but it's like I don't dare. I am afraid that something terrible will happen if I quit. It's the same as having to count the steps in the stairs when I go up or down. And I have to look at the stove, that no hotplate is on, before I go to bed. Sometimes I must go down again, even though it's dark, and look. Then I run up as fast as I can and count the steps one-two-three-four-five to fourteen. I am always afraid that a hotplate will be on, for once in the evening when I couldn't fall asleep because it tickled in my throat so I couldn't stop coughing and I went down to take some cough medicine, there was a hotplate on the stove that was red and shone like glow. "It's burning, it's burning!" I shouted and ran up to Mom and Dad. I knew it wasn't really burning, but I shouted that way because I got so scared. And Dad jumped up and ran down and turned it off. It was fortunate that I started coughing, because otherwise the whole house could have burned up. I usually never cough at night and never go down and take cough medicine, so that time you can almost believe that it was God who made me start coughing so that I would go down and could see that it was about to catch fire in the kitchen. In any case, if you believe in God, you can think that way.

When I was little, Mom said that God sees everything you do and hears everything you say and think, and I believed that. But how will he have time to look and listen to everyone all over the earth? So, I don't believe so anymore. But first, when Mom had said it, I became afraid that I would think things that are forbidden to think. Ugly words and stuff, I mean. Because you can't decide on thoughts. They are just coming. So, when it came an ugly word, I had to quickly think of another word to get rid of it.

Mom cooks, bakes, washes, cleans, and tidies up. Sometimes she knits. Before, she made cardigans for me and slipovers for Dad, but now she only knits socks.

Sometimes she plays the piano. I don't like that, because she doesn't play as you should but a little higgledy-piggledy, so there is no melody. Then I shout from my room that she should stop.

Dad bought the piano for me to learn to play. I take piano lessons in school. Kerstin does the same. Gun-Britt plays recorder and mandolin, but I don't know how to play those instruments.

If Mom and I are alone at home and there might come a pedlar or a tramp out on the road, she locks the doors and goes up to the bedroom and pretends that no one is home. She stands behind the curtains and peeks out until they have passed. If they come and knock on the door, she doesn't open. There are usually some named Jehovah's Witnesses and sellers who want you to buy brushes and whisks that the blind have made, that come. But Mom doesn't let them in. And if you don't want any brushes, you may not need to open for them. But I don't think they are dangerous. I think they just want to sell brushes.

Once when Dad was home and the door wasn't locked, someone came in anyway. Dad was down in the basement chopping firewood, and I was upstairs in my room with the door closed, so we didn't notice anything. Lady was up with me. I don't remember if she barked and wanted to go down, but at least I didn't let her go. Then Mom just pushed out the person standing there and slammed the door shut and locked it. It was a tramp or whatever it was. I heard that Dad was angry with Mom afterwards for doing it. I don't know why. The next day, which was my birthday, Mom was ill and vomited.

I have been given khaki trousers and a sweater with a collar that I often wear to school now. It's tough with khaki trousers, I think. But I don't want them to be too tight. Some girls in the sixth and seventh grade have very tight long trousers. A girl named Bibbi has sewn them in when she has had them on, so she can't take them off. When she wants to change to another pair of trousers, she must tear them open in the side seams. That's excessively done, I think.

Another exaggerated thing is that those who have a Brigitte Bardot hairstyle put a bun on the head and comb their hair over so it will be high. Instead of backcombing, they do that way. Then they spray it. I have heard of someone who had a bun in her hair, and on her there were mould and worms in the bun. I don't know if it's true, but I have heard it.

It's fun with nice clothes and things. As a girl named Marianne I would like to have. The cardigan back to front so that the buttons are on the back, and a shiny scarf that you first tie in the front under the chin and then in the back over the tip. I would like to have a light pink one. I also want a rock bag with strings that you hang over your shoulder and on which there is a picture of Elvis or Tommy. They are sharp, I think. If I get or buy one, I will have one with Elvis on.

My name is Gerda Zetterberg.
I am the wife of provincial doctor Holger Zetterberg
and mother of two adult children who now reside elsewhere.
As far as my age is concerned it is unimportant in this context.

Yes, what can I say? A small Uppland village is set in the centre for everyone's interest. A kind-hearted woman, who didn't hurt a fly during her hard-working life, has fallen victim to a brutal act of violence. The police investigations immediately revealed that it wasn't a natural death of a heart attack or the like, but a very unnatural death by external force, and this shook everyone deeply.

Many innocent people have been harmed and troubled by the outrage. People have their suspicions, and as always in events of this kind, the evil rumours can hit anyone. The police have explicitly stated that all checks have been made primarily for the purpose of getting people definitely sorted out as not suspects, but the gossip doesn't turn away for either reasons of fact or common sense.

I am thinking primarily of the poor farmhand Jan-Olof, who has been hit so hard by all the talk. He, like so many others, is unable to bear his liquor. Many have certainly testified that he has basically a peaceful nature, who struggles hard to make a living but prefers to go his own way. However, when he gets alcohol in his body, he can behave aggressively. Since he also is tall and extremely strong in his paws, none of his drinking companions have dared to oppose or strike back, and such inferiority can provoke jealousy and slander. As a doctor's wife, I am generally considered less suitable to be given simple gossip, but one thing and another has nevertheless reached my ears. In the village, many have spread the word about Jan-Olof's alleged temper and talked about how he, in a drunken state, has been on the rampage and behaved almost like a wild animal. One villager has said he has been threatened with death by him, and another has heard how he has walked around and bragged that he has killed a policeman with a pole.

When the days passed without the homicide commission being able to show any success in the form of, for example, an arrest, the bad rumours turned again against Jan-Olof. His alibi did nothing to counteract the compact storm of the people. Gossip can be so infinitely cruel. It cuts across all strata of society, flies relentlessly from mouth to mouth and blossoms into whispers and slander, which can eventually take the life out of even the strongest. Some people meant that such a great harm wasn't done after all, since the alleged person wasn't exactly an angel. But that has nothing to do with the matter at all. Especially not as none of his previous escapades could be compared to such a hideous crime as the one he is now accused of. If he is innocent, he has, in my opinion, compensation to claim, like any irreproachable citizen at all. But who would give it to him? He must be glad that he was released.

The police must try all the clues and it's inevitable that mistakes happen sometimes, but everything indicated Jan-Olof's innocence. His alibi was solid, and that should have been enough. But the suspicions continued to meet him everywhere, especially from older morally self-important women who accused him. It's almost impossible to definitively dispel such slander.

And the accusations against him finally took effect. The formerly so hard-working and friendly farmhand no longer dared to look people in the eye and began to withdraw from his surroundings. He suffered from phobias, and it was reported that he had visions. He had disclosed that Mrs. Johansson often appeared to him at night and that he used to have long conversations with her.

I think it's important to tell this, how a completely innocent person who is singled out by loose news gossip can be driven to the verge of insanity. To avoid such tragedy, everyone should keep their mouths shut and refuse to engage in malicious talk.

But everyone has their thoughts. I have that myself as well. For example, who came and knocked on our door at eleven o'clock in the evening, a few hours after the murder of Mrs. Johansson? I was alone at home and had gone to bed and slept for a while when I was awakened by the sound. At first, I didn't know if I would dare to open, because there are so many vagrants out along the roads nowadays. But after a few more knocks on the door, I got up. It could be a neighbour who was ill and needed help, I reasoned.

When I opened the door ajar, I saw an unknown man standing out there. I had never seen him before. I heard from his speech that he wasn't from the area. He asked how he would go to get to the main road. I was both dizzy and scared, so I told him about it and quickly closed myself in again. If I had known what had happened earlier in the evening, I would have immediately called the police. Afterwards, I thought that I might have met a murderer and that it could just as well have been me who had been killed.

This is the second time in my life that I have come in contact with a murder. The first time was almost twenty years ago, when a woman in town was murdered. She had opened a café, called Greta's Coffee Party, on Järnbrogatan in Uppsala. Her name was Greta Eriksson, and she was in her fifties. I visited her café quite often and became superficially familiar with her. She was incredibly interested in theatre, music, and opera and we discussed that. I got the impression that she was neat and tidy and liked by everyone. For the most part, she was happy and alert, but not always, because she was bad-tempered and could become so upset and aggressive that her eyes flashed. At the slightest complaint about the coffee or the bread, she could flare up.

Some I spoke to afterwards thought she had been kind and hardworking but bitter and grieved because of money worries and illness. She once told me that she had cancer and had to go to Radiumhemmet in Stockholm to get treatment.

Others claimed that she had been quite… erotic, but I had a difficulty believing that. She was a widow and had a son who was dead. Maybe that was why she was on such friendly terms with the young men who were studying theology at the Fjellstedska school, which was located very close to her café.

In any case, she was beaten, strangled, and choked to death in her room inside the café on Järnbrogatan. It was the last day of April 1940. She had a cat named Tusse, who probably witnessed it all. The police still haven't found the murderer and in seven years the period for prosecution has expired.

I hope it won't end in the same way with the murder of Mrs. Johansson, that the murderer will never be caught. It seems so strange that just this sweet person, who lived such a prudent and quiet life and could hardly have a single antagonist, would be murdered by an enemy unknown to everyone around her. It seems even more inexplicable because she had such a close circle of friends. There were only a few neighbours' wives about the same age as herself. In other words, there is nothing *mysterious* in the picture.

When the detectives went out to talk to the villagers, they met sheer honest citizens of the same splendid kind as Mrs. Johansson herself. That's why I think it must be a vagabond who has done it. A tramp or a gypsy or possibly a patient who had deviated from Ulleråker Hospital or Venngarn Alcoholic Institution.

I don't harbour these suspicions because of any discriminatory views because gypsies can generally be as useful citizens as anyone. But they have a hotter temperament than the average Swede and easily get the feeling of being less valuable, which can lead to a need for assertion which in turn can lead to violence. They are also extremely close to their relatives and would never betray a relative no matter what he or she has done. There are examples of how gypsies have been stabbed by relatives but not even on the deathbed wanted to reveal who did it. I mention this to better illustrate the difficulties the murder investigators have had in their hitherto vain attempts to find Mrs. Johansson's slayer.

When it comes to insane people, I just want to say that psychiatry is a science in its infancy, and that one shouldn't attach too much and decisive importance to the doctors' statements. There is no area of human knowledge where views can differ as much as in psychiatry. Different psychiatrists may have completely opposite views, so that one expert declares a person fully wise, while another considers the same man to be mentally ill, and in both cases, they refer to scientific findings. To blindly rely on science, I think, would be dangerous for the rule of law. And which one of us would actually measure up to a mental examination?

In order to enable the general public to have a not too inconvenient access to doctors everywhere, and to ensure cheap medical care, provincial medical services have long been established in our country. The doctors who hold these services are obliged to provide medical care to persons belonging to the area to which the service applies for a certain fee. The provincial doctor also has a special obligation to supervise general hygienic conditions, the open epidemic care, the health condition of minor workers and more.

A provincial doctor is employed and paid by the state. The only requirement to get a job is eight months' service in a hospital. For my own part, I had nine years of hospital experience when I started. Despite this, the salary was low, and the work was tiring and isolated with a great commitment to constant on-call duty. Over time, it has become increasingly difficult to recruit young doctors, who would rather be attracted by a career in a hospital with the opportunity for specialist training. Patients also prefer to go to the hospital's outpatient clinics because they rely more on specialists who have access to laboratory examinations, X-rays, and the like. In other words, the provincial medical service has found itself in a difficult crisis, and it's being discussed whether it should be abolished in order to expand open specialist care instead. Yes, we will see how it ends.

It was I who was summoned when Mrs. Lundin fell ill. A female relative later contacted me to get information about the disease in question. Of course, I couldn't discuss Mrs. Lundin's case in particular, but I gave general information about various mental illnesses and described common symptoms, so that she got answers to some of her thoughts and some of her worries could hopefully be allayed.

Schizophrenia, for example, can manifest itself in many different ways. The patient sometimes laughs suddenly for no reason, makes some strange movements, speaks for herself and answers questions more or less strangely and disorderly. You eventually notice that she hears voices that she answers or has hallucinations of another kind. In some cases, she claims to be exposed to rays, hypnosis, or mysterious devices. She is under the influence of a foreign will, which takes away her thoughts or gives her foreign thoughts. In other words, she falls victim to strange ideas or delusions – fixed ideas people generally call it.

For example, a young man thinks he is suspected of a murder committed in the area. At first, he does his job as before and appears orderly and decent, but eventually he becomes increasingly shy and suspicious. He thinks that people are watching him and pointing fingers at him, and he notices that the police are showing a clear interest in him. In the end, he clearly hears people whispering, "there goes the sex murderer". He starts to withdraw and avoid people, but it only gets worse; wherever he goes, the same thing repeats itself – everywhere one seems to know who he is and know his whereabouts. Unless his relatives take action in time, he will excel either by starting to assault strangers with a request for an explanation or by turning to the police for protection against his imaginary enemies or by causing other problems.

Another example: A sick woman comes up with the idea that her husband, who has been dead for five years, and at whose deathbed and funeral she was present, isn't dead at all. She goes from house to house, from door to door, knocking and asking: "Is this where my husband dwells?" It doesn't help to say that she herself was present when her husband died; she explains that when she moved away from the sickbed for a moment, they took the opportunity to put another man, who strongly resembled her husband, in his bed and that he is now assuredly alive.

The course of the disease is quite variable. Even after a long-term illness, there are opportunities for the patient to recover more or less. Through care in a mental hospital, one can often significantly improve the patient's condition. With intensive insulin treatment, in dosage leading to coma, one can in many cases achieve favourable treatment results by slowing down the disease process. During certain stages of the disease, electroshock treatment is effective.

Even if the patient doesn't come for medical attention, his situation is not entirely hopeless. The first signs of anxiety, whether in the form of a state of anxiety, or of confusion, or of catatonic symptoms, or of paranoid-like persecution ideas, usually subside after a while. The patient calms down and may eventually even return to easier work. But in his essence, as a rule, a lasting change has taken place; he isn't the same as before but slack, indifferent and without interest in life and its tasks. His feelings are more or less extinguished, and he has lost the ability to partake of life's sorrows and subjects for rejoicing.

As a provincial doctor and also a villager, I am not deaf to the talk that circulates in the farms. One would like to put the blame for Mrs. Johansson's death on people who in one way or another deviate from the usual pattern. I therefore want to take the opportunity and also briefly describe how the so-called imbecile and debilitated personality type works.

He has a fairly normal speech ability, and as an adult he has an intelligence development that roughly exceeds that of a six-year-old child but at most corresponds to a normal twelve-year-old child. Through teaching one can impart to him a certain amount of knowledge and teach him certain skills, but he isn't capable of independent professional activity. You must constantly show him the right way and watch over him at work. He is easily influenced by others, and if he isn't supervised, he can yield to shoplifting, prostitution and the like. He often acts in a ruthless and unthinking manner and is lying, unreliable, and insensitive to the suffering of others. From the very course of his actions, it can be concluded that his ability to assess the consequences of his actions, even with regard to himself, must be defective. If he is of the good-natured type, he may have a certain affection for people around him, but he doesn't have completely normal intelligence that can offset his ruthless and selfish disposition.

Merely due to the fact that a person suffers from insanity or debility, one can't suspect the person in question of having committed a violent crime. That would be both unfounded and unfair. No one should be suspected or accused if no concrete clues lead in that direction. Gossip, which often arises from ignorance and fear, shouldn't be allowed to brand innocent people. But unfortunately, it's not possible to stop it. As long as the culprit hasn't been caught and convicted of his guilt, it will inevitably continue.

Ingrid

I don't like it when Mom sits and whispers to herself, but I can't make her stop. She whispers and laughs at what the voices in her head are saying. *The one who whispers is lying and sucks on his thumb!*

Sometimes I lie even though it's forbidden. I have lied to Mom and said that I have only been out even though I have been with Gun-Britt and played. And once I lied about a reel of cotton that I had taken and pulled out the thread from because I wanted to see how long it was. Afterwards I didn't get the thread back on the reel again, and then I said to Mom that I didn't know where it was.

And I suck on my thumb though I am so old. I know it's wrong, but I must suck a little before I go to sleep. I can't help it. Kerstin doesn't know about it, so when I stay overnight with her I do it secretly, under the blanket. But it becomes so warm, and I am afraid it will be heard or that I will fall asleep before I have stopped sucking. Then maybe the blanket slides aside so she can see it if I have fallen asleep before her. I don't want that because I am ashamed that I suck on my thumb. But I have thought that I would say, if she would ask, that I don't know myself what I am doing when I am asleep.

I know I must quit, and I know I *will*, but I don't know *when*. In three years maybe, because then I am a teenager and then you don't want to do childish things.

Last time I was with Kerstin and stayed overnight, we came up with a secret club which we called the Maple Club, because we played under a big maple tree outside their henhouse. We also have maples in our garden, but none as big as the one at Kerstin's.

Later, when we had dinner with her parents, it became so painful, because I removed my plate when I was done and then Kerstin said: "Don't you want any afters?" We would get fruit salad. "Yes, I do," I said and was confused. And she said to her mom: "Mom, bring out other plates then!" She didn't dare tell me that they usually eat their starters and afters on the same plate in her family. She was ashamed of it, it seemed. But I didn't care. I just didn't think of it because we don't do so at our home. She might just as well have told me.

After dinner, we went into her big sister's room and read her magazines. We could do that because she wasn't home.

I wish I were as old as her sis, because then there would be so much fun to do. Knitting jumpers and putting on make-up and playing records and going to hops and stuff like that. But I don't want to get that kind of blood that girls get when they are teenagers. Menstruation or whatever it's called. Once I saw Mom's sanitary towel with blood on it, and it looked disgusting. "Are you on the rag?" a guy said to a girl. At that time, I didn't know what it meant, but I found out later.

Gerd was working on a light blue angora jumper that we inspected. Then we looked through her singles. She had *Diana* with Paul Anka and *Be Bop a Lula* with Gene Vincent and *Tutti Frutti* with Little Richard and several others. Kerstin likes some singers named Connie Francis and Cliff Richard best. Among Swedish ones, she likes Siw Malmkvist and Lill-Babs best. I also do that among the Swedish ones.

Gerd has Paul Anka as her idol. She has a large picture of him posted on the wall. I don't know who my idol is. Elvis Presley perhaps. There was a competition in *Bildjournalen* where you would vote for Elvis or Tommy, and then I voted for Elvis. Kerstin supported Tommy, and it was he who won.

215

When I was with Kerstin, we took a walk on their road and sang in canon. After that we sang English songs. I know *My Bonnie is Over the Ocean* and *It's a Long Way to Tipperary*. It's Gun-Britt who has taught me them.

It was dark outside when we walked on the road. Sometimes when I go with Dad and fetch the milk in the evening, it's also dark. Sometimes I walk with my face up, so I get completely tired in my neck after a while. I do this because I want to see the Charles's Wain in the starry sky. It was up where Laika was.

If we get to Lindberg's before they have stopped milking, we go into the cowhouse and wait. On the wall above each cow there is a small blackboard with the cow's name written in chalk. Stjärna and Majros and names like that they are called. Sometimes there are calves in a chain. Then I let them suck on my fingers.

I like it best when it's Aunt Lindberg who milks, because she is kind to the cows and doesn't swear at them like Uncle Lindberg does. He is angry at them all the time and pushes them even though they haven't done anything wrong. That's nasty, I think.

It seems hard to have cows. You must give them hay and muck in the cowhouse, and in the summer when they are out in the meadow you have to go and fetch them every night when they are to be milked. They have a farmhand who does that. Once when he came with them on the road and Dad was about to pass them with his car, it was a cow that threw herself sidewards and put the horns in the car so there was a big dent there. Then Dad got angry and scolded the farmhand.

When we get home with the milk, Mom first skims off the cream, then she pours it into a jug for my cornflakes. From

216

some milk, she sometimes makes sour milk. Dad, when he eats sour milk, breaks hard bread in it, but I don't like that. And I don't drink milk that has been in the larder and frozen to ice or is on the turn. Not boiled milk with skin on it either.

I am married to Göte Lindberg who owns the biggest farm here in the village.
My name is Astrid
and our children are named Birgit and Sven.

When Eivor died, Jan-Olof, our farmhand, had been with us for two years. He was hardworking and strong and always did what he was supposed to do. We had nothing to complain of about him. We didn't meddle with what he did in his spare time. There were some rumours about him, but I could never have believed that he would encounter so much suffering because of it.

Many villagers probably didn't mind that he was singled out as the murderer. Wasn't he punished before perhaps? Hadn't he killed another woman once? One he had lived with without them being married, and who he had put in the family way over and over again? You could expect anything from such a slacker! And the beauty of it was that he wasn't born here. He was an outcast. And he had been out that night and had plenty of time to attack.

In fact, he wasn't convicted of murder or assault, and he had never committed anything that could justify the villagers' negative view of him. Besides, how would he have had time with all that misery – still young as he was? But now he was suspected of murder, and then you could lay it on as thick as you wanted.

And it wasn't moderate how they went on. Blinded by rage, he all by himself had carried out the murder of Eivor, who had threatened to leave him. Because they had had hanky-panky together! Why would that be so unthinkable – that Mrs. Johansson had sought out an erotic partner outside of marriage and then chosen a young, strong man like Jan-Olof? That's how the talk went. It was nefarious how Eivor was blackened after her death!

These suspicions were immediately trumpeted forth and gossip runs especially easy when spiced with erotic elements. Jan-Olof was arrested, and the interrogations with him lasted virtually uninterrupted for five days. As a rule, he was awakened in the middle of the night for new hearings. Nocturnal hardships are apparently the specialty of the police. In addition, every opportunity is taken to intimidate and torment. And the interrogations were sharpened by throwing out false allegations, such as that there were witnesses who had seen him assault Eivor.

Jan-Olof declared his innocence, but it didn't help. Eventually he was so exhausted that he threw himself on the floor and cried. He was easily embarrassed and confused when asked to explain things. Usually, he just wanted to avoid talking when the conversation became too complicated. And if you watched him persistently, he looked down and then peeked furtively under his fringe. In situations he didn't master, he most resembled a big child. You could make him say anything just by looking sternly at him. So, when he sat in interrogation and noticed that the officers were angry with him, he probably confessed in order to get everyone happy with him.

Afterwards, he couldn't explain why he had taken the blame for the crime. But he said that it hadn't been done voluntarily but that the policemen had been repeating over and over again during the interrogations: "So and so you did, right?" Then he had finally answered in the affirmative. In addition, he had been tricked into believing that there were witnesses, and he was constantly assured that he would be allowed to leave as soon as he had confessed. Misleading a suspect by using false information is such a shabby police trick that it should be strictly forbidden. But they did so and made him confess something he hadn't done.

All this I later got to know from Jan-Olof himself. For the police, it was apparently a matter of portraying him as a rough customer who could commit any heinous crime. In support of this, it was stated that he had behaved both confused and uncontrollable during the interrogations. But that confusion the policemen themselves had aroused by treating him harshly and unpredictably.

Only once did I doubt his innocence. That was when I found an old jacket in the barn shortly after the murder was discovered. It was partly hidden under the straw and was of coarse cloth and bloody in front. A moment later Göte came in and saw what I had found. I asked him who owned the garment and he said it belonged to Jan-Olof. Then I shook off the jacket and asked Göte to go and get some paper to wrap it in.

At first, Jan-Olof didn't remember the bloody jacket when I showed it to him. He thought it was Göte's jacket. However, he had a bloody blouse, which he used when slaughtering pigs and calves, hanging in the stable. But the next day he remembered that he had had an old worn jacket that he used to wear during manuring and small slaughter or when he was out ploughing in bad weather. "I must have wiped the butcher knife on it, since it's stained in front," he said.

I handed the jacket over to the police, but they didn't attach any importance to it because the expert examination showed that the blood on it came from a pig.

It went badly for Jan-Olof, and it has gone badly for Sven, our son. It's like a curse resting on us, I think sometimes.

Already when Sven was little, we noticed that he was different. He is born with a completely different disposition than the rest of us. He is musical and eventually learned to play both violin and accordion. He isn't at all what people think and as it has been written in the newspapers.

When he was little, he had a very calm and nice way. He laughed and was happy. As he got older, he expressed an interest in nature and appreciated life in the woods. There was actually nothing wrong with him. But it wasn't possible to set him up according to any rules. He was born that way and he can't help it. He is a natural person and not interested in a structured life with time clocks. He wants to be free as air, as it's said.

Actually, he doesn't want to live in the woods, because it isn't so comfortable. But he isn't spoiled, so it has worked. And there is nothing forced on him. He has chosen it himself. I don't think he suffers from it. He has probably been able to get used to it. That he has chosen it depends on his way of being, and how you are you can't control. If he hadn't had that way, he wouldn't have done what he has done. When he started being chased by the police, I know that some people thought he was a parasite on society. He cost too much. If the police shoot him, it's to free society, I know there are those who think.

He takes some food in the summer cottages. He eats the food that is there and stays and sleeps for a while, and then there is nothing more to it. Just a broken door or a broken window and a bunch of empty cans. Otherwise, it's nothing. But as soon as there is a burglary in a summer cottage, he is accused of it. He becomes a suspect whether he has done it or not. The police have said he is dangerous and scares people. They magnify it to appear remarkable themselves. That's all it is. What they have talked about, that Sven has shot, I don't believe a bit. It was the police themselves who fired.

There have been writings in the newspapers. Everything has been magnified and made a sensation. What has been written hasn't been true, and we have tried to supress it. But it has been hopeless. As long as it sells, it will continue. And it isn't moderate what headlines it has become. Sven has been called a gangster and a desperado, and that's as wrong as it can be. The morning papers have adhered somewhat to the truth, but the evening papers have distorted and enlarged all of it. We who are involved and know how it really is think it's awful. It's like no kind at all to make Sven a giant desperado. He is just a poor boy who has withdrawn from society and wants to be at peace.

I don't know why it has become like this. I don't understand why it has been magnified so much. These are not remarkable things at all he has done. Just breaking into some summer cottages sometimes to get food. And it's society that has forced him into the life he lives. He has become more or less wild because he doesn't fit into society. So, it's not his fault, even if there is no excuse for him. But he can't help that he is such a person who can't adjust to time clocks.

The opinion demands his head. It's written that he is a crazy and desperate gangster. But it's the police who are desperate. They even tried to run him in for the murder of Eivor. He was questioned about it last autumn when he was at home, but then he wasn't a suspect at all. He didn't become one until the summer cottage burglaries came on the carpet and he began to stay away. I know he has nothing to do with the murder, and that's what I want to come out in the first place. So much has been written about him, but I know he could never hurt another human being. He is a forest man and an artist soul, who has never asked for anything but to live his life in freedom.

Yes, there have been hard days and nights. Anyone who hasn't had a loved one in such a desperate situation can hardly imagine how it feels.

Gun-Britt and I have a hut in the woods. We built it this summer between two large stones. All you had to do was to put sticks and branches as a roof and close the back, and then it was finished.

Mom doesn't like that I am in the woods. There are evil spirits there, who live under stocks and in the underworld, she says. They are called malignant elves. I don't know if she has made them up or if they are in fairy tales maybe. In any case, they don't exist in reality because I know that. So, I am in the woods anyway.

An uncle named Sven, who is the child of Aunt Astrid and Uncle Göte, lives in the woods. He has broken into summer cottages and fired a gun, they say, and the police have chased him with dogs. It has also been written about him in the newspaper.

Once when Gun-Britt and I arrived at the hut, a fox had taken a bird there. There was blood and a pile of feathers on the ground. At Gun-Britt's house a hen was taken once. The fox had dug itself in under the fence and caught it. I have seen foxes and I think they are cute. But everyone they have taken hens from is angry with them and would rather shoot them. Or they put a fox trap out in the woods. It's like iron rings with thorns in them, which they put on the ground and want the foxes to get caught in. If a fox comes running and happens to put a paw in the ring, it shuts so the thorns go into his leg. And he can't come loose because the ring is fastened to the ground. He has to stand there and wait until the hunter comes and shoots him. But some foxes gnaw off their bone and run away, so the only thing the hunter gets is a fox paw with blood and some meat sludge on it. That serves the hunter right, I think.

Squirrels and hares are also found in the woods. And deer and moose. Gun-Britt has seen a badger, but I haven't. They only appear when it's dark, I think, and then I am not there. But once when I was with Mom and Dad in the woods and picked lingonberries we got lost, and then we had to be there until it began to get dark. I was scared then, that we wouldn't find the way home. Dad said he knew how to go, but I noticed that he didn't, and then I got scared.

When I get really scared, it feels in my stomach, and my cheeks heat. In the evening, when it's dark outside and I am cycling, I am getting a little jumpy, because then you can hear strange noises in the ditches, and the bushes look like black men lurking. Then my legs pedal as fast as they can so that I will get out of there.

Once when I was down in the meadow, an old man came in the dark. Then I hid behind a large juniper bush so that he wouldn't see me. When he got closer, I saw that it was Uncle Edvin. But I didn't go forward because I didn't want him to see me.

What I am most afraid of is that it will start to burn and that I will feel sick and vomit. Snakes and being trapped I am also afraid of. When I was little, I was afraid of much more than I am now. Then, for example, I didn't dare answer the phone when it rang, because those who called never heard what I said. And I was afraid to flush with the water taps. Once when I had done that and wanted to turn it off again, I turned in the wrong direction so more and more water came out, and then I thought I couldn't make it stop. I didn't re-member in which direction to turn. After that I only dared to let it flow a little when I took water. If it didn't stop at once when I began to turn it off, I asked Mom to come and do it for me.

And I was afraid of elderly. There was an aunt named Hilma who lived next to Harald's then, and I didn't want to meet her. You got money and disgusting candies if you went in to her, and Gun-Britt always wanted to go in and get them.

Gun-Britt is afraid of murderers, but I am not. When Aunt Eivor was murdered, Dad said that the murderer had probably not done it on purpose and that it might have been an accident. I didn't have to be afraid, he said. But I am still a little scared when I am out when it's dark.

Sometimes it's fun to be scared. Like when we tell ghost stories and stuff. Then you *want* to be frightened because then you know that we are only pretending. If we talk about the Black Lady, for instance. But she exists, I think. It's an ordinary aunt who has gone crazy and walks around in black clothes and frightens people. She has bats in the belfry, Gun-Britt says. Once she put a baby on a baking sheet in the oven and fried it. They say so, but I don't know if it's true.

Nils Karlsson, freeholder
son of Harald and Beda
father of Solveig and Ragnar.
The missus' name is Britta.

Sven is a year younger than me, so we didn't go to the same class at school. But we met at home because we lived next door. Our parents socialized a little and I remember how the conversation went. Astrid was the one who tried to keep the family together. She fought like a female tiger for Sven and his rights.

Göte was the talk of the village because of his stinginess. It wasn't the usual thrift, the one that people have to resort to when there are many mouths in the family to feed, but he worshiped money for its own sake. He saved and scraped and piled up. That's why Sven and his younger sister were so badly dressed and looked so pale and thin. They got no new clothes and couldn't eat their fill. Astrid complained to my mother and said that in the beginning she had encouraged Göte's economy, but then it had become a tough battle between them for every penny she needed. When she saw that the money was kept in Göte's bed, she wasn't so happy about his thrift anymore. He had the money in a paper bag under the mattress. Astrid wanted him to at least deposit the money in a book, but he refused.

And it wasn't so little that he managed to skimp together over the years. He neither smoked nor snuffed, and the family's clothes had to be patched by Astrid until they barely held together anymore. She told people straight out that Göte was so stingy that he even begrudged her the clothes on her body. She was happy to embarrass him. It became like a task for her to walk around and be contemptuous of him. In that way, she got some revenge.

And she told my mother how sick he was. Once a week he counted his money. Then he wanted to be at peace and locked himself in with the bag and sat there thumbing the notes. It shone like madness in his eyes when he was dealing with his money, she said. Once she took a ten out of the bag to buy some coffee and food and socks for the children. When Göte discovered it, he went crazy. His eyes stared, and he came up to her with raised arms and wanted to strangle her. But she stood at the door and managed to run away.

Sometimes she cried for the sake of the children because they never got any new clothes or proper food. She came in to us and cried. She had disclosed Sven by standing and begging with another family and was told that he often used to walk like a starving stray cat and beg for food in the village. She felt ready to die of shame when she found out. She scolded him, but she didn't have the heart to beat him, she said.

But Göte often gave him a taste of the cane. He became anxious and nervous and began to bite his nails and wet his bed. He got bad grades in school and had to repeat.

But at home he and I played. We were in the woods. I am glad that I have grown up in the country and not on a street in town. You get a different view of life from being able to assimilate nature and enjoy it. It has been my brandy, I can say. The interest in nature has been inherited by our lad, and I am grateful for that because I know what relief nature can give a troubled mind. He has a brain injury, which he got at birth, and that's probably why I today have a certain understanding of Sven and his peculiarities.

As I remember it, he was good to play with and a decent friend. But he had no peace. If you started building a snow cave or something like that, he got tired quickly and didn't want to participate anymore. He was very musical and learned to play the violin. We were a few who played together, and he was with us sometimes with the violin. But when we had been playing for a while, he put the violin down and went out. That's how he was. He was restless, and it showed in everything he did. He couldn't put up with routines, and he didn't want to work with Göte on the farm. He hated hard manual labour and had a longing for a richer and freer life. With a different background and upbringing, he would most likely have become an artist or a musician.

He fled to the woods and began to live wilderness life. He probably came home from time to time, but for the most part no one knew where he was. When he started being chased for the summer cottage burglaries and had eluded the police long enough, it became newspaper headlines. He has often been described as a serious criminal and has been called both a gangster and a desperado. But the only thing he has done is to help himself with grub and things that he has needed to survive.

The police have been after him all summer. Many who are a little more familiar with it probably feel most sorry for him, I would think. There is a certain understanding for him as well. He lives a free life, and it appeals to people who may dream of doing the same thing themselves.

That it has become so big is probably mostly due to the way the press has treated it. When it was added that he might have stayed away due to the murder in the village, the journalists were partying for a while. The newspapers described it to make money, and desperados and killers are headlines that sell. But Sven isn't a dangerous armed gangster who hides in the woods and takes refuge in broken summer cottages and shoots wildly around him when the police approach. It's just what they write to increase the sales of single copies.

Sven's sister Birgit hasn't done so well either. She ended up in bad company already as a young woman and according to rumours she has continued to live a life of hustle and bustle. She lives in town now. Astrid and Göte never talk about her. They are ashamed of her way of life, I suppose. But it's probably most talk that things have gone wrong for her. I myself remember her as a lively girl, who grew up to be a comely skirt who was fun to hang out with. It's been a long time since I met her, but according to rumours, she should have been home visiting the same night that Eivor died. She should have been seen in the back of a motorcycle that roared along the road. But I don't know. People talk so much. Of course, the fact that she was alleged to be here made both her and her company suspected of the murder. I don't know how they get it together. There is no rhyme or reason in the speculations. The slightest deviation in a person's behaviour leads to suspicions. There are, for example, those who think that old Jansson is behind it, and that only because of his talk about elves and trolls, which he claims to have seen, and that he usually wanders around down in the meadow. But what reason would he have had to knock Eivor down? If he didn't mistake her for something he thought he had to defend himself against, that is, as some seem to believe.

Ingrid

I have been to Aunt Vera in Stockholm. Dad drove me to the train and then I went the rest of the way myself. I had some fruit and sweets with me and a comic paper that I read on the train. It wasn't scary to go alone.

Aunt Vera met me at the Central station, and we took a bus to her home. There is a subway in Stockholm, but we didn't take it. It's a kind of train that runs on tracks underground. Almost under the whole town there are tunnels in which these trains are running.

I have been to Aunt Vera before with Dad. Then we went to Skansen and Gröna Lund, but now we were only at her place. She has a room with a kitchenette where she lives. A kitchenette is a tiny kitchen where you can only stand and cook. You can't sit there and eat. She has her dining table in the hall. She also has her bed there. It looks like a shelf with a drapery at the bottom when it's folded up against the wall. I would also like to have such a bed.

I got to sleep on the sofa bed in Aunt Vera's room. When I had gone to bed, I lay and looked at all the things in there before turning off the light. Vera's husband, who is dead now, was an artist, and all his paintings were on the walls. You could barely see the wallpaper between the paintings. There was sunsets and trees and flower vases mostly. And there was a root that he had carved out and painted inside so that it looked like a cave. At the top he had attached a small lamp that could be lit. Another lamp he had made of a hand grenade or whatever it's called. Mom says that electricity is dangerous and that you should not go near the sockets in the wall. And the electricity is invisible, so it might seep out from the holes when the cord isn't plugged in. But I don't know.

Aunt Vera's furniture was sofa, table, armchairs, sideboard, bookshelf, and a table with glass on top. On that table stood Uncle Henry's pipe rack and a silver cigarette case and a large ashtray. It was his smoking table. On the bookshelf it was full of pictures in frames and fine ornaments that he had made of clay and pieces of wood and stones. There were also sculptures of faces and of a naked aunt on whom the arms were cut off.

When I grow up, I will have it like that at home. Full of paintings and vases and porcelain things and crowded with furniture and long curtains that can be drawn. On the wall I will have a violin, and then I will sit in an armchair and read magazines and listen to music.

Aunt Vera had a gramophone record called *Que sera sera* that we listened to. Another record she had was called *Only You*. It was with a Negro group. It wasn't exactly a hit song but not rock either, because it went smoothly.

In the fifth grade, we will start reading English in school. It's going to be fun, I think. I already know several English words. Only you, for example, I know what it means. And I know a few English songs. I have learned them from Gun-Britt.

When I was little, I believed that everyone on earth spoke the same language. I was very surprised when I found out that there are a lot of different languages. Why is it like that? Everything would be much easier if it were the same all over the world.

And in some countries, they are poor and starving. The food isn't enough for everyone. But then it's strange that they have children, I think. If they can't afford rubbers, they can just avoid doing a *certain thing*, and then they wouldn't have

any children. That's how I would do, anyway, if I were the
one who was poor.

My name is Edvin Jansson
and I have lived almost eighty years in this vale of tears.

I have toiled and moiled all my life, and now I am old and worn out and ready to be thrown on the dust heap. And never mind! I have done my part and have nothing more to look forward to. This modern time doesn't suit me. Atomic bombs and space rockets and satellites and televisions and everything they come up with. Damn shit! I say. The whole world is pissed and wretched. For me, it can just as well go to hell, so there was at least some change.

No one is worth a fig as long as he lives. But as soon as he has left, the tune is changed. "An unusually good and deeply grieved and missing person, too soon departed, leaving a void that can never be filled," it reads. It never happens that an evil person is immersed in the grave! But some must have been evil, because otherwise the world wouldn't look like it does. In other words, the posthumous reputation isn't true. Never so many lies are told as in obituary notices and at burials. Eivor was an exception, I suppose. In her case, the beautiful words probably corresponded with how she was when she was alive. Still, she had to end her life like a discarded old rag. Damn it all, I say, for everything rotten in this world!

And I can tell you… It was a late night in October, and I was on my way home across the meadow, when I suddenly saw a large herd of cows. All were black in colour and had resounding bells around their necks. They weren't Lindberg's cows, which are brown and of a different breed, and which are also not kept out so late in the autumn. It wasn't his cattle I saw, though I thought so at first. I didn't think much, but I liked the cattle, which were in good condition, and began to entice them to come to me. But they didn't want to obey. All of a sudden, I heard a strange moaning, and the whole cow flock went in that direction. I hurried after and had run a long distance when I saw the cows disappear into a large hill of grass. One by one they disappeared, and a dull thunder, as if from a rough door, was heard after them.

While I was standing there staring, a strange little man appeared in front of me. "Good day Uncle, where are Thou going?" I asked, for something I thought I ought to say. But I shouldn't have done that, because at the same moment I got a hard blow to the head, so I passed out and tumbled on to the ground. Afterwards I couldn't really remember if, or in what way, the old man had struck me, because he was no more than a handbreadth tall and shouldn't have been able to reach up. But it must have been a terrible blow because I didn't recover for a long time. When I finally woke up, the old man was gone.

What I want to say with this is that there is a lot in this world for which no reasonable explanation can be found. Who knows what Eivor encountered in the meadow? She might have been knocked down by the same little devil as me, I mean. She may also have caught sight of his cows, whom he was there to guard and defend. That the blow, in her case, took so badly that she didn't wake up again, was perhaps not the intention.

For those who doubt the supernatural, there are otherwise more objective theories to discuss. We have a couple of loutish young rascals here in the village that the police should inspect a little closer. Idlers who haven't been taught manners and who should actually be locked up in a reformatory. They don't know what hard work is, since they have never learned it. Young motor enthusiasts, that is. I both saw and heard a motorcycle roaring past the night of the murder, but of course it wasn't possible to see who was riding it. It was between six and seven. When I heard the sound, I went to the kitchen window and saw the lights sweeping past in the dark.

There is so much damned nuisance these days. For me, who has the means to defend myself, it works well, but it's worse for defenceless ladies, who live alone and don't have anyone nearby who can help them if there is a problem. I don't know how many times I have warned the old woman Sundelin. She can be murdered too, as lonely and isolated as she lives. She never locks herself in either. She should think a little more about her safety, I think. Especially if you consider that she is old and frail. But she has resisted when relatives and neighbours have offered her other opportunities. "I'm doing so well and feel so comfortable, because everyone is so kind to me," she says.

After Eivor's death, police officers came to her cottage and inspected. Outside the hen house, they found a chopping-block with brownish-red spots on it, which of course shone into their eyes. It was blood from slaughtered chickens, because Tekla had recently received help from a neighbour to neck a few. But no one could be absolutely sure. A lone log of wood, which was leaning against the firewood pile, had similar stains, and the police took it with them for safety's sake to investigate further.

My name is Tekla Sundelin and I am unmarried and childless.
But as I have been a primary school teacher, I think I have had
children anyway.

Yes, good Lord… This is a shambles. I have been a bit out of
sorts and haven't had the strength to go on as usual. That's
why it looks so awful in here. But I feel better now. And as
bad as it was last autumn it haven't been this time. It was in
October, the same month that Eivor was put to death. The
whole day before, I had felt uncomfortable. In the evening I
started to freeze and sweat and feel sick and got a chest pain.
Well, I thought, now it's my turn! It had been rough weather
all week and many people walked around coughing and
sneezing. Yes, now you will see that you are falling sick lying
here in solitude, I thought, because I didn't feel well at all.
And so it was. I got pneumonia and high fever and was deliri-
ous. I was close to perishing.

But it would take more than that to finish me off! Now I
am on my feet again. Imagine when your legs were so strong
that you could go out and ski in the winter! I often skied and
skated when I was a child. For skates, one took an old scythe
and let the blacksmith shape a couple of irons. Then one got
two boards to stand on and drilled holes for the lacing.

Skis used by children at that time were all homemade. Usually, it was a ski taken from a barrel. Oak skis were especially
sought after. A piece of leather was fastened in the middle,
into which the feet were inserted, and then it was just get going. Nowadays, the children have factory-made gear, but it
went well for us too, and I remember how fun I thought it
was to be out skiing.

Otherwise, it doesn't look so bright for us here in the village. It's as if after a carefree everyday life, you suddenly wake up and find that you are out on unknown ground when darkness falls. The unknown evokes anxiety, and the anxiety paralyzes the power. The incredible thing that has happened means that the darkness doesn't give way. That something so awful can happen! It's as if there is something underneath that we don't see. Nothing happens without a cause, and even here there are supposed to be reasons. Both nearby, which the guardians of law-and-order concern themselves with, and deeper, which can't be reached by the arm of the law but which the God of heaven sees and judges over.

You ponder and ponder, and the suspicions thrive. I have fought like a fool to get away from it, but your thoughts can't be controlled. There isn't a single corner that you can hide in to get away.

It's quite clear that someone in the village has done it. But who can be so devilishly evil? That's what I can't figure out. I have had my thoughts – not to say suspicions. Without knowing the slightest thing, I have guessed everything and had anxiety. I have felt the pressure of the unspoken as something that can become too much. Then I have fought like a fool to come up with better ideas. Finally, I have surrendered unconditionally and given up. I think God wants to test us with this. He wants to examine us and find out who we really are.

Everything reminds me of the horrible thing that happened in my hometown when I was young. It was 1911 when I served as a maid in Sandviken's industrial community. It was the same year that the famous artwork *Mona Lisa* was stolen from a museum in Paris. It was called "the world's biggest theft". Three years later, an Italian worker admitted that he had stolen the painting "for pleasure".

Yes, people were weird even then. And brutal murders were not uncommon at that time either. It's a murder I remember. It was a twelve-year-old girl who had to sacrifice her life. Her name was Elna Eriksson, and I knew who she was. A kind and quiet girl who was doing well at school and who was physically well developed for her age. I mention the latter because it may have mattered.

It was in the autumn, in September just like now, and she was on her way from Sandviken, to a chalet that her family had, and carried a package of clean towels with her. She was walking on the carriageway that winded through the forest, and it was about half past two. The weather was calm and sunny. When she still hadn't arrived in the evening, her father began searching for her. He followed the same path she had taken in the opposite direction to Sandviken. There he met an acquaintance who said he had seen Elna along the road at half past two. He continued by saying that at the same time he had noticed a tall, thin man who had walked the same path a short distance behind Elna.

In Sandviken, her father asked some acquaintances and relatives if Elna was there but received negative answers everywhere. He then made a report to the police, who gathered a number of volunteers for search. By that time, it had become dark, and it had started to rain. It really poured down, but the search continued, and around eleven o'clock in the evening Elna was found dead. She was lying on her back with her legs raised and apart in an open place next to a cairn a short distance from the country road where she had walked. She had had her carotid artery cut off and was hit in the back, on the chest, and in the stomach by a blow from probably an axe. She had bruises on her hands. Her one cut off thumb was found in the cairn. Yes, good Lord how awful it was! Torn stones and moss scattered about indicated that she had tried to defend herself. She was bruised in her face, and the towel package she had apparently used as protection was just in rags and pieces.

All of Elna's clothes were soaked with blood. Her hat's chin cord was cut off, and the hat was thirty meters further into the forest. The murderer must have thrown himself at her on the country road, and she had managed to escape a bit into the forest. There he overpowered her and tried to accomplish a first rape attack. With her utmost strength she managed to tear herself free and run back towards the country road, but she probably stumbled and fell on her stomach. The perpetrator then immediately threw himself at her and hit her with at least three cuts, before giving her the deadly slash across her throat. Finally, he tore her trousers and fulfilled his infamous intentions.

The details were so awful, and there was so much talk about it everywhere, that I still remember it today. Everyone was agitated about the bestial act. When Elna was buried, a large crowd of locals met up to accompany her to her final rest. I was there too. It was raining, I remember, and I recall the flower-covered coffin carried to the tomb where the vicar gave a moving speech that made many of the women and mothers burst into tears. School children from Sandviken sang, and then it was a choir that ended the ceremony. I remember it so clearly, although it's almost fifty years ago.

And I remember the upset atmosphere in society. Everyone suspected everyone, and anyone could be singled out. The rumours never wanted to end. It was like it's here with us right now, though much worse. When a tramp came and begged for food in a farm and one saw that his appearance corresponded to the description of the man who had walked behind Elna in the forest, it spread like wildfire through half the parish. People flocked in from all directions, and the tramp was surrounded by a crowd of angry peasants and hysterical women who in loud words wanted to make the process short with him. "Let us give equal for equal, eye for eye!" it was shouted. "Hang the killer, hang the killer!" There was a violent feeling of hostility, and no one knows how it would have ended if the sheriff hadn't come with a couple of parish constables and taken care of the tramp. He was to sit in jail for a couple of days while sturdy men with loaded rifles went on guard outside. But he had a solid alibi, it turned out, and was set free again.

Many were suspected and questioned by the police, but the evidence was never sufficient. Some even confessed to the murder, but no one was ever convicted of it.

Will it now go the same way here? No one has been held responsible for the murder of Eivor either. If only you could understand why it happened and who did it! Of course, the gossip seems to know, but it can't be trusted. Everyone has their own suspicions and theories. I have decided not to get involved in it. What you don't know anything about, you shouldn't comment on. "Let the police handle it," I say when it comes up.

Harry, who comes here and helps me when I am out of sorts, raises the issue sometimes. But then I just listen to him and don't make any comments of my own. According to him, it can be anyone who has done it. Even a woman, he says, and there he touches upon something that I try by all means to keep away from me. And I know what he thinks of tattling crones, so I carefully keep my counsel.

He is a jolly fellow, Harry, who is nice to meet. His philosophy of life is that you can just as well be happy, because life doesn't get a bit better from walking around and pondering. Easy for him to say, he who doesn't have a concern in the world! Although he became a widower a few years ago, it doesn't seem to have depressed him significantly. He was also a very good professional before he retired. And he is happy and cheerful all the time. Singing and joking and telling anecdotes like blazes. Preferably to a couple of drinks, which I offer him sometimes. He never gets drunk and unpleasant. It's proof of his good judgment that he has never been seen drunk by anyone around him. If he notices that it's getting a little too much of the spirits, he immediately says goodbye and goes home to avoid unnecessary frictions.

The only thing I have a little trouble with is his bragging. "You must believe that one is successful with the ladies," he usually says. "There are quite a few of them, believe me. And they visit me as often as they can. One is a married woman whose name I don't want to reveal. She often comes and stays until late at night, and then I usually arrange for me to get her down in the bedstraw." Yes, that's how he goes on when he has gotten a couple of drinks under his belt. "Today, you must believe that I am completely fagged out, because I have had a female with me all night and one isn't so young anymore. Who it was? No, I don't want to say that. It's like forbidden fruit because she is married". He is a real lady-killer. Or if it's all blather, because no one has ever seen any women at his house. But that he himself walks around to the wives in the cottages and allows himself to be invited and offered both one thing and the other, is something that's certain and true.

Ingrid

I have had my birthday. I am ten years old now. From Dad I got a drawing block and artist's colours as a gift and from Aunt Lilly I got a book and from Aunt Vera I got a spoon and a twin set, which is a jumper and cardigan in the same colour and of the same kind of fabric. From Mom I got red patent leather slippers with white silk tassels on them. It was Dad who bought them because Mom never goes to town nowadays. But they were from her.

Last time I had my birthday, Mom was sick and vomited. She had a bucket next to her bed that she vomited in. It was the day after Aunt Eivor was murdered. As a birthday present, I received a book about a family living in a shoe. I don't like that book now, just because Mom was sick when I got it. Only children can be sick sometimes, I think. Not grown-ups, because then they can't take care of everything they should. But if they are just a little sick in the head, they might cook and do the dishes and clean anyway.

Once at night, Mom got up and put on her Persian lamb coat over her nightgown and told Dad that she would go down to the river and look at all the dead people lying there. I woke up and heard it. But Dad stopped her.

Persian coats are made from dead lambs. The lambs are taken out before they are born, and then they kill them and rip off the skin. I don't think it should be allowed to make fur coats from animals. And it shouldn't be allowed to kill elephants to get hold of ivory either, I think.

It's fun to get presents when you have your birthday. But I already have so many things, so I almost don't need any more. I have the dolls, the doll's bed, the doll's pram, the ornamental animals, the hospital things, the little loom, the ukulele, the mouthorgan, the View-Master, the snowball, the painting things, the slate, the abacus, the marbles, the tin soldiers, the modelling clay, the paper dolls, the balls, the skipping rope, the yo-yo, the flying saucer, the windmill, the water pistol, the doll's house, the playhouse things... And I have a car and a bird and a rat made of sheet metal that can be screwed up. And books, scrapbooks, colouring books, drawing blocks, bookmarks, and movie stars. In the escritoire I have writing materials and stuff. Paper and notebooks and letter paper and pens. I have a real fountain pen that you fill with ink. And I have the poetry book and the diary. On the diary, there is a small lock that is like a heart. I write in the diary what I have played and about the weather sometimes. And I have my Esso pen. It's transparent at the top, and in it there is oil or whatever it is, and a gadget that says Esso. When you move the pen, it goes up and down in the oil. Dad has gotten it at a petrol station.

Gun-Britt has an autograph block that she got when she had her birthday, so now she collects autographs. She has Tage Severin, Jussi Björling, Dan Waern, Alice Babs, and several others. I don't know how she has gotten them. I would also like to have such a block.

When I turned eight, I got a work box from my aunt. It has red shiny fabric inside and a needle pad on the lid, and then there are sewing things in it. So, I have that too. And all my jewellery. There are earrings and bracelets and necklaces and hair slides and tiaras and brooches and rings. The comrade ring I wear all the time. And the wristwatch. That I got when I turned seven.

Every time I have my birthday, I get a silver spoon from

Aunt Vera. It's in a small box on pink paper and has a red bow around it. I will have them when I grow up and have coffee parties. As Christmas presents, I usually get vests and underpants from her. It's boring to get them. But she works in a clothing store, so we mostly get clothes from her. Mom gets aprons and cleaning coats, Dad gets underpants and undershirts, and I get vests and panties.

I have also received make-up things from my aunt. Lipstick, nail polish, perfume, and powder. I am getting things that are running out. Once I put on my best skirt and a white top, and then I took my red elastic belt with a gold buckle. Or it's just gold coloured. Then I painted my lips and nails and put on earrings and necklaces. But it looked sloppy, so I took it off again. You can have it when you play fine ladies, but not for real. Although it's fun to *have* makeup things and try them. It's about the same as with the fine things, that you only have them because you think they are nice. I have smooth stones and pearls and pieces of glass and unusual buttons and a glittery brooch. I have all of them in a cardboard box that has contained perfume. And then I have a fabric rose and a round metal thing with a pattern on it and a death's-head with red pearl eyes, that I have gotten from Tommy, and an empty perfume bottle with a silk tassel at the top. I don't count Pertussin bottles and Albyl boxes and Vicks jars, because those I have for hospital things.

Before I used to have a mania for playing hospital, but I no longer have that. At last, no one wanted to play it with me. It got too humdrum, they thought.

I have received several things from Tommy. One day when I was sitting alone in a seat on the bus, he came and sat down next to me with his back to me, while he was talking to Uffe.

After a while he turned around and looked surprised and said: "Oh, did I sit down next to *you*!" "Yes, obviously," I said. "Do you have any apples to offer then?" he said. Because I usually take apples from home and give to them on the bus. "Yes, I have," I said and opened the bag so that he could take one. "Then you can have this," he said and gave me a huge glass ball with a blue colour pattern in it. I didn't even have time to say thanks before he had gone to the back of the bus and sat down in another seat.

My name is Harry Rosendahl
and I am a retired merchant.
The children have left home
and the government, called Kristina, has passed away.

I have always respected women. I think they are the crowns of creation, regardless of whether they are called Madonnas or prostitutes. But they are a strange kind that is difficult to comprehend. They lack what we men have always had, namely power of action and courage. Instead, they chatter and gossip and muddle about, so you become completely confused. They feel satisfied in letting their tongues run and make one false rumour after another. It's endless speculations and slander and none of it can be trusted.

But nowadays, women are allowed to become clergymen, taxi drivers, and police officers. A woman in a clergyman's gown or in a uniform! If it weren't so damn cow dumb, one would laugh at the misery. They are of course not suitable for that!

When it comes to Eivor Johansson, her departure has become an interesting topic that can be discussed when the chatterboxes lack subjects. If a woman isn't allowed to talk, she probably falls away and dies like a potted plant without water in the absence of nutrition. The gossip runs through the village, flying with wagging chins from mouth to mouth, from cottage to cottage, from farm to farm. "Is Eivor dead? No, that can't be possible! We saw her earlier today, alive and in full health!"

And what about her death now? Suicide, one called it. Accident, suspected another. Stroke, was the third opinion, and she had already developed that theory the same evening in front of several neighbours. Among the women in the village, there was no one who, in the first uproar and confusion, even wanted to touch on the idea that Mrs. Johansson could have been the victim of a violent act. But according to the medical examiner and the police, it must be a case of manslaughter or murder.

The crone's mouths go, and there is no end to the speculations. Because if it's now the case that she has been killed, then you must ask yourself for what reason. The initiates are convinced that she was carrying a secret that would be fatal to someone if it were leaked. Either she knew something grave about someone, or she accidentally had witnessed a serious crime by accident. No one can know for sure, but in both cases, she appears as a dangerous witness. So, who was it that felt compelled to silence her?

No, that's not the case at all, says another. No, this perpetrator is certainly not a man with a dark secret whatsoever, but an ordinary man who has happened to kill by mistake and who is now going through a terrible time of insomnia, fear, and bad conscience! During the first hours after the drama, he certainly couldn't do anything at all – except possibly drink a lot of alcohol. In what cottage, or in what farm, did a man sit that night and got himself blind drunk? It should be possible to found out! In any case, he has killed, not murdered, or possibly under temporary confusion, beaten a human being to death. And he should take the responsibility for that crime by coming forth voluntarily. Instead of staying away, he should assist the police in solving the case. In any case, he will never get away from his own conscience, not even when the period for prosecution has expired.

Some declare: "No, I know nothing! I have no definite suspicions. I don't want that! And I don't take false considerations. Why should I take into consideration what I don't know what it is? I know nothing and have seen nothing. I don't suspect anyone!"

It may even have been a woman who did it: "Yes, can you imagine, it's she, they say, isn't that so you can crack! She is the one who killed Eivor! Yes, isn't that what we have always said, that she has always been a bit peculiar, and now her real self has shown! But you must understand that something has driven her. She must have had a reason! Yes, but which one, which one?"

And if the police should fail: "We have promised ourselves to go deeper into it. We will go as deep as we can! To the best of our ability, we will try to get to the bottom of it. If the police fail, we will continue until the case is either solved or must be considered unsolved forever!"

A middle-aged woman socializes in secret with a married man. When, some time after the drama, a divergency arises between them, she begins to spread rumours among the neighbours that the man may be the murderer. On the day in question, he is said to have angrily stated that "now no one is safe in the village". So, he has left, and when he returned to the woman later that night, she said that he had "blood stains on his hands and clothes and rushed straight into the bathroom to wash himself". Neighbours report what they have heard to the police, who visit the woman to have the information checked. But then she has changed her mind, because now it's not at all as the witnesses have claimed. "It's a lie every word they say, because I have never talked to anyone about that night!"

Yes, false statements are common in murder investigations

where the police don't find the right way. Injudicious people use the situation for their own purposes and to the great inconvenience of the authorities, who can never really know whether the accusations are true or not. The murder investigators must search further towards the truth until they manage to get hold of witnesses who can give the designated alibi. False designations are a damned nuisance that slows down the work of the police completely unnecessarily. It's true that there are laws that can lead to prosecution and punishment for false declaration, defamation, and so on, but then it must be proven that "malicious intent" exists, and also that the aggrieved party has suffered harm.

And who are then primarily engaged in such "pleasures"? Well, it's the women, these crowns of creation, who, without remorse and without any sensible thoughts of the consequences, let their poisonous tongues run.

My name is Gun-Britt Johansson and I am twelve years old.
Dad's name is Tore and Mom's name was Eivor
and I have two older siblings named Siv and Lennart.

Mom is dead. She was murdered. I was at the funeral, but I didn't cry. Dad and Siv cried but not Lennart and me. I have cried at home in my room and out in the woods sometimes. I don't want to show anyone that I am sad. I want to be as usual so that no one will feel sorry for me.

I listen to the radio, to Swedish Car Radio and Radio Luxembourg where they play music. Lennart likes jazz, but I like hits and rock better. Those who are at the top of the Barometer in *Bildjournalen* are good, I think. It's *Buona Sera* with Little Gerhard and *King Creole* with Elvis Presley and *Everybody Loves a Lover* with Doris Day.

I wish I could play and sing like them. I play recorder and mandolin, but it's guitar you should play, and you should sing along. Although Doris Day doesn't play, I think. It's probably an orchestra that does it for her. It's mostly guys, like Tommy and Elvis, who play themselves when they sing.

I don't have a good singing voice, so I could never become a singer. I know that. I might become a shop assistant or a clerk instead. Siv, my big sister, wants to be a nurse. I could never be that because I don't like hospitals. Ingrid was in the hospital for a very long time before she started school. She was there for five months. Mom and I sent her cards. And I made drawings that Mom took to Aunt Signe so that she could give them to Ingrid at the hospital. Children were not allowed to come and visit where she was.

I have become accustomed to Mom being gone. I don't think about her that much anymore. Nobody talks about her either. Only Siv sometimes. Judging by Lennart's behaviour, it seems as if she has never existed. And the police officers who would find out who killed her probably don't care anymore. I don't really know.

Ingrid and I play almost every day now but never at her house. Her mother doesn't allow her to let any children in, I think. Aunt Signe was angry with Mom and with me as well and didn't want Ingrid to play with me. I don't know why. But we are still playing now. Ingrid doesn't care what Aunt Signe says. I think that's good, because it would be so boring not to have her to play with. At school we have other friends, but at home it's mostly her and me.

Mother was sorry that Aunt Signe didn't want to see her anymore. She wanted them to be friends again. She went over to her several times and had a weekly magazine with her, but Aunt Signe didn't open when Mom knocked at the door. Mom wanted to talk with her and give her a magazine so that she might stop being angry, she hoped. She told me that.

Sometimes I think that Mom sees us even though she is dead. I don't exactly think she is an angel, but she may see us even though she isn't visible herself. I can't really explain what I mean. Every night when I lie in bed, I think through the goodnight verse she used to read to me when I was little and was to sleep. This is how it goes: *The star over there in the evening's lake, yes there over the ridge, is the island of dreams. There the sandman lives in a marble castle so high above the earth's weeping and sorrow. And yet the sandman travels down here every night in the quiet peace of twilight. He rides in a golden carriage on the silver sky, which ends right there at the edge of the ridge. And that, you can believe, is an elegant sight. Then he travels around the whole village. And just as they are about to crawl into bed, the little ones, in every cottage he comes in. He takes them in his arms, he carries them out, then they close their eyes without much ado. Then they fall asleep and soon on soft feathers they swing away.*

When I think of that verse, it almost feels like Mom is here again.

I am Birgit, vicious daughter of Astrid and Göte Lindberg.
I have a brother named Sven who isn't an angle either.

Arne and I have been hanging together for a while now and will surely get hitched up some fine day and get us a couple of kids. At least that's what I want. My folks don't like him, but I don't give a fuck. And he hasn't always been who he is now. When he was younger, he was well-behaved and had ambitions. He was confirmed when he was fourteen, and after primary school he worked as a delivery boy for two years. Then he started as a bricklayer apprentice on a building site and continued there until he was a trained bricklayer. After his military service, he started working as a bricklayer for real and joined the union and stuff like that. At that time, he was almost a teetotaller and was going steady with a decent girl. His mother has told me that. His goal was to study to be an engineer, either in the construction or motor industry. He saved up for a motorbike, and according to himself, the chicks queued to go with him.

I don't know why it went wrong for him later. He started boozing and taking days off and was sacked. That was before I met him.

He can be quite tough, Arne, but I like him sharply. Once when we had kicked up a row, he threw me down on the bed and strangled me. I could barely breathe and tried to get free. Then he landed me one in the breadbasket. I managed to get up and grabbed an iron that I threw at him. He got it on his leg, so it did no major damage. But he became shirty and started bumping on me with his fists. I thought I was going to die. I screamed so a neighbour heard it and called the cop. But they didn't get anything, because when the radio patrol car with the tough guys arrived there was only me left. I said that everything was a mistake and that nothing had happened. I would never snitch on Arne, you know.

The first time Arne and I met, he had just been released from the clink, and I was on the run from a girl's home. He had jacks left over from a break-in they hadn't discovered and bought booze and lots of presents for me. Then we were out with his bike all summer and camped and were on the spree. We were loaded almost the whole time. Sometimes I was scared shitless when I sat behind him on the bike because he drove like a lunatic at top speed and didn't give a damn that I was terror-stricken.

It's terrible what has happened in the village. It's said that Eivor's head was smashed to pieces with an axe. Who can do something like that? Arne has a buddy who has been in the States, and over there such things are not so remarkable. There you can get a murder fixed for thirty bucks. But here in Sweden, people don't usually do things like that. Arne and I were visiting my folks when it happened. Yes, not exactly at the same time, but approximately. We were in the village anyway, and of course the cops who knew who Arne is were interested.

Personally, I am not entirely unknown to them either. I have a reputation for being a woman of easy virtue and having a weak character. Sitting at home in the evenings has never been my style. I want to be where it swings and something happens. Before I met Arne, I was out dancing all the time. I like to wear posh clothing and loved to spruce myself up and make myself look good in a stunning party dress before I pushed along. I am doing that now as well. And I have always had an easy time connecting with guys. I never had to sit over a dance or go home alone at night. The hags in the village were horrified and called me loose-living and pleasure-seeking. The tittle-tattle said that I belonged to the women of the street. I was called both a streetwalker and a slut. But I have never received payment, I am just saying.

My folks did what they could to pull me away from the pleasures, but they didn't succeed. And the bitches on the Child Welfare Committee thought they understood: "Yes, unfortunately she drinks more than she can stand to deafen her bad conscience and try to feel less disgust over her shameful life as a mattress." They didn't get that I liked to dance and flirt and excite the guys, but that it was mostly a game with fire, because most of the time I didn't let them get what they wanted. Some became shirty, but it was worth it, because I liked to feel coveted and have power. I have always done that.

Christian people believe that there is a god and that you will come to heaven after death if you follow his commandments while you live. Anyone who doesn't obey the dictates can be punished, so it's important to stay on the narrow way: no divorces, no disobedience to parents, no abortions, no dishonesty, no slander, no premarital life together, not too much pleasure and entertainment. Otherwise, God Almighty on high will be huffy and sooner or later it will go to hell for the sinner.

When it comes to morality, you always come to the question of *why* you should act in a certain way when you may have the desire to act in another. The Christians believe that there must be a higher power that decides what is right and wrong and from which one can be informed. You should do so and so because God has said so! Fortunately, I don't believe in God and can do as I please in all situations. I have never cared about Mom's and Dad's moral sermons, and I don't obey any authorities. In that way, Arne and I are alike.

Someone had heard a motorcycle on the road around the time Eivor was killed. The cop arrested Arne and held him for a couple of days while they looked thoroughly into his affairs. When he got to know that he was suspected of murder, he was shocked. People thought he was guilty and began to slander him. It didn't help that he was released as soon as they found out that he had been with me all evening. The cops thought I was lying to fix him from suspicions, but there was no evidence, so they had to release him.

To a certain extent, he is to blame himself of being suspected. If he hadn't been in the police records, it would never have happened. But from burglary and car theft to murder, it's a fucking long step. And you might think that people would forget. But since then, he has never been called anything other than "Murder-Arne". As soon as a new acquaintance hears that he has been arrested for murder, they think: "Well, he couldn't have been that for no reason." He is just a simple thief who didn't manage to get away with it, and he has served his sentence and should obtain redress. Instead, he has been branded as a fucking killer.

We were in the village when it happened, but we had nothing to do with it. When we had had some grub with my folks, we took a ride on the bike to get some air. We went on the road along the river and met no one. In the middle of Tore's, we blew past a geezer who was out with a wheelbarrow, but otherwise it was dead. Out in the boondocks it's black as in the ass of a Negro once it has become dark. So, the only thing we could see was what the headlights hit.

When we came back, it was a little before seven, and by

then probably about half an hour had passed. During that time, according to the cops, Arne would have killed Eivor. Yeah, kiss my ass! For what reason would he have done that if you may ask. He didn't do it, and that's it! My old man tried to claim that we had been away longer, but he said that just because he can't stand Arne and wanted him back in the clink. But he is never going there again, I am just saying.

Of course, it's possible to commit a murder without being exposed. The easier and faster a crime is carried out, the less risk of detection. But one should beware of describing an unsolved crime as "perfect". It's usually either a question of a failure on the part of the police or that the perpetrator has had an incredible so-called luck of the devil.

In this murder mystery, we are currently without any clues. The murder detectives have been relentlessly stuck, which is largely due to the undeserved help given to the perpetrator by chance. We now have to trust that chance will also give us some help in the form of new ideas worth working with. In the time that has passed, there have been a number of telephone calls and letters from the public containing various notices, and we have checked all these tips, but without any clues of positive value. The extensive door-knocking operation that was initially carried out in the village also didn't yield what we had hoped for.

It's a fact that the longer the time that elapses, the more difficult it becomes to solve a murder. Witnesses' and other people's memories of what happened fade with time. Witnesses can be influenced by others, and this can result in misleading testimonies. It's often said that the reliability of a witness decreases with the square of time.

Another disadvantage is that the criminal staff who worked with the case from the beginning gladly stick to certain theories, even though they may be on the wrong track. In that situation, it can be good for new, healthy forces to be involved. On the other hand, additional valuable time is then wasted by new investigators having to read in the extensive material.

In any case, the documentation is extremely important. At the initial crime scene investigation, nothing must be forgotten. Every little detail, even the one that may seem insignificant, should be included. Everything must be photographed and described. What has been neglected or done by halves in the beginning, can seldom be repaired by ever so great efforts later on. Traces and other observable conditions, which may become evidence against a suspect or contribute to a reconstruction, usually change or disappear. By carefully studying the crime scene you can read how the crime took place. When we then get hold of the perpetrator, we compare his description of the incident with what we know from the site, and then we can determine if he is telling the truth or not.

In this case, we have unfortunately not been able to find the crime scene, which of course worsened our starting position, despite the fact that our turn-out went very quickly and immediately received the widest possible base. This may indicate that the murderer was given the opportunity to hide indoors at a short distance from the site or that he even lived nearby.

We have also not been able to find a reasonable explanation for why the murder took place. Mrs. Johansson evidently had no money on her, and she had not been subjected to infamous violence. It can hardly be about jealousy either, and we don't believe in revenge. This modest housewife appeared to be an unusually sterling woman with no enemies. If we had had motive and if we had got to deal with the real crime scene, we might have been able to solve the mystery, but that hasn't been the case.

Of course, it's very unfortunate that we haven't yet managed to uncover and arrest the murderer behind this evil deed.

He is still at large and has so far benefited from various random moments. But it's not certain that his luck will last all the years that remain until the period of prosecution has expired. We still hope to be able to solve the case and see to every new idea with renewed energy. The investigation hasn't been closed. A small criminal group is still prepared to step in as soon as new clues emerge. If necessary, our work can very quickly come into full force again.

Ingrid

Guess what Dad has bought for us? Yes, a telly! It's like a cupboard with legs underneath and two doors that can be opened and closed. And inside the doors is the viewing screen. Sometimes the picture rolls, but then you just turn a button, and it stops.

The telly is twenty inches, so it's bigger than Aunt Beda's and Uncle Harald's television set. Mom says that dangerous radiation comes out of it. At first, she didn't want to watch any programmes, but now she does it because she is curious. She puts on some cardigans, so that the radiation doesn't get into her so easily.

Sometimes when Mom writes messy notes that I don't want to read, I do it anyway, because I am curious. But they are so weird. It's no fun that she is writing those notes. And she hears voices inside her head that she is talking to. In the beginning, she said everything out loud, but I didn't let her, so now she whispers. She whispers and laughs and barely hears what I say because she has such thick things against her ears. I must force her to listen and answer if there is something I want. But for the most part, I just ignore her. There is no point in talking to someone who has bats in the belfry, I think.

Tommy has started knocking about with a girl in the fifth grade now. Her name is Anna. It's an ugly name, I think. He sits down next to her on the bus and wants to exchange stamps with her. She knows a sailor from whom she gets a lot of stamps. But that's not the only reason why he sits next to her. He does it because he likes her, and she likes him back. She seems to believe that she has a monopoly on him.

I have invented that I like a guy named Peter Westergren who lives in town, because otherwise Tommy might think that he is the only one for me, and I don't want him to think that, when I am not the only one for him. I write Peter's name on pieces of paper and draw hearts around it, and I have put his initials on my ruler so that Tommy can see it. I hope he will become a little jealous, since I am that way about Anna. I get so upset when I see him sit next to her on the bus. Just because she happens to have a lot of old stamps, he doesn't have to be with her every day! But I can't make him stop and come back to me. He likes her and doesn't care about me anymore.

But one day he took a note that I had. It was a heart with an arrow through and inside the heart I had written "Ingrid + Peter W = true" with another handwriting, so you would think I had received the note from someone who wanted to tease me. I pretended to get angry when he took it and tried to take it back, but I wanted him to read it. "Who is Peter W then?" he said. "A guy I know," I said. "What is his second name then?" he said. "It doesn't matter," I said. "You don't know him anyway." "Well, you never know," he said. "Yes, because he lives in town," I said. Then he said no more.

But it's Tommy who is Peter W. He is never going to know, because now that he is with Anna, I want him to believe that I don't like him anymore. But I do. Sometimes I think that maybe it's just on the outside he has changed, and that he still likes me just as much inside. Why would he otherwise take my yarn bird and place it on his desk as he did a day before? He had it there for a whole lesson. And another day before the bus came, he passed me and lifted his school bag and pushed it against me in the air. Then it felt like he liked me and wanted to be with me. Like he wanted to show it even though he couldn't say it. But I don't know. I am going to give that Anna a wallop between the glow-worms so she must take the pling-plong-taxi to the plaster house!

Sometimes girls can be beaten even though everyone thinks it's cowardly. You mustn't hit a girl and not attack one that is smaller and not be several against one. These are rules that exist. One day before, Uffe happened to hit Anette. First, he jumped around and teased her. Then he slapped her on her arm, and she ran away to the ball tower. Everyone followed, and she stood there behind it with her hands to her face. "Does she blubber?" Uffe said. "Yes, what do you think?" Barbro said. "You are nuts!" Then she said to Nettan: "Come, let's go and tell the master!" Then it seemed that Uffe was a little scared, but he didn't want to show it. "Can't you take a joke?" he said. "It was just for fun!"

If you peach on someone you can be teased. *Tell-tale-tit, your tongue shall be slit, and all the dogs in the town, shall have a little bit*, they say.

I think you should ignore everyone who is stupid and teasing. It's almost only Monika who tries to quarrel with me. Once during a handicraft lesson, when she was sitting and throwing pins at me, I turned around and said: "Little things please little minds!" Then I took no more notice of her. She didn't stop at once, but she had at least been told what I thought of her. She can go to blazes, I think.

It's mostly guys who fight. Girls can tease, but they don't fight. There is a difference between boys and girls. Not only that guys like to fight, but they also play other types of games. Guys, they like cars, boats, trains, aeroplanes, stamps, football, bandy, and ice hockey, and they play ball and angle and fly with kites and shoot with slingshots and cap pistols. They like to play war, and girls don't. And guys don't want to play with dolls. They think it's silly. But I think they are wrong, because war isn't needed, but taking care of children is needed. And it's the boys who will be the fathers later, so why don't they want to play with dolls?

I wouldn't like to be a boy if I could change, because if a boy gets the urge to do something that girls usually do, he can't. He doesn't dare because of his buddies. But if a girl wants to try things that boys do, everyone thinks she is tough. Girls have much greater freedom than boys and don't have to be afraid of what their mates will think.

I think some guys think they have to be strong and tough so that no one should be able to call them namby-pamby or yellow-belly. Like a guy in the seventh grade who has been rude and answered back to a teacher. Before, he also smashed a window and smoked in the boys' toilet. He is the school's black sheep and almost like a juvenile delinquent. He is a ding-a-ling, I think. *Idiot von Nitwit*, Tommy calls him. Now everyone has received a note to take home that says about the troublemakers. Because there are others too. In the sixth grade, for example, there are a few.

What is it that makes some people get rowdy and maybe pinch things and have to be put in the nick when they get older? I wonder. Why do they want to do things that can put them in jail? Because it can't be very fun to be locked in a cell and never be allowed to go out. They have nothing to play with either. Or they don't play, because they are old, but they have nothing to do. They may read a little but nothing else.

In the past, those who were in prison were given only bread and water to live on, but that's not the case nowadays. Now they get about the same kind of food that they are used to from home. They are not tortured either, as they used to be in the past. In a book that Dad has, there are drawn pictures of different kinds of torture. One gets boiling water into his throat, and one is tied to a stretching bench and is stretched out with a winch. Other punishments were to be thrown into a lion's pit or to be beheaded. Some were burned at the stake. Aunts they thought were witches were burned. And thieves had their hands cut off so they wouldn't be able to steal anymore.

Once when Uffe, Tommy, Gugge, and I were in town we went into Tempo, because there no one comes and asks what can I do for you, and then Uffe said that we would shoplift. I didn't want to, but Uffe said we would. Tommy went ahead and bought liquorice cigarettes, and while he was paying, Uffe pilfered a Roulette. Gugge stood in front of him, so that the aunt couldn't see it. Then she pilfered two lollipops. When we came out, we shared the Roulette, and I got a lollipop from Gugge. So, I haven't pilfered myself, but I have been present when others have done it and eaten pilfered sweets.

My name is Sten Hallgren.
I am married to Aina and we have three children.
I work as a carpenter at Anders Diös and is a fellow-worker with
the murder victim's husband Tore Johansson.

It's alleged that I was in the village at half past six on the night of the murder. I would have come riding in a northerly direction and had Åke's Chevrolet following behind me for just under a kilometre.

But that's completely wrong. At that time, I was still in Stockholm. I didn't come home until eight o'clock, as my wife can confirm. I was contacted by the police, of course, and had to report on my activities during the evening. The information about my car had aroused suspicion. But that misunderstanding could be quickly cleared up. Åke and his passengers must have simply made a mistake regarding the day.

Which shows how easy it can be to become innocently suspected. In this case, there have been plenty of suspicions in all possible directions, I have learned from my wife. Personally, I haven't dealt with the talk, but even the police have complained about the extensive spread of rumours, which of course has made their work more difficult.

It was Bengt, our son, who together with a friend of his found Eivor dead. He himself took it quite calmly, but his comrade, who is a couple of years younger, was afterwards extremely preoccupied with the incident and had fantasies about being able to help the police find the murderer. Which, of course, was just an expression of youthful lack of wisdom.

Not that the police didn't need help, one realizes today when more than a year has passed without their work having given positive results. We must probably accept that the case will never be solved. For Tore and his family, it's of course harder to give up hope. Tore has on several occasions expressed how impossible it is to accept that the murderer should escape. There are so many questions that he wants answered and that only the murderer can give. Anger has been linked to a desire to know the truth. It's difficult to determine whether it's the question of truth or anger towards the perpetrator that is strongest. But that's probably how many of us feel when facing murders and other violent crimes. We want to know the truth, and we want the perpetrator to be punished. No one, least of all the relatives of the victim, can have peace until the murderer is caught and has received his penalty.

Tore has told me about his thoughts on the murder and about the work of the police, which he expects to continue with undiminished force until the culprit is arrested. It's, of course, a vain expectation; the investigation has already been deescalated and will be phased out further. But to get peace and be able to shut out all brooding, he needs to get more information about what happened. If not, morbid fantasies can take root in him – dark thoughts that can be difficult to master and free himself from. He needs facts and information about the crime, from the moment it happened until today. Then it will be easier for him to move on. Therefore, one shouldn't save the resources in the investigation work after serious violent criminals. In the long run, it will be cheaper for everyone not to skimp. A lost human value is too high a price to pay. The culprit also feels better about being exposed and convicted, which of course he doesn't realize himself.

Ingrid

Soon it's Christmas. I really long for Christmas Eve when I can open the Christmas presents. Mom has baked cakes and made the house clean and tidy for Christmas, and she has polished the copper pans and changed curtains and taken out the Christmas tablecloths and put new paper in all the cupboards above the sink. Dad has set up a corn sheaf for the birds and chopped a spruce that we will take in on Christmas Eve and put candles and Christmas tree decorations in.

On Christmas Eve, Aunt Vera comes to us and brings hyacinths and Christmas presents with her. Then they first dip in the pot. I don't do that, because the liquid in which the loaf slices are dipped, is the same as the ham has been boiled in, and that mixture is very fat and disgusting.

At five o'clock we eat Christmas dinner. If I am to list everything we usually have then it's potatoes, ham, mustard, boiled ling, sauce, meatballs, spare ribs, rice pudding, milk, pickled herring, pickled gherkins, pickled Baltic herring, tinned sprat, Jansson's temptation, jellied veal, beetroot salad, aspic, wort loaf, ordinary loaf, crispbread, Christmas cheese, seed-spiced cheese, butter, small beer, lager, Christmas must, soft drink, snaps, liver paste, ox-tongue, salami-type sausage, chipolata sausage, other sausage, Christmas sausage.

On Christmas Eve, Mom sets the table with her finest plates and bowls and glasses. There is a white tablecloth on the table, and napkins with red Santas on, and a large wooden candlestick with lit candles that glows so that everything glitters.

It takes a very long time for the grown-ups to eat on Christmas Eve. I want it to go fast, so that the Christmas gift distribution can begin, but I have to wait and wait while they eat and drink and talk and clean the table and wash up and dry the dishes and put it all away.

At last, it's time for the Christmas presents. When I was little, Santa Claus came to us, but this year I am the one who will hand out the parcels. Last Christmas it was Dad. I can hardly remember what it was like last Christmas. An aunt that Dad knows came to us and cooked and baked gingerbread before Christmas. On the last sheet, the cakes were burnt, and then she asked me not to tell Mom about it. But I didn't like that aunt and didn't want to obey her. I didn't want her to stay with us in Mom's kitchen.

When I was little, we celebrated Christmas Eve with Gun-Britt's family, but now we no longer do. Sometimes we were in their house and sometimes in our house. It was Dad or Uncle Tore who dressed up as Santa and came in with a big sack with all the Christmas presents. Earlier, I believed in Santa Claus, but now I no longer do.

After the Christmas presents, we crack nuts and eat candy and light sparklers and listen to Christmas carols. Dad thinks you should think a little about Jesus when it's Christmas, because it was at Christmas time that the three wise men found the child Jesus in the manger. Then, when he was an adult, he was crucified and had to die because no one believed in him. You can feel sorry for him, but I don't think so much about him, because I think mostly about my Christmas presents and wonder what I will get. I have wished for books and a baby doll pyjama and a dressing table with a mirror and a jewellery box.

The Christmas presents that Mom and Dad will get from me are almost finished. I bought a comb for Dad, because his old one has broken and isn't so nice anymore. I bought a steel comb, because on such combs the tags can't be broken.

Mom will get a potholder that I am crocheting. At the bottom it's reasonably wide, but then it gets narrower and narrower with each round that goes. I will probably have to tear it up and start all over again.

Journal at Ulleråker Hospital's northern women's ward

23.11.1960: *Admitted to dept. 8. Care certificate issued by Dr. Evert Höglund. Previous medical records are available at pat., cared for in 1957 for less than a month under diagnosis of Schizophrenia, definitely discharged after another 2 months, since then no contact with the hospital.*

The care certificate announces: Anamnestic information through medical records Ulleråker Hospital and neighbour Tore Johansson. Heredity for mental illness where the mother and probably several siblings of 15 persons were cared for at Ulleråker Hospital. Married, 12-year-old daughter. Previously for the most part healthy, 1957 cared for at Ulleråker Hospital u.d. Schizophrenia with rather acute morbidity with confusion, high-grade anxiety, insomnia, visual and auditory hallucinosis, no disease insight. Discharged improved, then has had no contact with the hospital. Pat. is described by a neighbour after discharge as retiring, unsociable, sometimes when strangers have come, running into the woods.

Current: *Yesterday, the police and ambulance were alerted when the neighbour, who was not let in by the pat., saw through the villa window the husband lying motionless on the floor below the stairs to the upper floor. The husband was then unconscious and taken to hospital for treatment. The couple's 12-year-old daughter was at the time at school. The wife was found self-absorbed, difficult to contact, negative, probably hallucinating, talking to herself, giving pass over-answers, no concrete information could be obtained from her. Claimed that her husband was a strange man named Erik, but who wasn't her husband, and that one could certainly find several such strange men in the house. Her own husband, who is also called Erik, is at the slaughterhouse, since he is a butcher, she thinks. Lacks any form of disease insight, refuses any form of help, refuses to come along to the hospital.*

Somatic condition: Not further investigated.
Mental state: Not oriented to the time but formally to the situation. Motoric well - organized. Can't give any anamnestic information, in her self-absorbed condition negativistic, does not answer questions, gives omissions, inadequate smiles and periodically slightly dysphoric. The perception of reality is completely abolished, as is the emotional reactivity.

Summary: 48-year-old woman living with her husband and 12-year-old daughter, after the husband became acutely ill, admitted to hospital, where pat.1957 was treated at Ulleråker Hospital u.d. Schizophrenia and then showed probable defect healing or persistent tranquil symptoms. Unsociable, isolated, not left home for almost 3 years, clearly overprotected by her husband. She is not oriented to the time, completely abolished perception of reality, self-absorbed, with clear psychotic symptoms such as poisoning ideas, personal confusion ideas, incoherent world of thought, refuses hospital care, completely lacks insight into illness.
In the current family situation, the need for care seems to be urgent, as pat. due to mental illness probably of a psychotic nature cannot take care of herself and the daughter, when the husband is now in hospital.
Diagnosis: Psychosis with voice hallucinosis.

24.11.1960: Conversation (doc. Larsson): The undersigned had a conversation with this woman today, she was standing at the door and wanted to go out the whole the time. She was wearing six sweaters, old worn torn shoes, a turban on her head, wrapped ears. She didn't want to go to the ward and didn't understand at all why she must be here. She stated that she was 30 years old and also stated that she had a daughter and that her husband's name was Erik. He was at the slaughterhouse, where he worked with loading and removal of dead bodies, she thought. During the conversation very confused, made personal confusion between herself and the undersigned and present nurse. She was very tense to her staying here.

During the night she has slept on medication she has received, also in the morning ate some parts of the breakfast with persuasion. However, she has refused to take off her clothes and we will let her have her way for the time being. We have also not been able to physically examine her for that reason. She does not appear to be acutely physically ill.

26.11.1960: Conversation (doc. Larsson): It is announced that pat's husband Erik, born 07, died this morning, probably in a serious anaemia, secondary to some disease. The undersigned looks up pat. to inform her of this.

Pat. is sitting in the chair in her room self-absorbed. Can give the correct social security number but the wrong age, thinks she is 35 years old. Hears voices that she talks to from time to time during the conversation, often answering inadequately. Has some relevant near-memory fragments, such as that her husband was ill at home and apparently lay on the floor and was picked up by ambulance personnel. Also knows she is in hospital, thinks it is the University Hospital. The undersigned informs that her husband

274

has died. She comments on this with: "Was it the brawny-armed Erik?" Unclear how she receives the message.

Lilly Olofsson 1961

Throughout the whole first year after my sister's falling ill, I continued to visit her in her home. I missed our familiar conversations and hoped to reach her so that everything would be as usual again.

It was naive of me to think that I could overpower the disease. The contact I felt we still had was beyond words. She didn't reject me in a physical sense, but she couldn't have a conversation with me because she was fully occupied with listening to and answering her inner voices.

If Signe didn't seek my attention, Ingrid did it all the more. There was no end to her tirades. And I listened because I understood that was what she needed. That's how I by pure chance came across the truth about the neighbour wife's death. The solution was there in front of our eyes all the time.

The insight made me both sad and terrified. What should I do now? Go to the police and tell them?

No, what would be the point of that?

To put an end to all suspicions and bad rumours, I told myself.

So that the dead woman's family would no longer have to live in uncertainty.

So that the police could finally put an end to it.

But I didn't. I didn't tell a living soul what I suspected and hoped that everything would fade away and disappear by itself.

It was a vain hope.

And now it's too late to get my suspicions confirmed. I have kept quiet for over two years, and I still don't know if I did the right thing.

Erik is dead and Signe will never get well again.

Ingrid has lost both her parents, and no one knows how it will go for her in the future. She lives with me and my husband now, and we do everything we can to help her. I can't lay her new, fragile world in ruins just to do the right thing to others.

Or can I?

No, I must protect her. As long as she is a child, I must help and protect her, in the same way that Erik helped and protected Signe when he found the neighbour's wife pushed down and dead outside his door.